The son of a small landowner, **Nikolai Gogol** (1809–52) was educated at the Niezhin gymnasium, where he started a magazine and acted in student theatricals. In 1828, he went to St. Petersburg, obtained a government clerkship, and devoted himself to writing. In 1831–32, he published two volumes of *Evenings on a Farm Near Dikanka*, a collection of stories based on Ukrainian folklore that was enthusiastically received. He next planned to write a history of Russia in the Middle Ages. The work never materialized, but the planning of it served to win him a chair of history at the University of St. Petersburg. Meanwhile, he published "Taras Bulba" and a number of short stories, including "The Overcoat." On April 19, 1836, his famous comedy *The Inspector General* was produced. The play stirred up controversy, and critics hailed its author as the head of the Naturalist school. Gogol spent the next twelve years abroad, living mainly in Rome. During his voluntary exile, he completed *Dead Souls*, a panorama of Russian life. Published in 1842, the book was an immediate success. The next ten years Gogol spent writing and rewriting a sequel that was never to see publication.

Donald Fanger is Harry Levin Professor of Literature Emeritus at Harvard University. He is the author of *Dostoevsky and Romantic Realism: A Study of Dostoevsky in Relation to Balzac, Dickens, and Gogol*; *The Creation of Nikolai Gogol* (winner of Phi Beta Kappa's Christian Gauss Prize for Literary Criticism); *Gorky's Tolstoy and Other Reminiscences*; and numerous articles and reviews in *The Times Literary Supplement*, *The New York Times Book Review*, *The Los Angeles Times Book Review*, *The New Republic*, *The Nation*, and many professional journals. Before going to Harvard, he taught at Brown and Stanford. He is the recipient of many honors, among them a Guggenheim Fellowship and two residencies at the Rockefeller Center in Bellagio.

continued . . .

Andrew R. MacAndrew is the translator of numerous books, including *Notes from Underground* and *The Brothers Karamazov* by Fyodor Dostoyevsky, Gogol's *The Inspector General*, and *Selected Letters of Fyodor Dostoyevsky*.

Priscilla Meyer is Professor of Russian Language and Literature at Wesleyan University, She published the first monograph on Vladimir Nabokov's *Pale Fire, Find What the Sailor Has Hidden*, and edited Andrei Bitov's collected stories, *Life in Windy Weather*. She is coeditor of collections on Gogol, Dostoevsky, and Nabokov. Her most recent book is *How the Russians Read the French: Lermontov, Dostoevsky, Tolstoy*.

THE DIARY
OF A MADMAN
and Other Stories

Nikolai Gogol

Translated by Priscilla Meyer
and Andrew R. MacAndrew

With a New Introduction by
Donald Fanger
and an Afterword by
Priscilla Meyer

SIGNET CLASSICS

SIGNET CLASSICS
Published by the Penguin Group
Penguin Group (USA) Inc., 375 Hudson Street,
New York, New York 10014, USA
Penguin Group (Canada), 90 Eglinton Avenue East, Suite 700, Toronto,
Ontario M4P 2Y3, Canada (a division of Pearson Penguin Canada Inc.)
Penguin Books Ltd., 80 Strand, London WC2R 0RL, England
Penguin Ireland, 25 St. Stephen's Green, Dublin 2,
Ireland (a division of Penguin Books Ltd.)
Penguin Group (Australia), 707 Collins Street, Melbourne, Victoria 3008,
Australia (a division of Pearson Australia Group Pty. Ltd.)
Penguin Books India Pvt. Ltd., 11 Community Centre, Panchsheel Park,
New Delhi–110 017, India
Penguin Group (NZ), 67 Apollo Drive, Rosedale, Auckland 0632,
New Zealand (a division of Pearson New Zealand Ltd.)
Penguin Books (South Africa), Rosebank Office Park, 181 Jan Smuts Avenue,
Parktown North 2193, South Africa
Penguin China, B7 Jiaming Center, 27 East Third Ring Road North,
Chaoyang District, Beijing 100020, China

Penguin Books Ltd., Registered Offices:
80 Strand, London WC2R 0RL, England

Published by Signet Classics, an imprint of New American Library,
a division of Penguin Group (USA) Inc.

First Signet Classics Printing (MacAndrew Translation), January 1961
First Signet Classics Printing (MacAndrew and Meyer Translations), January 2005
First Signet Classics Printing (Fanger Introduction), March 2013
10 9 8 7 6 5 4 3 2 1

ALWAYS LEARNING   PEARSON

Contents

Contents

Introduction

Nikolai Gogol was nineteenth-century Russia's greatest writer of prose. Not its greatest prose writer—Dostoevsky (who launched his career by rewriting Gogol's most famous story), as well as Tolstoy, Turgenev, Chekhov, and others, all framed complexities that have no counterpart in their odd predecessor, and wrote on a scale that dwarfed his. They explored issues where he, at best, adumbrated them. They *used* a medium which he, over a brief eleven years, had fashioned and tuned to produce effects never before seen in Russian. The world of their writing gives the impression of having three dimensions, whereas Gogol's seems at the same time to have fewer and more.

Recognition of his qualities, in Russia and outside it, may have come only in the twentieth century, but that does not mean that he had to wait for fame at home; it came to him with his first collection of stories, *Evenings on a Farm Near Dikanka*, in 1831, when he was twenty-two, once and for all, illustrating in astonishing ways Rilke's observation that "fame is the sum of the misunderstandings that gather around a writer's name." But it was more than fame: that, after all, can be an external thing, whereas Russians, in his time and later, read and reread him, responding directly to his genius and celebrating it. The problem was that when they tried to account for that genius, to say what it was in the writing that so amazed and delighted them, for a very long time, they failed ludicrously. As one of his more percipient contemporaries put it, "Everyone saw in him what he wanted to see, and not what was really there."

The reason has to do with the radical originality of his

best writing, the way that, while most of the conventional categories by which fiction is interpreted *seem* to be applicable in his case, on closer inspection they cannot be said to control or organize individual works, turning out instead to be decoys or red herrings or—most baffling of all—genuine signposts that, unreconciled with one another, in the end point nowhere. This is as true of extratextual categories as it is of textual ones. Too precociously modern to be accounted for in terms of "romanticism" or "realism," Gogol's best work nonetheless bears the imprint of its time far too plainly to be comprehended by the kind of vocabulary appropriate to his twentieth-century continuators (symbolists, "neorealists," surrealists, absurdists). Some of his heterogeneous oeuvre can be caught in these nets, but not much. Small wonder that one of his best Russian critics, Andrei Biely, declared in 1909, a hundred years after his birth, "We still do not know what Gogol is."

The situation is the same when we consider internal categories. The Gogolian narrator, whether individuated or not, is protean, typically mixing levity and gravity, pathos and absurdity, observation of minute detail with disconcerting generalization while allowing none to dominate. Plot is liable to be inconclusive, and often circular, while character meets none of a reader's expectations. This can be seen in two stories that can fairly be taken as manifestos.

The first is "The Nose." It opens by referring to "an extraordinarily strange occurrence" (as if to distinguish it from an ordinarily strange one) and proceeds to veer off into a labyrinth of non sequiturs. The occurrence itself, we learn at length, is the unaccountable disappearance of the nose of an ambitious vulgarian, its metamorphic adventures while independent, and his frantic pursuit of it until it reappears mysteriously in place—a happy ending for a character who doesn't deserve one. The semipersonal narration is by a voice ostensibly omniscient, but it is full of gaps, lapses, and irrelevancies, ready to acknowledge oddity only at the end, and then with a disconcerting fitfulness. In preparing the story for publication, Gogol decided not to present it as a dream, thereby making it over into an experiment in absurdity, a puzzle without a key and a provocation to his readers. "No," the narrating voice concludes, "I don't understand this at all.

I absolutely don't understand! But what is stranger, what is least comprehensible of all, is how authors can choose such subjects. I confess, this is entirely inconceivable, it's exactly . . . no, no, I don't understand at all." And then the capper, added for the second edition of the story:

> But yet, with all this, although, of course, one may admit this, that and the other, may even . . . and after all, where aren't there incongruities? But all the same, when you think about it, there is something, really, in all this. No matter what anyone says, such things happen in the world, rarely, but they happen.

With this subtle adjustment of the closing emphasis, the authorial voice moves from articulating the reader's rational objections to playing with them, unreliably, and so ends by pointing beyond the creative mystery to an ontological one. The censor charged with passing the story for its third publication—in 1854, two years after Gogol's death—proved an ideal reader. "The aim of the author is obscure and capable of being interpreted in various ways," he observed, "and so approval of the story requires the permission of the chief censorship authority."

The censor's point is an unwitting tribute to a quintessentially Gogolian masterpiece, in which the quest for experience is displaced from the experience related *in* the work to the reader's experience *of* the work, whose artistry not only sustains the comic effect but compels assent to the narrator's insistence that "all the same, when you think about it, there is something, really, in all this." Readers in search of profundity have found it there by following their own noses, seeing the story as an indictment of physicality, an orthodox Freudian castration fantasy, a sermon against godlessness, a symbolic comment on the drift away from Orthodox observance, and so on. Most of these interpretations are plausible and justified to a point, but each is unconvincing because too much of the text escapes it. Here as elsewhere, Gogol has created a puzzle that many keys may fit but none opens, a trap for the unwary.

"The Nose" may be called a manifesto because the story as a whole mocks a serious attitude toward accepted notions of significant form, mocks ordinary assumptions about intentionality (the very notion of artistic language as the carrier of messages), insists openly on the mockery, and at the end encourages the beleaguered reader's assumption that just the same there must be something in all this. And there is—only not within the story, but in the very fact of its existence. Misled by fragments of meaning and the semblance of an adventure, the reader may be cheated of vicarious experience, but he emerges enriched by his own linguistic and imaginative experience, delight, bafflement, and all.

What is at work in most of Gogol's all-but-plotless stories can be seen in the shortest of them all, "The Carriage," where virtually nothing happens. At a drunken dinner, a provincial landowner hyperbolizes on the theme of an incomparable carriage he has bought—"You could put a whole bull in the side pockets!"—and invites an incredulous visiting general to dine with him and inspect it on the following day. The landowner oversleeps and, reminded of his promise only by the arrival of his guests, pretends not to be at home, but they, deciding to have a look anyway, discover the carriage to be a quite ordinary one—and, curled up in it, their host. "Aha! You are here!" says the amazed general, and that, in the terms of Gogol's artistic strategy, is the point. It is in effect what he is saying about so many of his characters.

All the same, as stern a judge as Tolstoy called "The Carriage" "the peak of perfection in its kind." The perfection in question is clearly not to be sought in "content," or in anything that can be indicated by paraphrase, but rather in the narration itself, which constitutes the verbal equivalent of a one-man band, showing a liveliness and complexity inversely proportional to its objects. It is the subtle modulations of its rhythms, the arresting oddities of expression, the tantalizingly suggestive details, the abortive but not quite self-canceling gestures toward larger significances, that work together to provoke something like aesthetic bliss in the baffled reader. Throughout his short career, Gogol had consistently expressed a horror of "mere existence," regarding it as something that needed to have value and significance conferred on it. In the period of unself-conscious writing that ended with *Dead Souls*, such redemption had been primarily aesthetic; later it was to be primarily moral. But, early and late, his concern was with the transformative power of art, which alone could confer significance—on his own existence no less than on the objects of his depiction.

What went unacknowledged in all his pronouncements on these matters was the countervailing strength of what the poet Annensky perceived as Gogol's own ecstatic love for existence: "not for life but precisely for existence." So many of his characters are not merely mired in the trivial but are happily mired, happily and, however odd the word may seem, consciously warmed by the comfort of mindless routine, privy (as their author himself must have been) to the contentment that lies in the blank contemplation of things.

As must be clear by now, Gogol is a purveyor of paradox, the chief paradox being that things simultaneously are and are not what they seem. In the matter of character, the standard quest for dimensionality and complexity is doomed to utter failure. And yet his characters are memorable, both the central and the peripheral ones. They throb with a weird vitality, and though they can tell you virtually nothing useful about their time and place or about human psychology, they display a constant capacity to surprise. Approached as people, they tend to be cretins and automata; approached as symbols, they disappoint no less. Kafka (whose "Metamorphosis" is a lineal descendant of Gogol's "Nose") and Beckett doubtless made it easier for readers in the twentieth century to accept the strange ontology of Gogol's characters. Here, for example, is Beckett, writing to a director staging *Waiting for Godot* in 1953:

> The characters are living creatures, only just living perhaps, they are not emblems. I can readily understand your unease at their lack of characterization. But I would urge you to see in them less the result of an attempt at abstraction, something of which I am almost incapable, than a refusal to tone down all that is at one and the same time complex and amorphous in them.

But it is Gogol himself who has shown us the astonishingly narrow limits of what we can legitimately say about

his characters. In "The Carriage" it boils down to the state-
ment: "Aha! You are here!" The same point is embedded
unforgettably in his supreme comedy *The Government Inspector*, where, when a harebrained young stranger is taken
by the inhabitants of a remote provincial town to be an
important personage from the capital city of St. Petersburg,
one of the local landowners approaches him with a request:

> **Bobchinsky:** I humbly beg you, when you go back to Pe-
> tersburg, tell all the various nobles there, senators
> and admirals: Do you know, your Excellency or High-
> ness, in such and such a town there lives one Pyotr
> Ivanovich Bobchinsky.
>
> **Khlestakov:** Very well.
>
> **Bobchinsky:** And if you happen to be with the sover-
> eign, then tell the sovereign too: Do you know, your
> Imperial Majesty, in such and such a town lives one
> Pyotr Ivanovich Bobchinsky.
>
> **Khlestakov:** Very well.

Gogol's greatest achievement in the short story form,
"The Overcoat," shows the radically original nature of
theme, character, and narration that I have been stressing,
but with a new depth and power. Like "The Nose," this
story invites the reader to find "something in it"—and this
time the something can be recognized and named. The
themes of urban impersonality, bureaucracy, poverty and
comfort, meekness and pride, justice, love, Christian char-
ity, and literature itself all make their appearances in the
text. Those who claim that "The Overcoat" is not "about"
these things are demonstrably mistaken, though hardly
more so than those who claim that it is. The serious themes
of "The Overcoat" are unprecedentedly numerous—that is
what marks the story as belonging to Gogol's later period—
but they still make their fleeting appearance in an arbitrary
narration whose tendency is to move on, rather than to develop, reconcile, or resolve them. Reading the story is thus
like looking through a kaleidoscope: the constituent elements of the changing patterns are limited in number; one
can recognize them, and wonder at their variety, while not-
ing how the recurrence of certain patterns appears more

than fortuitous but less than primary. In this kaleidoscope's successive patterns, we see images that prompt reflection; these are related, we may come to realize, to other, less arresting images. Each turn contributes to a growing familiarity with the separately enigmatic shapes, and so intensifies the search for that perpetually elusive yet constantly potential pattern that might fix them all in positions of analyzable beauty.

There is, of course, no such fixity in Gogol's story. That was the point first seen by one of his best twentieth-century critics, Boris Eikhenbaum, who insisted on seeing "The Overcoat" as pure performance. But there is no such purity either. Gogol may not satisfy the reader's conventional expectation that a story should ultimately be comprehensible from a single dominant point of view, but he keeps that expectation alive enough to make sport of it. Once this is recognized as an index of the story's peculiar mode of being, it becomes possible to see that there is, after all, an ultimate, stable, and inclusive theme. "The Overcoat" is "about" not the questions it contains but the questions they finally evoke in the bemused reader. Which is to say that it is about significance and nonsignificance *as such*. The familiar themes it contains function, in their fluidity and incompleteness, only as cues pointing toward this larger understanding.

The radical novelty of this problematic text, in other words, lies in the way it provokes a quest for significance, for the sense in which humble phenomena may contain it, for the criteria by which it may be identified. And this quest—the more tantalizing because it is presented with seeming randomness, like a game of blindman's buff—is enacted in the narrative, whose arbitrary shifts of level and perspective represent the obstacles in that search. A hermeneutic challenge, intrinsically elusive and endlessly evocative, it is Gogol's monument to the poetic power of prose art.

Basically the function of this power is to supply the emphatically positive counterpart to its emphatically banal targets: freshness, vitality, surprise, freedom of action, freedom from time and place and constraint of all kinds, freedom from the ordinary logic of language itself—all embodied in a language that alters a reader's experience once having entered it. Here is the fundamental displacement in his art of displacement: scratch a Gogolian character and you are likely to find bare verbal tissue; examine a Gogolian phrase and you are likely to find the energy of human aspiration, human contradiction.

This ultimate paradox of literary art is Gogol's ultimate message. The rest is implication—and of the most various sorts: psychological, social, ethical, moral, religious—all encoded, demonstrably and at the same time incompletely, in the texts. One's sense, explicitly abetted by the narration, that there is "more to these works than what they are" (Andrei Sinyavsky's phrase about Gogol's characters) leads legitimately and inevitably to a search for allegorical meaning. Only if the search be for singleness and consistency is it doomed. Far more than most fictions, Gogol's seem to illustrate the principle of complementarity, according to which certain basic lines of interpretation are at once necessary and mutually exclusive. Moreover, because the data that sustain them are primitive and fragmentary, to trace large patterns of meaning requires extrapolating beyond what can be shown as textually warranted. The interpreter is placed in a double bind: he misses the point if he ignores allegorical meaning, and errs if he embraces it. Perhaps it is enough to conclude that the bedrock allegory of his art concerns the mystery and miracle of its own existence.

At this point a brief clarification is in order. Gogol's best work, which I have tried to characterize in these remarks, includes the first four items in the present collection, but not *Taras Bulba*, which, like many of his other Ukrainian tales, is a more conventional thing, being an exercise in pseudohistorical fiction where they tend to be exercises in pseudofolkloric fiction. There are exceptions, but by and large these works, though they contain brilliant passages and memorable scenes, show his talent rather than his genius; they are the product of an informing imagination that is adolescent, catering to the sort of audiences who today flock to Disney films and their many television spinoffs. When they succeed it is as popular art, confected of familiar ingredients but lacking the thoroughgoing originality that Gogol was to achieve elsewhere to such deep and lasting effect.

—DONALD FANGER

THE DIARY
OF A MADMAN
and Other Stories

The Diary of a Madman

An extraordinary incident occurred today. I got up rather late in the morning, and when Mavra brought me my cleaned boots I asked what time it was. Hearing that it had already long ago struck ten, I hurried to dress as quickly as possible. I confess, I wouldn't have gone to the department at all, knowing in advance what a sour face the chief of our division would make. For a long time he's been saying to me: "How come, brother, your head's always in such a muddle? Sometimes you run around like a lunatic, you get your work so tangled up that Satan himself couldn't make it out, you write a small letter in the heading, you don't put in either the date or the number." The damn heron! He probably envies me for sitting in the director's study and sharpening quills for His Excellency. In a word, I wouldn't have gone to the department if it weren't in the hope of seeing the treasurer and somehow getting even a little of my salary in advance out of that Jew. What a creature! For him ever to give money a month in advance— my God, the Judgment Day will come sooner. Beg him, tear your hair, be desperate—he won't give it, the gray-haired devil. But at home his own cook slaps him in the face. The whole world knows that. I don't understand the advantages of serving in my department. There are absolutely no resources. In the provincial civil and treasury offices it's a completely different matter: there, you look, someone is squeezed into a tiny corner and writing. His wretched frockcoat is vile, his snout makes you want

I

to spit, but just look at the dacha he rents! Don't bring him a gilded porcelain cup: "That," he'll say, "is a present for a doctor," but give him a pair of trotters, or a droshky, or a beaver coat at three hundred rubles. He looks so quiet, speaks so tactfully: "Lend me your little knife to sharpen my little quill," and then he'll so clean out a petitioner that he'll leave him only his shirt. True, on the other hand our work is respectable, there is such cleanliness everywhere as a provincial office will never see: the tables are mahogany, and all the superiors use the formal form of address to us. Yes, I confess, if it weren't for the respectability of the work, I would have long ago left the department.

I put on my old overcoat and took my umbrella because it was pouring rain. There was no one on the streets; I saw only peasant women covering their heads with their skirts and Russian merchants under umbrellas, and coachmen. As for the respectable classes, only a fellow clerk was plodding along. I saw him at the intersection. As soon as I saw him I said to myself: "Aha! No, my dear, you're not going to the department, you're hurrying after that woman who's running along ahead of you and you're looking at her legs. What a beast our fellow clerk is! I swear to God, he's worse than any officer: some female goes by in a little hat and he's bound to attach himself. While I was thinking this, I saw a carriage drive up to the store I was passing. I recognized it at once: it was our director's carriage. But he has no reason to go to the store, I thought: probably it's his daughter. I pressed myself against the wall. A footman opened the doors, and she fluttered out of the carriage like a little bird. How she glanced left and right, how she flashed her brows and eyes. . . . My God! I was lost, completely lost. And why did she have to go out at such a rainy time? Now try to tell me women don't have a great passion for all those rags. She didn't recognize me, and anyway I deliberately tried to wrap myself up as much as possible, because I had on a very dirty overcoat, and an old-fashioned one at that. Now they wear cloaks with long collars but mine were little short ones one on top of the other; besides, the cloth wasn't at all rainproof. Her little dog, not managing to leap in the door of the store, remained on the street. I know that little dog. They call her Madgie. I hadn't been there a minute when I suddenly heard a thin little voice: "Hello, Madgie!" How do you like that! Who's speaking? I looked around and saw two ladies walking under umbrellas: one an old lady, the other a young one; but they had already passed, while near me again sounded: "Shame on you, Madgie!" What the devil! I saw that Madgie was exchanging sniffs with the little dog which had been following the ladies. Aha! I said to myself, hang on, am I drunk? Only that, it seems, rarely happens to me. "No, Fidèle, you're wrong to think that," I myself saw Madgie say, "I was, bow wow! I was bow wow wow! very sick." Oh you little dog! I confess, I was very surprised to hear her speaking human language. But later, when I thought this all out thoroughly, I stopped being surprised. Actually, a great number of such things have already happened in the world. They say that in England a fish swam up which said two words in such a strange language that scholars have been trying to identify it for three years already and still to this day haven't discovered a thing. I also read in the papers about two cows that came into a shop and asked for a pound of tea. But, I confess, I was much more surprised when Madgie said: "I did write to you, Fidèle; Polkan probably didn't bring you my letter!" Well I'll forfeit my salary! Never yet in my life have I heard of a dog that could write. Only a nobleman can write correctly. Of course, some shopkeeper-bookkeepers and even serfs do a little writing sometimes, but their writing is mostly mechanical: no commas, no periods, no style.

This surprised me. I confess, recently I've begun to hear and see such things sometimes as no one has seen or heard before. I think, I said to myself, I'll follow that little dog and find out what she is and what she thinks. I folded up my umbrella and set off after the two ladies. They crossed to Gorokhovoy, turned into Meshchansky, then to Stolyarny, finally to Kokushkin Bridge and stopped in front of a large house. I know this house, I said to myself. This is the Zverkov house. What a thing! What people live in it: how many cooks, how many Poles! and our fellows, the clerks, sit one on top of the

other like dogs. I have a friend there who plays the
trumpet well. The ladies went up to the fifth floor. Good,
I thought: I won't go in now, but I'll remember the place
and won't fail to make use of it at the first opportunity.

Today is Wednesday, and therefore I was in our
chief's study. I deliberately arrived a bit early and, having sat down, sharpened all the quills. Our director must
be a very intelligent man. His whole study is lined with
books. I read the titles of some of them: all scholarliness,
such scholarliness that for one of my ilk there's no approaching it: it's all either in French or in German. And
when you look him in the face: foo, what importance
glows in his eyes! I have never yet heard him say a
superfluous word. Only perhaps when you give him a
paper, he'll ask: "What's it like out?" "Damp, Your Excellency." Yes, not a match for our ilk! A statesman.
I've noticed, though, that he particularly likes me. If only
the daughter too . . . ekh, rascalry! . . . Never mind,
never mind, silence! I read *The Northern Bee*. What a
stupid people the French are! Well, what do they want?
I'd take them all, I swear to God, and birch them! There
I also read a very pleasant description of a ball written
by a Kursk landowner. Kursk landowners write well.
After that I noticed that it had already struck twelve-
thirty, but our man hadn't come out of his bedroom. But
around one-thirty an incident occurred which no pen can
describe. The door opened, I thought it was the director,
and I leapt from my chair with some papers; but it was
she, she herself! Holy fathers, how she was dressed! Her
dress was white as a swan: foo, how luxurious! And how
she gazed: the sun, I swear to God, the sun! She bowed
and said, "Has Papa been here?" Ai, ai, ai! What a
voice! A canary, really, a canary! Your Excellency, I
wanted to say, don't command me to be executed, but
if you want me executed, execute me with your little
aristocratic hand. Yes, the devil take it, somehow my
tongue wouldn't obey and I only said: No, Miss. She
looked at me, at the books, and dropped her handker-

chief. I rushed after it, slipped on the damn parquet and almost knocked my nose off, however, I recovered myself and got the handkerchief. Saints, what a handkerchief! The most delicate, batiste—ambergris, absolute ambergris! It simply exudes aristocracy. She thanked me and smiled slightly so that her sweet little lips almost didn't move, and after that she went out. I sat for another hour when suddenly a footman came in and said: "Go home, Aksenty Ivanovich, the master has already gone out." I can't stand the footman set; they're always lounging around the front hall and won't even make the effort to nod to you. As if that weren't enough: once one of these beasts took it into his head, without even getting up from his place, to offer me some snuff. Do you know, you stupid serf, that I'm a clerk? I'm of noble origin. However, I took my hat and put on my coat myself, because these gentlemen will never help you on with it, and went out. At home I mostly lay on my bed. Then I copied out some very good little verses:

> *Not having seen my love an hour,*
> *I thought at least a year had passed;*
> *And finding that my life'd grown sour,*
> *Do I not live in vain, I asked.*

Must be Pushkin's work.* In the evening, wrapped up in my overcoat, I walked to the entrance of Her Excellency's house and waited for a long time to see if she wouldn't come out to get into her carriage so that I could have another little look at her—but no, she didn't come out.

November 6th

The chief of the division was furious today. When I arrived at the department, he called me in and began to talk to me like this: "Well, tell me please, what are you doing?" "What do you mean what? I'm not doing anything," I answered. "Well, think it over carefully! After

*In fact by N. P. Nikolev (1758–1815).

all, you're over forty, it's time you got smart. Who do you think you are? You think I don't know all your tricks? You're chasing the director's daughter! Well, look at yourself, just think, what are you? You're a zero, nothing more. You don't have a cent to your name. Just take a look in the mirror at your face, how can you think about that!" The devil take it, just because he has a face that looks a little like a druggist's bottle, and a clump of hair on his head curled into a pompadour, holds his head in the air and smears it with some kind of rosette oil, he thinks that only he can do anything he wants. I understand, I understand why he's angry at me. He's jealous; maybe he's seen the preferential signs of approbation shown me. Well I spit on him! So what if he is a court councillor! He gets a gold chain for his watch, orders boots at thirty rubles—and the devil take him! Am I some plebian, some tailor or subaltern's child? I'm a nobleman. I can rise in the service too. I'm still forty-two—the time when service only really begins. Just wait, friend! We too will become a colonel, or maybe, if God's willing, something a little higher. We too will get ourselves a reputation even better than yours. How did you get it into your head that except for you there just isn't a single decent person? Just give me a fashionable frockcoat tailored by Ruch and let me put on a tie just like yours—then you won't hold a candle to me. I have no means—that's the problem.

November 8th

Was at the theater. They did the Russian fool Filatka. Laughed a lot. There was also some vaudeville with amusing verses about clerks, especially about a certain collegiate registrar, quite freely written, so that I was surprised that the censorship let it through, and they say right out about merchants that they deceive the people and that their sons are debauched and climb into the nobility. There was also a very amusing couplet about journalists: that they love to rail against everything and that the author requests protection from the audience. Very funny plays authors are writing nowadays. I love going to the theater. As soon as there's a penny in your pocket—you can't keep from going. But among our fellow clerks there are such swine: he absolutely won't go to the theater, the peasant; only maybe if you give him a free ticket. One actress sang very well. I remembered the one who . . . ekh, rascalry! . . . Never mind, never mind . . . silence.

November 9th

At eight o'clock I set off for the department. The head of the division pretended he hadn't noticed my arrival. I too for my part, as if there had been nothing between us. I looked over and folded some papers. Went out at four o'clock. Passed the director's apartment but no one was in sight. After dinner mostly lay on my bed.

November 11th

Today I sat in our director's study, sharpened 23 quills for him, and for her, ai! ai . . . for Her Excellency four quills. He really likes a lot of quills around. Ooh! What a brain he must be! Always silent, but in his head, I bet, always deliberating. I would like to find out what he thinks about most; what's going on in that head. I would like to have a closer look at the life of these gentlemen, all these equivoques and court doings, what they're like, what they do in their set—that's what I'd like to find out! Several times I've thought of starting a conversation with His Excellency, only, the devil take it, my tongue just doesn't obey: you only say it's cold or hot out, and you absolutely won't get out anything more. I would like to get a glimpse of the living room, which you only sometimes see through into still another room. Ekh, what rich decor! What mirrors and porcelain. I'd like to get a glimpse of the half where Her Excellency is, that's what I'd like to see! The boudoir, how all those little jars and bottles are arranged, such flowers that it's terrifying even to breathe on them, how her dress lies thrown down there, looking more like air than a dress. I'd like

to get a glimpse of the bedroom . . . there, I bet, are
marvels, there, I bet, is a paradise such as is not even
to be found in the heavens. To have a look at the little
stool she stands on getting out of bed, at her little foot,
at how she puts on her little stocking white as snow on
her little foot . . . ai! ai! ai! never mind, never mind . . .
silence.

   Today however it came to me in a flash: I remembered
that conversation between the two dogs that I heard on
Nevsky Prospect. Fine, I thought to myself: Now I'll find
out everything. I have to seize the correspondence those
rotten little dogs were carrying on. There I'll probably
find out something. I confess, I once even called Madgie
over and said: "Listen, Madgie, here we are alone now,
if you want, I'll even lock the door so no one will see,
tell me everything you know about your mistress, what's
she like? I swear to you I won't tell anyone." But the
sly dog tucked her tail under her, doubled up and quietly
went out as if she hadn't heard a thing. I have long
suspected that dogs are much smarter than people; I was
even sure that they can talk, but that they just have a
kind of stubbornness in them. They're exceptional politi-
cians: they notice everything, a person's every step. No,
no matter what, tomorrow I'll go to the Zverkov house,
interrogate Fidèle and, if possible, seize all the letters
Madgie wrote her.

November 12th

   At two o'clock in the afternoon I set out to see Fidèle
without fail and to interrogate her. I can't stand cabbage,
the smell of which pours out of all the small shops on
Meshchansky; furthermore such hellishness wafts out
from under the gates of every house that I wrapped up
my nose and ran as fast as I could. What's more, the
foul craftsmen let out such a quantity of soot and smoke
from their workshops that it's absolutely impossible for
a respectable person to take a walk here. When I made
my way up to the sixth floor and rang the bell, a not
completely bad-looking girl with little freckles came out.
I recognized her. It was the same one who had been

walking with the old lady. She blushed a bit, and I suspected at once: you, dearie, want a fiancé. "What do you want?" said she. "I need to speak with your dog." The girl was stupid! I knew at once she was stupid! At that moment the dog ran up with a bark; I wanted to grab her but, the vile thing, she almost grabbed me by the nose with her teeth. However, I saw her basket in the corner. Ah, that's just what I need! I went up to it, rummaged in the straw in the wooden box and, to my singular satisfaction, pulled out a small packet of little papers. The loathsome dog, seeing this, first bit me on the calf, and then when she had sniffed out that I'd taken the papers, began to whine and fawn, but I said: "No, dearie, good-bye!" and ran off. I think the girl took me for a madman, because she was extraordinarily frightened. Having come home, I wanted to get to work at once and decipher those letters because I see a little badly by candlelight. But Mavra decided to clean the floor. These stupid Finns are always inappropriately clean. And therefore I went to take a walk and think over this occurrence. Now I'll finally find out all their affairs, designs, all those springs, and I'll finally get to the bottom of everything. These letters will reveal everything to me. Dogs are an intelligent lot, they know all the political relationships and therefore probably everything will be there: a portrait and all the affairs of that husband. There'll also be something about her . . . never mind, silence! Towards evening I came home. Mostly lay on my bed.

November 13th

Well, let's see: the letter is pretty legible. However, there's something sort of doggy in the handwriting. Let's read it:

> Dear Fidèle, I just can't get used to your bourgeois name. Couldn't they have given you a better one? Fidèle, Rose—what vulgar taste, however, that's beside the point. I'm very glad we decided to write to each other.

The letter is written very correctly. The punctuation and even the spelling is right everywhere. Even our division chief couldn't write that simply, though he says he studied in a university somewhere. Let's look further:

> *I think that sharing one's thoughts, feelings and impressions with another is one of the great blessings in the world.*

Hm! The thought is taken from some composition translated from the German. I don't recall the title.

> *I say this from experience, although I haven't been around the world further than the gates of our house. Doesn't my life flow pleasurably? My mistress, whom Papa calls Sophie, loves me madly.*

Ai, ai! . . . never mind, never mind. Silence!

> *Papa also pets me very often. I drink tea and coffee with cream. Akh, ma chère, I should tell you that I just don't see the pleasure of the big gnawed bones which our Polkan gobbles in the kitchen. The only good bones are from gamebirds, and then only when no one has sucked the marrow out of them yet. It's very good to mix several sauces together, only without capers and without greens; but I don't know of anything worse than the custom of giving dogs little balls rolled out of bread. Some gentleman or other sitting at the table who's held all sorts of trash in his hands will start mashing bread with these hands, call you over and shove a little ball in your teeth. To decline is somewhat impolite, so you eat it; with disgust, but you eat it. . . .*

The devil only knows what that is. What nonsense! As if there weren't a better subject to write about. Let's look on another page. Maybe there'll be something a bit more sensible.

> *I'm quite ready and willing to inform you about all the events going on at our house. I've already told you*

something about the chief gentleman, whom Sophie calls Papa. He's a very strange person.

Ah! At last! Yes, I knew it: they have a political view of every subject. Let's see what Papa is like:

> . . . . *a very strange person. Mostly he is silent. He speaks very seldom; but a week ago he talked to himself incessantly: Will I get it or won't I get it? He would take a paper in one hand, close the other empty one and say: Will I get it or won't I get it? Once he even turned to me with the question: What do you think, Madgie? Will I get it, or won't I get it? I couldn't understand anything at all, I sniffed his boot and went away. Then, ma chère, a week later. Papa came home overjoyed. All morning gentlemen in uniforms came to see him and congratulated him for something. At the table he was merrier than I've ever seen him, told anecdotes, and after dinner held me up to his neck and said: "Look, Madgie, what's this?" I saw some little ribbon. I sniffed it, but found absolutely no aroma; finally, on the sly, I licked it: a little salty.*

Hm! That little dog, I think, is a bit too . . . she ought to be whipped! Ah! So he's ambitious! This must be taken into account.

> *Farewell, ma chère! I must run and so on . . . and so on. . . . Tomorrow I'll finish the letter. Well, hello! Now I'm back again. Today my mistress Sophie . . .*

Ah! well, let's see what Sophie is like. Ekh, rascalry! Never mind, never mind . . . we will continue.

> . . . *my mistress Sophie was in an extraordinary flurry. She was going to a ball and I was delighted that I could write to you in her absence. My Sophie is always extraordinarily glad to go to a ball, although she almost always gets angry while dressing. I simply can't understand, ma chère, the pleasure of going to balls. Sophie comes home from balls at 6 a.m., and I almost always deduce from her pale and exhausted face that they*

haven't given her anything to eat there, the poor dear. I confess, I could never live like that. If they didn't give me gravy with grouse or hot chicken wings . . . I don't know what would become of me. Gravy with kasha's good too. But carrots, or turnips, or artichokes will never be any good . . .

Extraordinarily uneven style. It's immediately clear that a person didn't write it. She'll begin properly but end in dogginess. Let's have a look at another little letter. A bit longish. Hm! The date's not even given.

Akh! My dear, how one senses the approach of spring! My heart beats as if it kept waiting for something. There's a perpetual noise in my ears. So that I often stand several minutes with lifted foot listening at the doors. I'll confide to you that I have many suitors. I often watch them as I sit on the windowsill. Akh, if you knew what freaks there are among them. One coarse mongrel, terribly stupid, stupidity is written on his face, goes along the street importantly and imagines that he is the most distinguished individual, he thinks that everyone will turn to look at him. Not at all. I didn't even pay any attention, as if I hadn't even seen him. And what a terrifying Great Dane keeps stopping in front of my window! If he were to stand on his hind legs, which, the boor, he probably can't do, he would be a whole head taller than my Sophie's Papa, who is also rather tall and fat. That blockhead must be awfully arrogant. I growled at him but he couldn't have cared less. If he'd at least frowned! He stuck out his tongue, hung his huge ears and looked in the window—such a peasant! But do you really think, ma chère, that my heart is indifferent to all seekers—akh, no . . . if you were to see one cavalier named Trésor climbing over the fence of the next house. Akh, ma chère, what a dear little snout he has!

Foo, the devil with it! . . . What trash! . . . And how can one fill letters with such stupidities? Give me a person! I want to see a person; I demand food of the kind that would nourish and delight my soul; but instead such trivia. . . . Let's skip a page, maybe it'll be better:

. . . Sophie was sitting at the table and sewing something. I was looking out the window because I like to watch the passersby. Suddenly the footman came in and said "Teplov!" "Ask him in," cried Sophie and ran to hug me. "Akh, Madgie, Madgie! If you only knew who that is: dark-haired, a court chamberlain, and what eyes! Black and bright as fire!" And Sophie ran to her room. A minute later a young court chamberlain with black sidewhiskers walked in; he went up to the mirror, arranged his hair and looked around the room. I growled and sat down in my place. Sophie soon came out and gaily bowed to his heel-clicking; but I continued looking out the window as if not noticing anything; however, I bent my head slightly to the side and tried to hear what they were talking about. Akh, ma chère, what nonsense they were talking about! They were talking about how some lady did one figure instead of another in a dance; also about how some Bobov looked very much like a stork in his ruffled shirt and had almost fallen down; that some Lidina thinks she has blue eyes, whereas they're green—and the like. What, I thought to myself, if you compared the court chamberlain with Trésor! Heavens! What a difference! First of all, the court chamberlain has sidewhiskers all around a completely smooth broad face as if he had tied it up in a black handkerchief; but Trésor has a slender little snout and a white patch on his forehead. And there's no comparing Trésor's waist with the court chamberlain's. And his eyes, ways, manners are completely different. Oh, what a difference! I don't know what she finds in her court chamberlain. Why is she so enraptured by him? . . .

It seems to me too that there's something wrong here. It's impossible that a court chamberlain could so fascinate her. Let's look further:

It seems to me, if she likes that court chamberlain, she'll soon start liking that clerk who sits in Papa's study. Akh, ma chère, if you knew what a freak he is. A real turtle in a sack. . . .

What clerk could that be?

*He has the strangest name. He always sits and sharp-
ens quills. The hair on his head looks a lot like hay.
Papa always sends him out instead of a servant. . . .*

It seems to me that this vile cur is alluding to me.
Since when is my hair like hay?

*Sophie just can't keep from laughing when she looks
at him.*

You lie, you damn dog! What a vile tongue! As if I
didn't know that it's a matter of envy. As if I didn't
know whose doings these are. These are the doings of
the division chief. After all, the man's sworn himself to
unbending hatred—and so he attacks and attacks, at
every step he attacks. Let's look, however, at another
letter. Perhaps the matter will become clear by itself.

*Ma chère Fidèle, forgive me for not writing for so
long, I have been in utter ecstasy. Truly did some writer
say that love is a second life. Furthermore, there are
big changes at our house. The court chamberlain is
here every day now. Sophie is madly in love with him.
Papa is very gay. I even heard from our Grigory, who
sweeps the floor and almost always has conversations
with himself, that soon there'll be a wedding; because
Papa absolutely wants to see Sophie marry either a
general or a court chamberlain, or a colonel. . . .*

The devil take it! I can't read any more. . . . Everything's either a court chamberlain or a general. Everything that's best in the world, everything goes to court
chamberlains or generals. You find yourself some poor
treasure, you think it's within arm's reach—and a court
chamberlain or a general grabs it from you. The devil
take it! I'd like to become a general myself, not to win
her hand and so on. No; I'd like to be a general only in
order to see how they dangle around doing all these
various court routines and equivoques, and then tell
them I spit on both of you. The devil take it. It's irritat-
ing! I tore the stupid dog's letters to bits.

December 3rd

It can't be. Rumors! There won't be a wedding! What if he is a court chamberlain? After all, that's nothing more than a position; not some visible thing you could hold in your hands. After all, just because you're a court chamberlain you don't get a third eye in your forehead. After all, his nose isn't made of gold, but it's just like mine, like everyone's; after all, he uses it to smell with, and not to eat with, to sneeze with, not to cough with. I've wanted several times to figure out where all these differences come from. Why am I a titular councillor and why should I be a titular councillor? Maybe I'm some count or general, and only seem to be a titular councillor? Maybe I don't know myself who I am. After all, there are so many examples in history: there's some simple guy, not quite a noble, but simply some bourgeois or even a peasant—and suddenly it's discovered he's some magnate, and sometimes even a ruler. When a peasant sometimes turns out like that what might a noble turn out to be? Suddenly, for example, I come in in a general's uniform: an epaulette on my right shoulder and an epaulette on my left shoulder, a blue ribbon across my chest—what'll happen? What tune will my beauty sing then? What will Papa himself say, our director? Oh, what an ambitious man! A mason, certainly a mason, although he pretends to be this and that, but I noticed at once that he's a mason: if he gives someone his hand, he only sticks out two fingers. And can't I this very minute be appointed governor general or commissary or some other thing? I'd like to know why I'm a titular councillor? Why precisely a titular councillor?

December 5th

Today I read the newspapers all morning. Strange things are going on in Spain. I couldn't even really figure them out. They write that the throne is vacant and that they are having difficulty trying to choose a successor and therefore insurrections are taking place. This seems extraordinarily strange to me. How can a throne be vacant? They say that some donna is supposed to ascend the throne. A donna can't ascend the throne. She just can't. A king should be on the throne. But they say there is no king. It can't be that there is no king. A government can't be without a king. There is a king, only he's incognito somewhere. It might be that he's right there, but either some family reasons or threats on the part of neighboring powers, France and other lands, are somehow forcing him to hide, or there are some other reasons.

December 8th

I was quite ready to go to the department, but various reasons and considerations kept me. I just can't get the Spanish affairs out of my head. How can it be that a donna should become a queen? They won't permit that. And, in the first place, England won't permit it. And furthermore political affairs of all Europe: the Austrian emperor, our sovereign . . . I confess, these events have so exhausted and shaken me that I absolutely couldn't do anything all day. Mavra kept remarking to me that I was exceptionally distracted at the table. And actually, it seems I threw two plates on the floor out of absent-mindedness which instantly broke. After dinner I walked up to the hills. Couldn't get anything instructive out of it. Mostly lay on my bed and thought about the Spanish affairs.

Year 2000 43rd of April

Today is a day of the greatest jubilation! There is a king in Spain. He has been found. I am this king. Only just today did I find out about this. I confess, it struck me suddenly like lightning. I don't understand how I could think and imagine that I was a titular councillor. How could this mad thought get into my head? It's a good thing no one thought of putting me in the madhouse at the time. Now everything has been revealed to me. Now I see everything clear as day. But before, I don't understand, before everything was in a kind of fog before me. And it all, I think, comes from the fact that people imagine that the human brain is located in the head; not at all: it is brought by the wind from the direction of the Caspian Sea. At first I revealed who I am to Mavra. When she heard that the King of Spain was standing before her, she threw up her hands and almost died of fright. The stupid woman had never seen a King of Spain before. However, I tried to calm her and tried to assure her in gracious words of my good favor, and that I wasn't the least angry that she sometimes cleaned my boots badly. After all they're a benighted lot. They can't talk about lofty subjects. She was frightened because she is convinced that all kings in Spain look like Philip II. But I explained to her that there is no resemblance between me and Philip and that I don't have a single Capuchin. . . . Didn't go to the department. The devil with it! No, friends, you won't entice me now; I'm not about to copy your foul papers!

Marchtober the 86th
Between day and night

Today our messenger came to get me to go to the department since I haven't been going to work for more than three weeks already. I went to the department just for kicks. The division chief thought that I'd bow to him and start apologizing but I looked at him indifferently, not too angrily and not too graciously, and sat down in my place as if not noticing anyone. I gazed at the whole office scum and thought: What if you knew who's sitting among you. . . . My God! What a hubbub you'd raise, and the division chief himself would start bowing low to me the way he now bows to the director. They put some papers before me for me to do an extract of them. But I didn't even lift a finger to them. After a few minutes everything flew into a flurry. They said the director was coming. Many clerks ran up and vied with each other to show themselves to him. But I didn't budge. When he passed through our division everyone buttoned up their frock coats; but I didn't do a thing! What's a director! I'm supposed to stand up for him—never! What kind of director is he? He's a cork, not a director. An ordinary cork, a simple cork, nothing more. The kind they stop bottles with. What amused me most was when they thrust a paper at me to sign. They thought that I'd write on the very bottom of the sheet: clerk so-and-so, what else? But in the most important place where the director of the department signs, I wrote: "Ferdinand VIII." You should've seen what an awed silence reigned; but I just waved my hand, saying: "No signs of allegiance are necessary!"—and went out. From there I went straight to the director's apartment. He wasn't home. A footman didn't want to let me in, but I said such things to him that he simply gave up. I made my way straight to her dressing room. She was sitting before a mirror; she leapt up and retreated from me. However, I didn't tell her that I was the King of Spain. I only said that such happiness awaited her as she couldn't even imagine and that, despite the machinations of our enemies, we would be together. I didn't want to say anything more and went out. Oh, what a perfidious creature is woman! Only now have I comprehended what woman is. Until now no one has yet discovered whom she's in love with: I'm the first to discover it. Woman is in love with the devil. Yes, no joking. Physicists write stupidities, that she's this and that—she loves only the devil. You see over there, in the first tier of boxes, she's focussing her lorgnette. You think she's looking at that fat man with the medal? Not at all, she's looking at the devil who's standing behind his back. Now he's hiding in his medal. Now he's beckoning to her with his finger! And she'll marry him. She will. And all these people, all their high-ranking fathers, all these who fawn in all directions and climb into court circles, and say they're patriots and this and that: rents, rents are what these patriots want! They'd sell their mother, father, God for money, ambitious creatures, Christ-sellers! It's all ambition and ambition comes from a little bubble under the tongue and in it there's a small worm the size of the head of a pin, and it's all done by some barber who lives on Gorokhovaya. I don't remember his name; but it's certainly true that he and a certain midwife want to spread Mohammedanism throughout the whole world and therefore, they say, the majority of the people in France already profess the faith of Mahomet.

No date at all.
The day was dateless.

I walked incognito along Nevsky Prospect. The imperial sovereign drove by. The whole city took off their hats and I did too; however, I gave no sign whatsoever that I was the King of Spain. I considered it indecorous to reveal myself right there in front of everyone because my tall confrère would probably have asked why the King of Spain had not yet been presented at court. And indeed one should present oneself at court first. The only thing that stopped me was that I still don't have a king's raiment. At least if I could get a royal mantle. I wanted to order it from the tailor, but they're complete asses, besides they're utterly careless with their work, they're addicted to fraud and mostly cobble stones on the street. I decided to sew myself a royal mantle out of my new uniform which I'd only worn twice. But so that those scoundrels couldn't ruin it, I decided to sew it myself, locking the door so that no one would see. I cut it all up with the scissors because it was necessary to redo it entirely and give the whole cloth the appearance of ermine tails.

Don't remember the date.
There was no month either.
Devil knows what there was.

The royal mantle is completely ready and sewn. Mavra screamed when I put it on. However, I still haven't decided to present myself at court. There's still no delegation from Spain. It's improper without deputies. There'll be no weight to my dignity. I expect them any hour.

The 1st date

The extraordinary slowness of the deputies surprises me. What reasons could be detaining them? Not France? Yes, that's the most unfavorably disposed power. I went to the post office to find out if the Spanish deputies hadn't arrived. But the postmaster was extraordinarily stupid, he doesn't know anything: no, he says, there aren't any Spanish deputies here, but if you want to write letters, we'll take them at the established rate. The devil take it! What's a letter? A letter's nonsense. Druggists write letters. . . .

Madrid. Februarius the thirtieth

And so I'm in Spain, and it happened so quickly that I could hardly regain my senses. This morning the Spanish deputies came to me and I got into a carriage with them. The extraordinary speed seemed strange to me. We drove so fast that in half an hour we reached the Spanish border. However, there are now cast-iron roads all over Europe and steamboats go extraordinarily fast. Spain is a strange land: when we entered the first room I saw a number of people with shaved heads. However, I guessed that these must be either Dominicans or Capuchins because they shave their heads. The conduct of the State Chancellor who led me by the arm seemed extraordinarily strange to me; he pushed me into a small room and said: Sit here and if you keep calling yourself King Ferdinand I'll beat that whim out of you. But, knowing this was nothing more than a test, I answered negatively, for which the Chancellor hit me twice with a stick on the back so painfully that I almost screamed, but I restrained myself, remembering that this was a custom of the knights on entering high rank, because in Spain even to this day knightly customs are maintained. Remaining alone, I decided to occupy myself with affairs of state. I discovered that China and Spain are absolutely one and the same country, and it's only from ignorance that they're considered different nations. I advise everyone to write down Spain on paper, and it'll come out

China. But I was exceptionally grieved by an event which will take place tomorrow. Tomorrow at 7 o'clock a terrible phenomenon will be accomplished: the earth will mount the moon. The famous English chemist Wellington writes about it. I confess, I felt real anxiety when I imagined the unusual delicacy and frailty of the moon. The moon after all is usually made in Hamburg; and is most poorly made. I'm surprised that England pays no attention to this. A lame cooper makes it, and it's clear the fool hasn't the least conception of a moon. He used tarred rope and part olive oil; and therefore there's a terrible stench all over the earth so that you have to hold your nose. And therefore the moon itself is such a delicate sphere that people simply can't live there and now only noses live there. And that's why we can't see our own noses, for they're all on the moon. And when I realized that the earth is a heavy substance and by mounting could grind our noses into flour, such anxiety possessed me that, putting on my shoes and socks, I hurried into the State Council hall in order to give an order to the police not to let the earth mount the moon. The Capuchins of whom I found a great number in the State Council hall were a very intelligent lot and when I said: "Gentlemen, let us save the moon; because the earth wants to mount it," everyone at once ran to carry out my monarchal will and many climbed the wall in order to get the moon; but at that time the great Chancellor came in. Seeing him, everyone scattered. I, as the King, remained alone. But the Chancellor, to my surprise, struck me with a stick and chased me into my room. Such power do folk customs have in Spain!

January of the same year,
occurring after February

I still don't understand what kind of a country Spain is. The folk customs and court etiquette are quite unusual. I don't understand, I don't understand, I absolutely don't understand anything. Today they shaved my head, despite the fact that I shouted with all my might about my unwillingness to be a monk. But I can't even

remember anymore what happened to me when they
began to drip cold water on my head. I have never felt
such hell. I was ready to fly into a frenzy, so that they
could hardly restrain me. I just don't understand the
significance of that strange custom. The custom is stupid,
senseless! The folly of the kings who haven't yet abol-
ished it is incomprehensible to me. Judging by all proba-
bilities, I wonder: haven't I fallen into the hands of the
Inquisition, and the one I took for the Chancellor, isn't
he the Grand Inquisitor himself? Only I still can't understand how a king could be subject to the Inquisition. It's
possible, true, on France's part and especially Polignac's.
Oh, that beast Polignac! He's sworn to harm me to the
death. And now he pursues and pursues me; but I know,
friend, that you're being led by the Englishman. The
Englishman is a great politician. He bustles about everywhere. It's already known to the whole world that when
England takes snuff France sneezes.

date 25th

Today the Grand Inquisitor came to my room but,
hearing his steps when he was still at a distance, I hid
under the chair. Seeing that I wasn't there, he began to
call me. At first he shouted: "Poprishchin!" I didn't say
a word. Then: "Aksenty Ivanov! Titular councillor! Nobleman!" I keep silent. "Ferdinand VIII, King of
Spain!" I was about to stick out my head, but then I
thought: No, brother, you won't fool me! We know you:
you're going to pour cold water on my head again. However, he saw me and chased me out from under the
chair with a stick. The damn stick hits extraordinarily
painfully. However, today's discovery rewarded me for
all that: I found out that every rooster has a Spain, that
it is found under his feathers. The Grand Inquisitor,
however, left me in a rage and threatening me with some
punishment. But I completely disregarded his impotent
malice, knowing that he is acting like a machine, as a
tool of the Englishman.

No, I have no more strength to endure it. God! What they're doing to me! They pour cold water on my head! They don't listen to, don't see, don't hear me. What did I do to them? Why are they tormenting me? What do they want from poor me? What can I give them? I don't have anything. I don't have strength, I can't bear all their torments, my head burns and everything whirls before me. Save me! Take me away! Give me a troika with horses swift as a whirlwind! Take your seat, my coachman, ring, my bells, soar up, steeds, and bear me away from this world! Further, further, so that nothing, nothing is visible. There the heavens swirl before me; a little star twinkles in the distance; the forest rushes past with dark trees and the moon; a blue-gray fog spreads out beneath my feet; a chord rings in the fog; on one side the sea, on the other—Italy; over there Russian huts can be seen. Is that my house showing blue in the distance? Is that my mother sitting at the window? Mother, save your poor son! Shed a tear on his sick head! Look how they torment him! Press your poor orphan to your bosom! There is no place for him in the world! They're chasing him away! Mother! Have pity on your sick child! . . . And did you know that the Dey of Algiers has a bump right under his nose?

The Nose

1

On March 25th in Petersburg an extraordinarily strange occurrence took place. The barber Ivan Yakovlevich, who lives on Voznesensky Prospect (his surname has been lost, and even on his signboard—where a gentleman is depicted with a soaped cheek and the inscription: "We also let blood"—nothing more is stated), the barber Ivan Yakovlevich woke up rather early and detected the smell of hot bread. Raising himself up a bit in his bed, he saw his wife, a rather respectable lady who was very fond of drinking coffee, taking from the oven some freshly baked rolls.

"Today, Praskovya Osipovna, I will not drink coffee," said Ivan Yakovlevich, "but instead I would like to eat a bit of hot bread with onion." (That is, Ivan Yakovlevich would have liked both the one and the other, but knew that it was quite impossible to ask for two things at once, for Praskovya Osipovna very much disliked such whims.) "Let the fool eat bread; so much the better for me," thought his wife to herself, "there'll be an extra portion of coffee left." And she threw one roll on the table.

For decency's sake Ivan Yakovlevich put his tailcoat on over his nightshirt and, sitting down at the table, sprinkled salt, prepared two onions, took a knife in hand and, assuming a significant expression, proceeded to cut the bread. Having cut the bread into two halves, he looked into the middle and, to his surprise, saw something white. Ivan Yakovlevich poked carefully with the knife and felt with his finger. "Solid!" he said to himself, "what sort of thing could it be?"

He thrust in his fingers and pulled out—a nose! . . .
Ivan Yakovlevich was dumbfounded; he began to rub
his eyes and to feel it: a nose, precisely, a nose! And
furthermore, it seemed to belong to someone he knew.
Horror was expressed on Ivan Yakovlevich's face. But
this horror was nothing next to the indignation which
seized his wife.

"Where did you cut off a nose, you beast?" she
shrieked with rage. "Scoundrel! Drunkard! I'll denounce
you to the police myself. What a bandit! I've already
heard from three people that you yank their noses so
hard while shaving them that they hardly stay on."

But Ivan Yakovlevich was more dead than alive. He
realized that the nose belonged to none other than the
collegiate assessor Kovalyov whom he shaved every
Wednesday and Sunday.

"Wait, Praskovya Osipovna! I'll wrap it in a rag and
put it in the corner. Let it lie there a little bit, and later
I'll take it away."

"I won't hear of it! I'm supposed to let a cut-off nose
lie around my room? You dried-out bread crust! He only
knows how to strop his razor, but soon he won't be in
a condition to fulfill his duty at all, the trollop, the good-
for-nothing! I'm supposed to answer to the police for
you? . . . Oh you filth, you blockhead! Out with it! Out!
Take it where you want! Don't let me set eyes on it
again!"

Ivan Yakovlevich stood exactly as if he had been
beaten. He thought and thought—and didn't know what
to think. "The devil knows how that happened," he said
at last, scratching behind his ear with his hand.
"Whether I came home drunk yesterday or not, I really
can't say for sure. But by all indications it should be an
impossible occurrence: for bread is a baked affair, while
a nose is something entirely different. I can't make anything of it! . . ." Ivan Yakovlevich fell silent. The thought
that the police would discover the nose on him and in-
dict him threw him into a total frenzy. The crimson collar beautifully embroidered in silver, the sword, already
flashed before him . . . and he shook all over. At last he
got his underwear and boots, put on all this rubbish and,
accompanied by the unlovely remonstrations of Prasko-

vya Osipovna, wrapped the nose in a rag and went out onto the street.

He wanted to slip it somewhere: either into the post by the gate, or simply to drop it accidentally somehow and then turn into a side street. But to his misfortune some acquaintance or other kept happening along who would begin immediately with the inquiry: "Where are you going?" or "Whom are you going to shave so early?"—so that Ivan Yakovlevich couldn't find the right moment. On another occasion he actually dropped it, but a policeman at some distance off pointed to it with his halberd, saying: "Pick it up! You've dropped something there!" And Ivan Yakovlevich had to pick up the nose and hide it in his pocket. He was seized with despair, all the more since the crowd on the street constantly increased as the stores and shops began to open.

He decided to go to the Isakievsky Bridge: wouldn't he manage somehow to fling it into the Neva? . . . But I am somewhat remiss in that up to now I have said nothing about Ivan Yakovlevich, an honorable man in many respects.

Ivan Yakovlevich, like every decent Russian workman, was a terrible drunkard. And although every day he shaved other people's chins, his own was forever unshaven. Ivan Yakovlevich's tailcoat (Ivan Yakovlevich never wore a frockcoat) was motley, that is, it was black, but covered with brownish-yellow and gray blotches; the collar shone, and instead of the three buttons only threads dangled. Ivan Yakovlevich was a great cynic, and when the collegiate assessor Kovalyov would say to him as usual while he was being shaved: "Ivan Yakovlevich, your hands always stink!" Ivan Yakovlevich would reply with the question: "Why should they stink?" "I don't know, brother, only they stink," the collegiate assessor would say, and Ivan Yakovlevich, having taken a pinch of snuff, would soap him for this both on the cheek and under the nose and behind the ear and under the beard, in a word, wherever he wanted.

This respectable citizen found himself already on the Isakievsky Bridge. First of all he looked around; then he leaned over the railing as if to look under the bridge to see whether there were many fish running, and stealthily flung in the rag with the nose. He felt as if five hundred pounds had fallen off him at once; Ivan Yakovlevich even grinned. Instead of going to shave officials' chins, he started off for an establishment with the sign "Food and Tea" to ask for a glass of punch, when he suddenly noticed at the end of the bridge a police inspector of noble appearance with full sidewhiskers, in a three-cornered hat, with a sword. He froze; however, the inspector crooked his finger at him and said:

"Come here, my good man!"

Ivan Yakovlevich, knowing good form, took off his cap when he was still at a distance, and, approaching gracefully, said:

"I wish your honor good health!"

"No, no, brother, not your honor; say, what were you doing standing on the bridge?"

"I swear to God, Sir, I was going to shave someone, and I only looked to see if the river was flowing quickly."

"You're lying! You're lying! You won't get off with that. Kindly answer!"

"I'm prepared to shave your grace two times a week or even three, without any objection," answered Ivan Yakovlevich.

"No, friend, that's a trifle! Three barbers shave me, and furthermore they consider it a great honor. But now kindly tell me what you were doing there?"

Ivan Yakovlevich paled. . . . But here the event is entirely covered in fog, and of what happened further, absolutely nothing is known.

2

The collegiate assessor Kovalyov woke up rather early and went "Brrr" with his lips, which he always did when he woke up, although he himself could not explain for what reason. Kovalyov stretched, and ordered the small mirror standing on the table to be brought to him. He wanted to look at the pimple which had popped up on his nose the evening before, but to his great amazement, he saw that instead of a nose, there was an entirely smooth space! Taking fright, Kovalyov ordered water to be brought and rubbed his eyes with a towel: precisely, no nose! He began to feel with his hand to ascertain: isn't he asleep? It seems he's not asleep. The collegiate assessor Kovalyov leapt out of bed and shook himself: no nose! He ordered his clothes to be brought at once and flew off directly to the chief of police.

But meanwhile it is essential to say something about Kovalyov, so that the reader might see what sort of collegiate assessor he was. The collegiate assessors who receive that title with the help of academic certificates may in no way be compared with those collegiate assessors who used to be appointed in the Caucasus. These are two entirely distinct breeds. Learned collegiate assessors. . . . But Russia is such a wondrous land, that if you talk about one collegiate assessor, all collegiate assessors from Riga to Kamchatka are sure to take it personally. Of course the same is true of all titles and ranks. Kovalyov was a collegiate assessor from the Caucasus. He had so far only enjoyed that title for two years and therefore couldn't forget it for a minute; but in order to give himself nobility and weight, he never called himself a collegiate assessor, but always a major.* "Listen, my dear," he would usually say upon meeting a woman selling shirtfronts on the street, "you come to my house; my apartment is on Sadovaya; just ask: Does Major Kovalyov live here? Anyone will show you." If he met some pretty little thing, he would give her a secret instruction as well, adding: "You ask, my sweet, for Major Kovalyov's apartment." For this very reason we too will henceforth call this collegiate assessor "major."

Major Kovalyov had the habit of strolling along Nevsky Prospect every day. The collar of his shirtfront was always exceptionally clean and starched. His whiskers were of the sort which even now can still be seen on provincial and district surveyors, architects and regimental doctors, also on the directors of various police functions and in general on all those men who have full, ruddy cheeks and play Boston very well: these whiskers

*The equivalent military rank to the civil service title of "collegiate assessor."

go along the very middle of the cheek and go straight up to the nose. Major Kovalyov wore a quantity of seals; cornelian, and with crests, and those on which was engraved: Wednesday, Thursday, Monday, and so on. Major Kovalyov had come to Petersburg on business, namely to look for a position befitting his title: if he were successful, a vice-governor's, if not—an executor's in some conspicuous department. Major Kovalyov was not against even marrying, but only on the condition that the bride come with two hundred thousand in capital. And by this the reader can now judge for himself what was the situation of this major when he saw instead of a rather attractive and moderate nose a ridiculous, level and smooth space.

To his misfortune, not one coachman showed up on the street and he had to go on foot, wrapped in his cloak and covering his face with a handkerchief, giving the impression that he was bleeding. "But maybe I just imagined it: it's impossible that a nose would disappear out of sheer stupidity," he thought and went into a pastry shop expressly in order to look in the mirror. Fortunately there was no one in the pastry shop; little boys were sweeping the rooms and arranging the chairs; some with sleepy eyes were bringing out hot meat pies on trays; yesterday's coffee-spattered newspapers were scattered around on the tables and chairs. "Well, thank God no one's here," he said, "now I can have a look." He shyly approached the mirror and looked. "The devil with it, what rubbish!" he said, spitting. "At least if there were something in place of a nose, but nothing! . . ."

Biting his lip with annoyance, he went out of the pastry shop and decided, contrary to his habit, not to look at anyone or to smile at anyone. Suddenly he stopped by the doors of a house as if rooted to the spot; before his eyes an inexplicable phenomenon occurred: a carriage stopped in front of the entrance; the doors opened; bending over, a gentleman in a uniform jumped out and ran up the stairs. What was the horror and at the same time astonishment of Kovalyov when he realized that this was his own nose! At this unusual spectacle it seemed to him that everything whirled before his eyes; he felt that he could hardly stay on his feet; but he, all trembling as if in a fever, decided at any cost to wait until the nose returned to his carriage. In two minutes the nose did in fact come out. He was in a uniform embroidered in gold with a high-standing collar; he wore buckskin breeches, at his side a sword. From his plumed hat one could conclude that he held the rank of state councillor. From everything it was evident that he was going visiting somewhere. He looked to both sides, shouted to the coachman: "Let's go!" got in and drove off.

Poor Kovalyov almost went out of his mind. He did not know how even to think about such a strange occurrence. How could it be, indeed, that a nose, which just yesterday was on his face, couldn't ride or walk—was in uniform! He ran after the carriage, which, fortunately, did not drive on very far and stopped before the Kazan Cathedral.

He rushed into the cathedral, made his way through a row of old beggar women with wrapped-up faces with two holes for the eyes, whom he used to laugh at so, and went into the church. There were few worshippers inside the church; they all stood just by the entrance in the doorway. Kovalyov was in such a distressed state that he had no strength whatsoever to pray, and he cast his eyes about all the corners in search of that gentleman. At last he saw him standing to one side. The nose had entirely hidden his face in the high-standing collar and was praying with an expression of the greatest piety.

"How to go up to him?" thought Kovalyov. "From all appearances, from the uniform, from the hat, it's evident that he is a state councillor. The devil knows how to do it!"

He began to cough a bit in his vicinity; but the nose did not for a minute abandon his pious attitude and kept bowing low.

"My dear sir . . ." said Kovalyov, inwardly forcing himself to take courage, "my dear sir. . . ."

"What do you want?" answered the nose, turning around.

"I'm surprised, my dear sir, it seems to me . . . you should know your place. And suddenly I find you, and where?—in church. You must agree. . . ."

"Excuse me, I cannot make sense of what you are pleased to be talking about . . . explain yourself."

"How am I to explain to him?" thought Kovalyov, and, summoning his courage, began: "Of course I . . . however, I am a major. For me to go around without a nose, you will agree, is unseemly. Some marketwoman who sells peeled oranges on Voskresensky Bridge can sit around without a nose; but I, having the intention of attaining . . . furthermore being acquainted with ladies in many good families: Chekhtaryova, the state councillor's wife, and others . . . Judge for yourself. . . . I don't know, dear sir. . . . (At this Major Kovalyov shrugged his shoulders.) Excuse me. . . . If one looks at this according to the rules of duty and honor . . . you yourself can understand. . . ."

"I understand absolutely nothing," answered the nose, "explain yourself more satisfactorily."

"My dear sir . . ." said Kovalyov with a sense of his own dignity, "I don't know how to understand your words. . . . The whole matter, it seems, is perfectly obvious. . . . Either you want . . . why, you are my own nose!"

The nose looked at the major, and his brows knit somewhat.

"You are mistaken, dear sir. I'm on my own. Furthermore there cannot be any close relations between us. Judging by the buttons on your uniform, you must work in another department." Having said this, the nose turned away and continued to pray.

Kovalyov was utterly confused, not knowing what to do and even what to think. At this moment the pleasant sound of a woman's dress was heard; a middle-aged woman came up, all done up in lace, and with her a slim little thing, in a white dress very prettily describing her slender waist, in a pale-yellow little hat, light as a pastry. Behind them a tall footman with big side-whiskers and a whole dozen collars stopped and opened his snuffbox.

Kovalyov drew nearer, stuck out the batiste collar of his shirtfront, arranged his medals dangling on a golden chain and, smiling to all sides, turned his attention to the light little lady who, like a spring flower, inclined slightly and brought her little white hand with its semi-transparent fingers to her brow. The smile on Kovalyov's face spread still further when he saw from under her hat

her little round chin of bright whiteness and part of a
cheek flushed with the color of the first spring rose. But
suddenly he leapt back as if burned. He remembered
that in place of a nose he had absolutely nothing, and
tears came to his eyes. He turned around in order to say
straight out to the gentleman in the uniform that he was
only posing as a state councillor, that he was a swindler
and a scoundrel and that he was nothing more than
merely his own nose. . . . But the nose was already gone:
he had managed to gallop off, probably again to visit
someone or other.

This plunged Kovalyov into despair. He went back
and stopped for a minute under the colonnade, attentively looking in all directions in case the nose might
turn up somewhere. He remembered distinctly that the
hat he was wearing had a plume and his uniform was
embroidered in gold; but he hadn't noticed his overcoat,
nor the color of his carriage, nor the horses, nor even
whether he had some kind of servant in the rear and in
what livery. Furthermore such a quantity of carriages
flew back and forth, and with such speed, that it was
difficult even to distinguish them; but even if he had
distinguished one of them, he would have had no means
whatsoever of stopping it. The day was fine and sunny.
On the Nevsky it was thick with people; an entire flow-
ery waterfall of ladies flowed along the whole sidewalk,
from the Police to the Anichkin Bridge. There went a
court councillor he knew whom he called "colonel," particularly if they happened to meet in the presence of
outsiders. There too was Yaryzhkin, the head clerk in
the senate, a great friend, who always lost at Boston
when he bid eight. There too was another major who
had received his assessorship in the Caucasus, waving
his hand so that he would come up to him. . . .

"Oh, the devil take it!" said Kovalyov. "Hey coachman, take me straight to the chief of police!"

Kovalyov got into the droshky and merely shouted to
the coachman, "Full speed ahead!"

"Is the chief of police in?" he cried, entering the hall.

"Not at all," answered the doorman, "he just left."

"How do you like that!"

"Yes," added the doorman, "not even so long ago,

but he left. If you had come just a minute earlier, then, perhaps, you would have found him at home."

Kovalyov, not taking the handkerchief from his face, got into the carriage and shouted in a despairing voice:

"Let's go!"

"Where?" said the coachman.

"Straight ahead!"

"What do you mean straight ahead? There's a turn here; right or left?"

This question stopped Kovalyov and made him think again. In his position he ought first of all to consult the Board of Security, not because it had direct connection with the police, but because its disposition of the affair might be much quicker than in other places; to seek satisfaction from the heads of the place in which the nose claimed to work would be senseless, because from the nose's own answers one could already see that for this person nothing was sacred and he could be lying in this case as he had lied in asserting that he had never associated with him. So, Kovalyov was already going to order the coachman to drive to the Board of Security, when the thought again came to him that this swindler and cheat who already at their first meeting had acted in such an unscrupulous manner, could again, conveniently making use of the time, somehow slip out of town, and then all searches would be in vain or could continue, which God forbid, for a whole month. Finally, it seemed, heaven itself brought him to his senses. He decided to go straight to the newspaper office and place a timely ad with a detailed description of all the specifications so that anyone meeting the nose could at that very minute present him to him or at least let him know of his where-abouts. So, having decided on this, he ordered the coach-man to drive to the newspaper office and didn't stop pummelling him on the back with his fist, the whole way repeating, "Faster, you scoundrel, faster, you rogue!" "Ekh, master!" the coachman would say, shaking his head and lashing with the reins at the horse whose coat was as long as a lapdog's. The droshky at last stopped, and Kovalyov, gasping for breath, ran into a small recep-tion room where a gray-haired clerk in an old tailcoat and glasses sat at a table and, holding a pen in his teeth, was counting the small change that had been brought in.

"Who here takes notices?" shouted Kovalyov. "Oh, hello!"

"My respects," said the gray-haired clerk, raising his eyes for a minute and lowering them again to the distributed piles of money.

"I wish to print. . . ."

"If you please. Kindly wait a bit," said the clerk, marking a figure on the paper with one hand and advancing two beads on the abacus with the fingers of his left hand. A servant with gold braid and an appearance showing he lived in an aristocratic house stood by the table with a note in his hands, and saw fit to show his worldliness. "Would you believe it, sir, that the mutt isn't worth eight kopeks, that is I wouldn't even give eight kopeks for her, but the countess loves her, I swear to God she loves her, and so the one who finds her gets a hundred rubles! To put it decently, that is, the way you and I are now conversing, people's tastes are entirely incompatible; if you're a hunter then keep a pointer or poodle; don't spare five hundred, pay a thousand, but at least let it be a good dog."

The worthy clerk listened to this with a significant air and at the same time made up the estimate: how many letters were there in the note brought in. At the sides stood a quantity of old ladies, merchant assistants and porters with advertisements. In one it was advertised that a coachman of sober conduct was released for service; in another—a little-used carriage imported in 1814 from Paris; there a housemaid of nineteen experienced in laundering, suitable also for other kinds of work, was available; a solid droshky missing one spring; a fiery young dapple-gray horse seventeen years old; new turnip and radish seeds received from London; a dacha with all conveniences: with two stalls for horses and a place where one could start an excellent birch or pine grove; there too was a summons to those wanting to buy old shoe soles with the invitation to appear at the bidding every day from eight to three o'clock in the morning. The room in which all this company was contained was small, and the air in it was exceptionally thick; but collegiate assessor Kovalyov couldn't smell anything because he covered himself with the handkerchief and because his actual nose was God knows where.

"Dear sir, allow me to ask you . . . I badly need . . ." he said at last with impatience.

"Right away, right away! . . . 2 rubles 43 kopeks! In a minute! One ruble 64 kopeks!" the gray-haired gentleman was saying, throwing advertisements in the faces of the old ladies and the porters. "What do you want?" he said at last, turning to Kovalyov.

"I beg you . . ." said Kovalyov, "a swindle or a hoodwinking has occurred, I am still quite unable to find out which. I ask you only to print that he who presents that scoundrel to me will receive a suitable reward."

"Permit me to ask, what is your name?"

"No, why my name? I can't tell it. I have many acquaintances: Chekhtaryova, the state councillor's wife, Pelageya Grigorievna Podtochina, the staff officer's wife . . . they might find out, God forbid! You can simply write: collegiate assessor, or still better, one being of the rank of major."

"And the one who ran off was your house serf?"

"What house serf? That wouldn't even be such a big swindle! What ran off was . . . my nose. . . ."

"Hm! What a strange name! And did this Mr. Nosov steal a large sum from you?"

"My nose, that is . . . you don't understand! My nose, my own nose, has disappeared somewhere unknown. The devil wanted to play a joke on me!"

"But in what way did it disappear? There's something I can't quite understand."

"But I can't tell you how; the main thing is that he's now driving all over town and calling himself a state councillor. And therefore I ask you to announce that anyone capturing him should immediately present him to me as soon as possible. Judge for yourself, after all, how am I to go around without such a prominent part of the body? It's not as if it were some little toe which I can stick in a boot—and no one will see if it's missing. I go to the state councillor's wife Chekhtaryova on

Thursdays: Podtochina Pelageya Grigorievna, the field officer's wife, and she has a very pretty daughter, are also very close acquaintances, and you yourself can judge how I feel now. . . . Now I can't show myself to them."

The clerk pondered this, which his firmly compressed lips attested.

"No, I cannot place such an advertisement in the papers," he said at last after a long silence.

"What? Why?"

"Because. The newspaper might lose its reputation. If everyone starts writing that his nose has run away, then. . . . Even so they already say that a lot of absurdities and false rumors are printed."

"But in what way is this matter absurd? Here, it seems, there is nothing of the sort."

"It seems to you that there isn't. But last week there was just such a case. A clerk came in, the same way you came in now, brought in an advertisement, the bill came to 2 rubles 73 kopeks, and the whole advertisement consisted in the fact that a poodle with a black coat had run away. You'd think, what could be the harm in that? But it turned out to be a libel: that poodle was a treasurer, I don't remember of what department."

"But after all I'm not asking you to advertise about a poodle, but about my own nose: that is, almost the same thing as about me myself."

"No, I can in no way put in such an announcement."

"Even when my nose has, precisely, disappeared!"

"If it has disappeared, then it's a doctor's affair. They say that there are such people who can stick on any kind of a nose you want. However, I remark that you must be a man of merry nature who loves to have a joke in society."

"I swear to you, as God is holy! Perhaps, if it's come to that, I'll show you."

"Why trouble yourself!" continued the clerk, sniffing snuff. "However, if it's no trouble," he added with a gesture of curiosity, "then it would be desirable to have a look."

The collegiate assessor took the handkerchief from his face.

"Indeed, extraordinarily strange!" said the clerk, "an entirely smooth space, as if it were a freshly fried pancake. Yes, flat to an incredible degree!"

"Well, are you going to argue even now? You see for yourself that it's impossible not to print it. I will be particularly grateful to you; and I'm glad that this incident has given me the pleasure of meeting you. . . ." The major, as is evident from this, decided on this occasion to be a little low.

"Printing it, of course, is a trivial affair," said the clerk, "only I don't foresee any advantage for you in it. If you really want, give it to someone who has an artful pen to describe it as a rare phenomenon of nature and print the little article in *The Northern Bee* (here he again took a pinch of snuff) for the edification of youth (here he wiped his nose) or simply for general curiosity."

The collegiate assessor felt completely hopeless. He lowered his eyes to the bottom of the newspaper where the information about performances was; his face was already ready to smile on encountering the name of an actress, very attractive, and his hand felt for his pocket: did he have a five-ruble note on him, because field officers, in Kovalyov's opinion, should sit in the best seats—but the thought of his nose ruined everything!

The clerk himself, it seemed, was touched by Kovalyov's difficult position. Wishing to lighten his grief somewhat, he saw fit to express his sympathy in a few words: "It is, to be sure, very distressing to me that such a funny thing should have happened to you. Wouldn't you like to take a pinch of snuff? It dispells headaches and melancholy moods: it's good even in regard to hemorrhoids." Saying this, the clerk offered his snuffbox to Kovalyov, rather deftly opening the lid with a portrait of some lady in a hat.

This thoughtless action made Kovalyov lose all patience. "I don't understand how you can see fit to joke," he said with feeling, "can't you see that I don't have precisely that with which I could sniff? The devil take your snuff! I can't even look at it now, and not only at your wretched *Beryozinsky*, but even if you offered me rapé itself." Having said this, he went out of the newspaper office deeply vexed, and set off for the district police

superintendent, an extraordinary lover of sugar. In his
house the whole foyer, it and the dining room, was
stacked with sugar loaves which merchants had brought
him out of friendship. The cook at that moment was
taking off the district superintendent's regulation
Wellington boots; his sword and all his martial armor
already hung peaceably in the corners, and his three-
year-old son was already fingering his formidable three-
cornered hat; and he, after a fierce fighting life, was preparing to taste the pleasures of peace.

Kovalyov went in to him at the moment when he
stretched, grunted, and said, "Ekh, I'll sleep gloriously
for two hours!" And therefore one could predict that
the arrival of the collegiate assessor was entirely mis-
timed. And I don't know, even if he had brought him
several pounds of tea or some cloth at this time, he
would not have been received too joyfully. The superintendent was a great patron of all arts and manufactur-
ings, but he preferred the government banknote to
everything. "That's the thing," he would usually say,
"there's nothing better than this thing: it doesn't ask for
food, takes up little space, will always fit in the pocket,
you drop it—it won't break."

The superintendent received Kovalyov rather drily
and said that after dinner was not the time to carry on
an investigation, that nature herself had ordained that,
having eaten, one should rest a bit (from this the collegiate assessor could see that the pronouncements of the
ancient wise men were not unknown to the district superintendent), that they don't pull the nose off a respectable man and that there are plenty of all sorts of majors
in the world who don't even have their underwear in
decent condition and who hang around all sorts of indecent places.

That is, right between the eyes! It is necessary to remark
that Kovalyov was a man exceptionally easy to offend. He
could forgive anything which might be said about himself, but he could not forgive it at all if it related to
rank or profession. He even considered that in theatrical
presentations one could permit anything which related
to field officers, but one ought not to attack superior
officers in any way. The reception of the superintendent

so disconcerted him that he shook his head and said with a sense of dignity, somewhat spreading his arms: "I confess, after such insulting remarks on your part, I have nothing to add . . ." and went out.

He came home scarcely able to stand on his feet. It was already dark. His apartment seemed sad or exceedingly disgusting to him after all these unsuccessful searches. Entering the foyer he saw on the dirty leather divan his servant Ivan, who, lying on his back, was spitting at the ceiling and kept hitting the same spot rather successfully. The indifference of the man enraged him; he struck him on the forehead with his hat, saying: "You pig, you're always doing stupid things!"

Ivan leapt up suddenly from his place and rushed full speed to help him off with his cloak.

Going into his room, the major, tired and sad, threw himself into an armchair and at last after several sighs, said: "My God! My God! Why such a misfortune? Were I without an arm or a leg—it would still be better; were I without ears—wretched, but still more bearable; but without a nose a man is the devil knows what: neither fish nor fowl; simply take him and throw him out the window! And at least if it had been cut off at war or in a duel, or if I myself had been the cause: but it actually disappeared for no reason at all, disappeared for nothing, not for a kopek! . . . Only no, it can't be," he added, having thought a bit. "It's incredible that a nose should disappear; incredible by any means. This, probably, is either a dream or simply a daydream; perhaps somehow by mistake I drank the vodka I rub my beard with after shaving instead of water. Ivan, that fool, didn't take it away and I, probably, picked it up." In order really to convince himself that he wasn't drunk, the major pinched himself so painfully that he shrieked. This pain completely convinced him that he was acting and living in a waking state. He stealthily approached the mirror and at first shut his eyes tight with the thought that perhaps the nose would appear in its place; but at this very minute he leapt back, saying: "What a libellous appearance!"

This was, precisely, incomprehensible. If a button had disappeared, a silver spoon, a watch or something like that; but to disappear, and from whom to disappear?

And furthermore in his own apartment! . . . Major Kovalyov, weighing all the circumstances, considered it almost the closest of all to the truth that the blame for this should belong to none other than the field officer's wife Podtochina, who wished him to marry her daughter. He himself liked to flirt with her, but he avoided a final resolution. When the field officer's wife announced to him straight out that she wanted to marry her to him, he quietly weighed anchor with his compliments, saying that he was still young, that he had to serve for about five years so that he would be exactly forty-two. And therefore the field officer's wife, probably for revenge, had decided to ruin him and hired some kind of peasant sorceresses for this, because it was in no way possible to suppose that the nose had been cut off—no one came into his room; the barber Ivan Yakovlevich shaved him only on Wednesday, and all during Wednesday and even all Thursday his nose was whole—this he remembered and knew very well; besides he would have felt pain, and, without doubt, a wound wouldn't heal so fast and be flat as a pancake. He made plans in his head; either to summon the field officer's wife to court in the formal manner or to go to her himself and expose her. His deliberations were interrupted by a light shining through all the chinks of the door which indicated that the candle in the foyer had already been lit by Ivan. Soon Ivan himself appeared, carrying it in front of himself and brightly illuminating the whole room. Kovalyov's first gesture was to grab the handkerchief and cover the place where yesterday his nose had still been, so that the stupid man would not indeed start gaping, seeing such a peculiarity in his master.

Ivan hadn't managed to go off to his lair when an unfamiliar voice was heard in the foyer saying, "Does collegiate assessor Kovalyov live here?"

"Come in—Major Kovalyov is here," said Kovalyov, leaping up quickly and opening the door.

There entered a police officer of handsome appearance, with sidewhiskers not too light and not too dark, with rather full cheeks, the very same one who at the beginning of the story was standing at the end of the Isakievsky Bridge.

"You were pleased to lose your nose?"

"Just so."

"It is now found."

"What did you say?" cried Major Kovalyov. Joy made him lose his tongue. He stared at the officer standing before him, on whose full lips and cheeks the flickering light of the candle flashed brightly. "How?"

"By a strange coincidence: they caught him almost on the road. He had already gotten into a stagecoach and wanted to go to Riga. And his passport has been issued long ago in the name of a certain official. And the strange thing is that I myself at first took him for a gentleman. But, fortunately, my glasses were with me, and I at once saw that this was a nose. You see, I'm nearsighted and if you stand in front of me, I see only that you have a face, but I notice neither nose nor beard nor anything. My mother-in-law, that is, the mother of my wife, doesn't see anything either."

Kovalyov was beside himself.

"Where is he? Where? I'll go at once."

"Don't trouble yourself. I, knowing that you needed it, brought it with me. And the strange thing is that the chief accomplice in this affair is that scoundrel the barber on Voznesensky Prospect, who is now sitting in prison. I have long suspected him of drunkenness and thievery and only the day before yesterday he filched a dozen buttons in a certain shop. Your nose is exactly as it was." With this the officer dipped into his pocket and took out the nose wrapped in a piece of paper.

"That's it!" cried Kovalyov, "exactly it! Have a cup of tea with me today."

"I would consider it a great pleasure, but I couldn't possibly: from here I have to drop in on the House of Correction. . . . The high prices of all supplies have risen very greatly. . . . I have living in my house both my mother-in-law, that is, the mother of my wife, and the children; the eldest especially gives great promise: a very smart little boy, but there are absolutely no means whatsoever for his education."

Kovalyov caught on and, grabbing a ten-ruble note from the table, thrust it into the hands of the policeman who, having bowed, went out the door and almost at that very moment Kovalyov already heard his voice on the street, where he was admonishing with his fists a certain stupid peasant who had ridden right onto the boulevard with his wagon.

The collegiate assessor, upon the departure of the policeman, for some minutes remained in a kind of undefinable state and after some minutes hardly regained the ability to see and feel, to such oblivion had the unexpected joy reduced him. He carefully took the restored nose in both cupped hands and once again inspected it attentively.

"That's it, exactly it!" said Major Kovalyov. "Here is even the pimple on the left side which popped up yesterday." The major almost burst out laughing from joy.

But there is nothing enduring in this world, and therefore even joy in the second minute is already not as acute as in the first; in the third minute it becomes still weaker and finally merges unnoticeably with the usual condition of the soul, as a circle on the water, caused by the fall of a pebble, finally merges with the smooth surface. Kovalyov began to think and realized that the affair was still not finished: the nose was found, but after all it had to be attached, put in its place.

"And what if it won't stay put?"

At such a question, posed to himself, the major paled.

With a feeling of inexpressible terror he dashed to the table, brought the mirror over in order not to somehow put the nose on crooked. His hands trembled. Carefully and cautiously he laid it on its former spot. Oh, horror! The nose wouldn't stick! . . . He brought it to his mouth, warmed it slightly with his breath and again applied it to the smooth spot situated between his two cheeks; but the nose would in no way stay on.

"Come on, come on now, get on, you fool!" he said to it. But the nose was as if wooden and fell on the table with such a strange sound, as if it were a cork. The major's face contorted spasmodically. "Will it really not grow back on?" he said in fright. But however many times he brought it to its proper place, his efforts were unsuccessful as before.

He called Ivan and sent him for the doctor who rented the best apartment in the same house on the ground floor. This doctor was a fine-looking man, had beautiful pitch-black sidewhiskers, a fresh, healthy wife, ate fresh apples in the morning and kept his mouth in a state of unusual cleanliness, rinsing it every morning for almost three quarters of an hour and brushing his teeth with five different sorts of brushes. The doctor appeared right away. Having asked how long ago the misfortune occurred, he lifted Major Kovalyov by the chin and gave him a flick with his thumb in the very place where his nose had formerly been, so that the major had to throw his head back with such force that he hit the back of his head against the wall. The medic said that this was nothing, and, advising him to move away from the wall a bit, ordered him to bend his head at first to the right side and, having felt the place where his nose had formerly been, said: "Hm!" Then he ordered him to bend his head to the left side and said: "Hm!" And in conclusion again gave him a flick with his thumb so that Major Kovalyov jerked his head like a horse whose teeth are being inspected. Having performed this experiment, the medic shook his head and said:

"No, it's impossible. You had better just stay like that, because it might make it even worse. It can, of course, be attached; I could, probably, attach it right now for you; but I assure you that it would be worse for you."

"That's a fine thing! How am I to remain without a nose?" said Kovalyov. "It can't be any worse than it is now. This is simply the devil knows what! Where can I show myself with such a libel? I have important acquaintances: even today I have to be at parties in two houses. I am acquainted with many: the state councillor's wife Chekhtaryova, Podtochina the field officer's wife . . . although after her present action I have no further business with her other than through the police. Do me a favor," said Kovalyov in a pleading voice, "isn't there a way? Stick it on somehow; even if not so nicely, just so it would hold; I can even prop it up slightly with my hand in dangerous situations. Furthermore I don't even dance, which might harm it by some careless motion. As regards appreciation of the visit, rest assured, as much as my means permit. . . ."

"Would you believe," said the doctor in a voice nei-

ther loud nor soft, but exceptionally persuasive and hyp-
notic, "that I never practice out of self-interest? That is
against my principles and my art. True, I take money
for my visits, but solely in order not to offend by refusal.
Of course, I could attach your nose; but I assure you on
my honor, if by now you don't believe my word, that it
will be much worse. Better leave it to the action of nature herself. Wash more often with cold water, and I
assure you that you, not having a nose, will be just as
healthy as if you had one. And the nose I advise you to
put in a bottle with spirits or still better to pour in two
tablespoons of strong spirits and heated vinegar, and
then you can get considerable money for it. I'll even
take it myself, if you don't set too high a price."

"No, no! I won't sell it for anything!" shrieked the
despairing Major Kovalyov. "Better let it disappear!"

"Excuse me!" said the doctor, bowing his farewell, "I
wanted to be of help to you . . . what can one do! At
least you have seen my effort."

Having said this, the doctor walked out of the room
with a majestic air. Kovalyov didn't notice even his face
and in deep numbness saw only the cuffs of his shirt,
white and clean as snow, peeking out of the sleeves of
his black frockcoat.

The next day he decided, before registering a complaint, to write to the field officer's wife to see if she
would agree without a fight to return him what was
proper. The letter was of the following content:

Dear Madam,
            Alexandra Grigorievna!
    I cannot understand this strange action on your part.
Rest assured that, acting in this way, you will gain nothing and will in no way force me to marry your daughter. Believe that the affair relating to my nose is
completely known to me, equally as is the fact that you
are the chief accomplice in this, and no one else. Its
sudden separation from its place, its escape and mas-
querade, first in the form of a certain official, and then
finally in its own form, is nothing more than the consequence of sorcery effected by you or by those who
practice similar noble pursuits. I for my part consider

it my duty to forewarn you that if the above-mentioned nose is not in its place this very day, I will be obliged to seek the defense and protection of the law.

However, with complete respect for you, I have the honor to be

Your faithful servant
Platon Kovalyov

Dear Sir,
    Platon Kuzmich!
Your letter surprised me exceedingly. I, I confess to you openly, in no way expected this, in particular as regards the unjust reproaches on your part. I wish to inform you that I have never received the official whom you mentioned in my house either masquerading or in his real form. It is true that Filipp Ivanovich Potanchikov has been coming to my house. And although he, precisely, sought the hand of my daughter, being himself of good, sober conduct and great erudition, I never gave him any hope. You also mention a nose. If you mean by this that I wanted to lead you by the nose, that is to give you a formal refusal, then it surprises me that you yourself speak of this when I, as you know, was of the entirely opposite opinion, and if you pledge yourself to my daughter in legal fashion right now, I am ready to satisfy you at once, for this has always been the object of my most heartfelt desire, in the hope of which I remain always at your service

Alexandra Podtochina

"No," said Kovalyov, having read the letter. "She is clearly not guilty. It can't be! The letter is written in a way a person guilty of a crime couldn't write." The collegiate assessor was an expert in this because he had several times been sent on investigations when still in the Caucasus. "By what means, then, by what fates did this happen? Only the devil can make this out!" he said at last, in despair.

Meanwhile rumors about this extraordinary occurrence were spreading around the entire capital and, as always, not without certain additions. At that time everyone's minds were particularly disposed to the extraordinary: recently experiments with the effects of hypnotism had been occupying the whole town. Furthermore the story of the dancing chairs in Konyushennaya Street was still fresh, and therefore there is nothing surprising in the fact that they soon began to say that collegiate assessor Kovalyov's nose takes a stroll on Nevsky Prospect exactly at three o'clock. A multitude of curious people flocked there every day. Someone said that the nose was to be found in Junker's store; and next to Junker's there was such a crowd and a press that even the police had to intervene. One speculator of respectable appearance, with sidewhiskers, who sold assorted dry pastries at the entrance to the theatre, purposely set up excellent solid wooden benches on which he invited the curious to stand for 80 kopeks per visitor. One estimable corporal left his house early just for this purpose and with great difficulty made his way through the crowd; but, to his great indignation, he saw in the window of the store, instead of a nose, an ordinary woolen sweater and a lithograph which depicted a girl adjusting her stocking, and a dandy with an open waistcoat and a small beard looking at her from behind a tree—a picture which had been continually hanging in the same place for already more than ten years. Walking away, he said with annoyance: "How can one fool people with such stupid and improbable rumors?" Then the rumor went around that Major Kovaliov's nose was strolling not on Nevsky Prospect, but in the Tauride Gardens, that he had already been there a long time, that when Khozrev-Mirza* still lived there he used to be very surprised by this strange trick of nature. Some of the students of the surgical academy set off thither. One aristocratic, respectable lady asked the keeper of the garden in a special letter to show her child this rare phenomenon with, if possible, an explanation instructive and informative for the young.

Exceptionally delighted by all these events were all the men about town, the indispensable frequenters of soirées, who liked to amuse the ladies and whose re-

---

*A Persian prince, in Petersburg in 1829 in connection with the murder in Persia of the Russian ambassador, the writer A. S. Griboedov. He stayed in the Tauride Palace.

sources at that time were entirely exhausted. A small portion of respectable and well-intentioned people was exceptionally dissatisfied. One gentleman said with indignation that he didn't understand how in our present enlightened century absurd inventions could spread, and that he was surprised that the government paid no attention to it. This gentleman, as is evident, belonged to the number of those gentlemen who would like to involve the government in everything, even in their daily fights with their wives. Following this. . . but here again the whole event is covered in fog, and what happened next is absolutely unknown.

3

Perfect nonsense goes on in the world. Sometimes there is absolutely no plausibility whatsoever: suddenly that very nose which had been riding around with the rank of state councillor and caused so much fuss in the town showed up again, just as if nothing had happened, in its place, that is, precisely between the two cheeks of Major Kovalyov. This happened already on the seventh of April. Waking up and inadvertently glancing in the mirror, he sees: his nose! Feel it—a nose exactly! "Ehe!" said Kovalyov and in his joy almost danced the gopak all around his room barefoot, but Ivan coming in deterred him. He ordered him to give him his washing things at once and, washing, glanced again in the mirror: a nose. Wiping himself with the towel he again glanced in the mirror: a nose!

"Look, Ivan, it seems I have sort of a pimple on my nose," he said, meanwhile thinking, "It would be awful if Ivan said: Oh no, sir, not only no pimple, but there's no nose!"

But Ivan said: "It's nothing, sir, no pimple: a clean nose!"

"Great, the devil take it!" said the major to himself and snapped his fingers. At that moment the barber Ivan Yakovlevich peeked in the door, but as timidly as a kitten which has just been whipped for stealing lard:

"Tell me first: are your hands clean?" Kovalyov shouted to him when he was still at a distance.

"Clean."

"Liar!"

"I swear to God they're clean, sir."

"Well, look out."

Kovalyov sat down. Ivan Yakovlevich covered him with a napkin and in one instant, with the help of a brush, turned his whole beard and part of a cheek into cream such as they serve at merchants' name-day parties. "Look at that!" said Ivan Yakovlevich to himself, looking at the nose, and then he turned his head to the other side and looked at it sideways. "There it is! How do you like that!" he continued and looked at the nose for a long time. At last, lightly, with a caution which can only be imagined, he raised two fingers in order to seize it by the tip. Such was Ivan Yakovlevich's system.

"Now, now, now, look out!" screamed Kovalyov. Ivan Yakovlevich simply dropped his hands, stopped dead, and grew embarrassed as he had never been embarrassed. At last, he carefully began to tickle him under the beard with the razor, and although it was difficult and not at all handy for him to shave without holding onto the olfactory part of the body, nonetheless, somehow or other bracing himself with his rough thumb against the Major's cheek and lower jaw, he at last overcame all obstacles and finished shaving him.

When everything was ready, Kovalyov hurried to dress right away, took a cab and drove straight to the pastry shop. Entering, he called out still from a distance: "Boy, a cup of chocolate!" and the same minute turned to the mirror: there's the nose. He gaily turned around and with a satiric expression looked, somewhat squinting, at two soldiers, one of whom had a nose not the least bit bigger than a vest button. After this he set off for the office of the department where he was soliciting a vice-governor's job, or in case of failure, an executor's. Going through the reception room he glanced in the mirror: there's the nose. Then he went to see another collegiate assessor or major, a great scoffer, to whom he often said in answer to various nosy remarks: "Well, you, I know you, you're a sharp one!" On the way he thought: "If even the Major doesn't burst out laughing on seeing me, then it's a sure sign that everything, whatever it be, sits in its own place." But the collegiate assessor didn't say anything. "Great, great, the devil take it," thought Kovalyov to himself. On the way he met the field officer's wife Podtochina together with her daughter, bowed to them and was met with joyous exclamations, it must be all right, he hadn't undergone any damage. He talked with them for a very long time, and deliberately taking out his snuffbox, kept stuffing his nose at both entrances for an extremely long time in front of them, adding to himself, "There you are, womankind, stupid hens! And all the same I won't marry the daughter! Simply for fun, *par amour*—by all means!" And from then on Major Kovalyov went about as if nothing had happened, on Nevsky Prospect, to the theatres, and everywhere. And the nose too, as if nothing had happened, sat on his face, not giving even the appearance that it had been running around elsewhere. And thereafter Major Kovalyov was always seen in a good humor, smiling, pursuing absolutely all the pretty ladies and even stopping on one occasion in front of a stall in the Gostiny Dvor and buying the ribbon of some order, it is not known for what reason, because he himself was not the chevalier of any order.

That's the kind of incident that happened in the northern capital of our vast empire. Only now, on thinking it all over, we see that there is much that is implausible in it. Not to mention the really strange supernatural separation of the nose and its appearance in various places in the form of a state councillor—how could Kovalyov not realize that one cannot advertise for a nose through the newspaper office? I don't here mean it in the sense that it seemed to me a lot to pay for the advertisement; that's nonsense, and I am not at all one of those mercenary people. But it's indecent, indelicate, improper! And then again—how did the nose appear in a baked bread and what about Ivan Yakovlevich himself? . . . No, I don't understand this at all, I absolutely don't understand! But what is stranger, what is least comprehensible of all, is how authors can choose such subjects. I confess, this is entirely inconceivable, it's exactly . . . no, no, I don't understand at all. In the first place, it is of absolutely no benefit to the fatherland; in the second place . . . but even in the second place there's also no benefit. I simply don't know what it is. . . .

But yet with all this, although, of course, one may admit this, that and the other, may even . . . and after all, where aren't there incongruities? But all the same, when you think about it, there is something, really, in all this. No matter what anyone says, such things happen in the world; rarely, but they happen.

The Carriage

The little town had grown much livelier since the cavalry regiment had been quartered there. It had been incredibly dull before. When you drove through the town, the sour expression with which the dirty little houses stared out into the street depressed you in a way difficult to convey: you felt as though you'd been cleaned out at cards or had made a terrible fool of yourself. In a word, you did not feel good. Plaster had fallen off the houses, turning them from white to piebald. The roofs were thatched with reeds as in most of our southern towns. And, a long time ago, one of the town's mayors had ordered the front gardens done away with to make things look neater. You ran little risk of meeting anyone, except perhaps some rooster that happened to be crossing the street—a street as soft as a pillow with dust, the kind that turns to mud with the lightest rain. And with rain, the streets would become crowded with fat animals which the mayor liked to refer to as "Frenchmen." They sat in their mud baths, thrusting their great snouts out and grunting so loud that a traveler thought of nothing but whipping up his horses and getting away. But at that time only very few travelers passed through the town at all.

Occasionally, very occasionally, some landowner with about eleven serfs on his estate and wearing an alpaca coat would rattle over the cobblestones in something looking like a cross between a cart and a carriage, peering out from among flour bags and urging on his bay mare, beside which trotted a colt. Even the marketplace was gloomy. The tailor's shop, idiotically enough, is not

53

parallel with the street but sticks out into it at an angle. On the other side, some sort of stone building with two windows has been under construction for fifteen years. Further, there is a wooden stall standing by itself, painted gray to match the mud, which was originally intended as a model for others. It is the creation of the mayor when he was still young, before he had taken to afternoon naps and drinking a concoction with dried gooseberries in it in the evenings.

For the rest, in the marketplace, wattle fencing takes the place of stalls. In its center stand the smallest shops in which you were always sure to see a dozen pretzels on a string, a peasant woman in red kerchief, forty pounds of soap, a few pounds of bitter almonds, buckshot, lengths of cotton material, and two shop assistants who spent their time playing quoits in front of the door.

But after the arrival of the cavalry regiment, all this changed. The streets came to life, gained color, in a word, became unrecognizable. Now the low houses would often see some elegant officer with plumed headgear going to see a brother officer, to discuss promotion, good tobacco, and sometimes, in secret from the general, to play cards, staking the carriage which might as well be described as regimental since it was owned by all the officers in turn: one day it was the major who rolled off in it, the next it was to be found in the lieutenant's stable, and, the day after that the major's orderly was greasing its axles once more. The wooden fences between the houses were decorated with soldiers' caps hanging in the sun. A gray greatcoat would somehow be hanging on a gate. In the small streets, one came across soldiers with mustachios as stiff as boot brushes. These mustachios were to be seen in all sorts of places. No sooner did a few housewives of the town gather in the marketplace, than a mustachio was sure to be peeking over their shoulders.

The officers brought life to society, which, until then, had consisted only of the judge, who was living with some deacon's wife, and the mayor, who was a fairly reasonable man but who slept literally all day long— from lunch to supper and from supper to lunch.

And social life became still more active and interesting

when the staff of the Brigadier General was quartered in the town. The landowners from all around, of whose existence no one would have guessed before, started coming into the little town. They wished to spend some time in the company of the officers, to play bank occasionally, a game which, until then, had been a mere blur in heads stuffed with crops, errands for wives, and the shooting of hare.

I am sorry I cannot remember the occasion which moved them to give a great dinner. The preparations were awe-inspiring. The clatter of the knives in the general's kitchen could be heard out beyond the edge of town. All the produce of the market was requisitioned for the dinner so that the judge and his deacon's wife were forced to eat flour-and-water pancakes with some fruit jelly. The courtyard of the house occupied by the general was crowded with all kinds of carriages. It was a strictly male affair, a dinner for the officers and the neighboring landowners.

Of the landowners, the most remarkable was Pythagoras Pythagorasovich Chertokutsky, a leading member of the local aristocracy. He made more noise than anyone else at the nobility's elections and drove a very elegant turnout. He had served in a cavalry regiment and had been one of its prominent and respected officers. At least, he was always to be seen at the regimental parties and gatherings, wherever the regiment happened to be quartered. But that can be verified with the ladies of the provinces of Tambov and Simbirsk. Possibly he would have extended his glory to other provinces had he not resigned because of a matter such as is usually referred to as an unpleasant business. Whether it was he who slapped someone or whether someone slapped him, I cannot say for sure, but he was asked to resign. This, however, did not affect his standing in the slightest.

Phythagoras Pythagorasovich always wore high-waisted, military-looking coats, spurs, and mustachios so that the local gentry should not be led to believe that he had served in the infantry, to which he referred scornfully as the footfantry, or sometimes the foottrottery. He never missed the many crowded fairs to which the heart of Russia, nannies, children, daughters and fat landowners, flocked to have a good time. They arrived in landaus, carriages, tarantasses, broughams, and vehicles such as no one has ever dreamt of. He would sort of smell out where the cavalry regiment was stationed and always came to see the officers. He would jump down very gracefully from his light calash or carriage and introduce himself with great ease of manner. During the last election he had given the gentry an excellent dinner and promised that if they elected him as their leader, he would set a tone of the utmost respectability. In a word, he behaved like a gentleman, as they put it in the provinces. He had married someone quite pretty and had acquired, along with her, an estate with two hundred serfs and a few thousand in capital.

The capital was immediately put to use in the acquisition of six really excellent horses, gilt locks for his doors, a tame monkey for the house, and a French butler. As to the two hundred serfs that had come with the dowry, they, like the two hundred he had had before, were mortgaged to finance a number of commercial ventures. In a word, a landowner.

Besides him, at the general's dinner, there were a few other landowners, but there is nothing to say about them. The rest were all officers of the regiment plus two officers from the general staff: a colonel and a very fat major. The general himself was there, a big, stout man who nevertheless had a reputation as a good commanding officer. He spoke in a rather thick, important bass voice.

The dinner was magnificent. The sturgeon, the white-fish, the asparagus, the quail, the partridges, and the mushrooms made it evident that the cook had not consumed any liquor since the day before. And the four soldiers assisting him had worked throughout the night, knives in hand, on the fricassee.

The myriads of bottles, the tall ones with claret, the short-necked ones with Madeira, the bright sunny day, the wide-open windows, the plates of ice chips in various spots on the table, the crumpled shirtfronts of the civilians, the brilliant conversation dominated by the general's voice and besprinkled with champagne—everything was in perfect harmony. The dinner over, they all rose from the table with a pleasant heavy feeling. The gentlemen lit their pipes and went out onto the terrace to drink their coffee.

"Now we can have a look at her," the general said. "Please, my dear fellow," he said, addressing his adjutant, a rather smart, pleasant-looking young man, "have the bay mare brought here." Then he turned back to the others. "You'll see for yourselves," he said.

At this point the general puffed at his pipe and let out a stream of smoke.

"She's not quite in shape yet. There's no decent stable in this damned backwater of a town. But she's—puff-puff—a very acceptable horse."

"How long have you had her, sir, puff-puff-puff?" Pythagoras Pythagorasovich asked.

"Puff-puff-puff, well . . . puff, not very long. I only got her from the stud farm a couple of years ago."

"Was she broken in when you got her, sir, or did you have her broken in here, sir?"

"Puff, puff, poo, poo . . . oo . . . ff . . . here," the general said, and disappeared in a cloud.

At that moment a soldier emerged from the stable, within which a trampling of hoofs could be heard. Then another soldier appeared who wore huge mustachios and a white smock and was leading by the bridle a quivering, nervous mare. Suddenly raising her head, she almost lifted the soldier, mustachios and all, off the ground, and he had to squat down to hold her.

"Come, quiet, Agrafena Ivanovna," the soldier said, leading the mare toward the porch.

The mare's name was Agrafena Ivanovna. She was strong and wild like a South-Russian beauty. Her hoofs drummed against the wooden porch and she suddenly stopped still.

The general took the pipe out of his mouth and started to look over Agrafena Ivanovna with obvious satisfaction. The colonel stepped down from the porch and personally took her by the muzzle. The major followed him out and patted the mare's leg. The rest of them clicked their tongues.

Pythagoras Pythagorasovich walked over toward her from behind. The soldier who was holding the horse by the bridle drew himself up, staring fixedly into the eyes of the guest as though he were about to jump on Pythagoras' back and gallop off.

"Very, very fine indeed," Pythagoras said, "a capital horse! And, sir, I suppose she's a wonderful trotter?"

"She goes well, to be sure . . . but . . . I'll be damned . . . that stupid vet gave her some kind of pill and since then she's been sneezing—for two days without letup."

"A very, very pretty beast. And may I ask, sir, do you have a carriage to go with her?"

"A carriage? But she's a riding horse."

"Of course, sir. I asked because I wondered whether you have carriages for your other horses?"

"Well, I must say I'm not too well fixed as far as carriages are concerned. . . . I must admit that for some time I've been hoping to get a modern calash. I wrote to my brother in St. Petersburg to that effect, but I don't know whether he'll send me one or not."

"I would think, sir," the colonel said, "that there are no better calashes than the Viennese ones."

"You're quite right, puff-puff-puff, to think so."

"I have, sir, a superlative calash of Viennese manufacture," Pythagoras Pythagorasovich said.

"Which one? The one you came in?"

"Oh no, sir. That one is just . . . to go places, that sort of thing. But the other . . . it is incredible how light it is. Like a feather. And, if you stepped into it, if you'll allow me to say so, sir, you'd feel as though your nanny were rocking you in your cradle."

"I suppose it's quite smooth then?"

"Very, very smooth. You know, pillows, springs, like a picture."

"Good, good."

"And it holds an incredible amount, sir. Personally, I've never seen anything like it. When I was an officer, sir, I managed to pack into its luggage space ten bottles of rum and twenty pounds of tobacco, six dress uniforms, underwear and two longest pipes imaginable. Moreover, sir, in the glove compartment, sir, there is room enough to stow a whole carcass of beef."

"Sounds good."

"I got it for four thousand, sir."

"Judging by the price, it must be a good one. You bought it yourself?"

"Oh no, sir, I got it by a stroke of luck. It was bought by a friend of mine, a childhood playmate, an exceptional man whom you'd have liked very much, sir, I'm sure. He and I, we were very close, sir. His or mine, it made no difference, you see, sir. I won the calash from him at cards. Won't you, sir, do me the honor of dining at my house tomorrow and at the same time having a look at the calash?"

"I don't know what to say. Alone . . . I feel rather, you know . . . Perhaps you would like me to come with other officers. . . ."

"I beg them to come too. It would be a great honor for me, gentlemen, to see you in my house."

The colonel, the major and the other officers thanked Pythagoras with well-mannered bows.

"I myself, sir, am of the opinion that if one buys a thing it should be good, and if it is not good it is not worth the trouble of getting it. And when you do me the honor of being my guest tomorrow, I will be bold enough to show you some items which I have introduced on my estate."

The general looked at him and puffed out some more smoke.

Pythagoras was very pleased at having invited the officers. He was already mentally working out the menu for the dinner—the meat pies, the sauces—while he looked gaily at his guests for the morrow. And they, on their part, became twice as amiable toward him, as could be gauged from their eyes and certain slight bodily movements such as little half bows, etc. Pythagoras, from then on, spoke with more familiarity and his voice acquired the languorous note of a man wallowing in satisfaction.

"And, sir, you will make the acquaintance of the mistress of the house."

"I'll be delighted," the general said, stroking his mustache.

At this point, Pythagoras would have liked to return home immediately to prepare everything for the next day's reception. He already had his hat in his hand, but somehow it happened that he stayed a little longer. In the meantime card tables were set out and the entire company broke up into groups of four and games of whist started in different parts of the room.

Candles were brought in. Pythagoras hesitated for a while over whether to sit down to a card table or not. But since the officers invited him to do so, he thought it would be unsociable to refuse. He sat down. Somehow a glass of punch appeared in front of him which, without thinking, he proceeded to empty. After a couple of rubbers, Pythagoras found another glass of punch at his elbow which, still absently, he downed, having said, "Really, gentlemen, I must be off." But he went on playing.

In the meantime, the conversations in various corners of the room became altogether individual. The players were quite silent. It was those who were not playing who talked among themselves.

In one corner a captain, sprawled on a sofa with a pillow under his ribs and a pipe between his teeth, was quite freely and smoothly relating his amorous adventures. He managed to hold the attention of the circle gathered around him. A remarkably fat landowner with very short arms, which looked rather like elongated potatoes, was listening to him with an understanding expression, only now and then attempting to pull his tobacco pouch out of the pocket of his coattail; his arm proved too short and his backside too wide. In another corner, a quite lively argument started on the subject of artillery drill, and Pythagoras, who had already played a knave for a queen twice, butted into this private discussion, shouting from his corner phrases like, "In what year was that?" or "In what regiment?" Frequently his questions had nothing to do with the subject under discussion.

Finally, a few minutes before supper, the actual game of whist stopped, although it continued in words. Pythagoras remembered distinctly that he had won quite a lot but somehow his hands had nothing to hold and when he got up from the table he stood like a man who has not even a handkerchief in his pocket. In the meantime, supper was served. Obviously, there was no shortage of wine and Pythagoras was forced by circumstances, almost involuntarily, to fill his own glass because there was always a bottle standing to the right and left of him.

The conversation was drawn out for a very, very long time. But it took rather a strange course. A landowner, who had been in the army during the 1812 campaign against Napoleon, told his listeners of a very hot engagement, so hot in fact that it had never taken place. And then, for completely unobvious reasons, he seized the stopper of the decanter and thrust it into a pie. In short, when the guests began to leave it was already close to three and the coachmen of certain personalities had to grab their masters as one grabs a package of groceries, and Pythagoras Pythagorasovich, for all his aristocratic background, bowed right and left with such zest as he was driven home that he arrived there with two thistles in his mustachio.

At home, everything was asleep. The coachman had trouble finding the valet, who saw his master across the drawing room and handed him over to a chambermaid, with whose help Pythagoras managed to reach his bedroom, where he collapsed next to his pretty young wife, lying there in a delightful pose in a snow-white nightgown. The commotion created by the fall of her husband woke her up. She stretched herself, raised her eyelashes, three times squeezed her eyes closed, then opened them with a half-angry smile. But seeing that her husband definitely was not disposed toward any amiabilities at that time, she turned over on her other side, resting her fresh cheek on her hand, and went back to sleep.

It was already beyond the hour which is considered early in the country when the young wife woke up next to her snoring husband. Remembering that he had come home at four in the morning and not wishing to awaken him, she slipped her feet into the slippers Pythagoras had ordered for her by mail from St. Petersburg. Then, clad in a white dressing gown which draped her like the waters of a fountain, she went into her bathroom, washed in water as fresh as herself and glanced into the mirror. She had a couple of peeps at herself and saw that she did not look at all bad that morning. This fact, which may seem insignificant, caused her to sit in front of the mirror for a little over two hours. Finally she dressed herself, with very good taste at that, and went out into the garden to get some fresh air.

As if on purpose, the weather was as superb as can be imagined, even for a summer day. The sun had reached the meridian and was heating the air with the full power of its rays. But it was cool on the shady paths, and the flowers, warmed by the sun, trebled their fragrance. The pretty lady of the house completely forgot that it was past noon and that her husband was still asleep. She could hear the snores of two coachmen and one groom who were already taking their afternoon nap in the stable beyond the garden. But she continued to sit in the thick shade from which the road could be seen, gazing absentmindedly at its emptiness.

Suddenly her attention was caught by a light cloud of dust rising in the distance. Soon she made out several carriages in single file coming toward her. The one in front was a light, two-seat calash and in it sat the general, his fat epaulets gleaming in the sun, with the colonel next to him. Behind was a four-seater with the major, the general's aide-de-camp, and two other officers facing. Behind it was the regimental chaise, mentioned earlier, now owned by the major. Behind that there was another four-seater of the type known as a *bon-voyage*. It contained five officers, one of them sitting on the knees of a comrade. Finally, behind it, there were three officers on three fine bays.

"Can they possibly be coming our way?" the young mistress of the estate thought. "Good heavens, they're actually turning off the main road."

She let out a little cry, clasped her hands and flew straight over the flower beds, trampling the flowers, into her husband's bedroom. He was sleeping like a log.

"Get up, get up, quickly!" she shouted, pulling him by the arm.

"Ah-ah," Pythagoras said without opening his eyes.

"Get up, sugar angel, come on, do you hear me? We have guests."

"What . . . what guests?" Having said that, he let out a restrained mooing like that of a calf trying to find his mother's teat. "Mmmm . . . give me . . . give me your neck, lovey-dovey, I want to kiss it."

"Pussycat, get up, for heaven's sake. Quick. The general and his officers. Oh, goodness me, you have a thistle in your mustachio."

"The general? He's already on his way? Why the hell wasn't I awakened? And the dinner . . . Now, is everything ready for the dinner?"

"What dinner?"

"The dinner I ordered."

"You ordered? But you came in at four in the morning and you didn't even answer when I spoke to you. And if I did not wake you up, lambkin, it was because I knew you hadn't slept all night, you poor dear. . . ."

These final words were uttered in a very languorous and beseeching tone.

Pythagoras Pythagorasovich lay in bed popeyed and motionless. Then he jumped up in just his nightshirt, forgetting that he was not even decent.

"I am nothing but a dumb horse," he exclaimed, slapping himself on the forehead with the palm of his hand. "I invited them to dinner. What are we going to do? How far are they?"

"I don't know . . . but they'll be here any minute."

"Hide yourself, love. Hey there, you, girl, come here, you fool! What are you afraid of? Some officers are about to arrive. You go and tell them that the master is not at home. Tell 'em he's not expected back, that he drove off early in the morning, you hear? And warn all the servants, understand?"

Having said this, he rushed to hide in the coach house. He had thought he would be quite safe, but as he stood in a corner, he began to fear that he might be found there too. A better idea flashed through his head. He let down the steps of the calash that stood there next to him, jumped inside, closed the door, and as a further precaution covered himself with the leather apron. And there, doubled up in his dressing gown, he remained completely silent.

In the meantime the cavalcade had driven up to the front porch.

The general got out first and shook himself. The colonel followed him, smoothing the plumes of his hat. Then the fat major jumped out of the four-seater, gripping his sword under his armpit. Then the slim lieutenants and the sublieutenant who had been sitting on someone's knees skipped out of their carriage. And finally the riders who had been showing off their bays got down too.

"The master is not at home," said a servant appearing on the porch.

"What do you mean not at home? Still, he'll be in for dinner, I suppose."

"No, sir. He left for the day and I don't expect him back before, perhaps, this time tomorrow."

"Well, I'll be damned," the general said. "How is that possible?"

"I must say it's quite some joke," the colonel said, laughing.

"No, but I still don't understand," said the general with obvious displeasure. "Goddammit! . . . If he can't receive us, why did he invite us?"

"I really don't understand, sir, how people can do such things," said one of the young officers.

"What?" said the general, who always used that interrogative when speaking to young subalterns.

"I was saying, sir, how is it possible to behave like that?"

"Naturally, naturally . . . Well, something may have happened. . . . Should have let us know at least—or then not invite us."

"Well then, sir, what can we do? Let's go back," the colonel said.

"Of course. There's nothing else left to do. But wait, we can still have a look at the calash. We don't need him for that. He can't have taken it with him. Hey, you there, come over here."

"Yes, sir?"

"You a stableman?"

"I am, sir."

"Then show us the new calash your master bought recently."

"If the gentlemen will be kind enough to follow me."

The general and his officers followed the stableman into the coach house.

"Here, sir. Shall I roll it out a bit? It's rather dark in here."

"All right, all right . . . that's good enough. Thank you."

The general and the officers walked all around the calash, carefully examining the wheels and the springs.

"Well, I don't see anything special about it," the general said. "Quite an ordinary calash, I'd say."

"Nothing much," the colonel said, "nothing remarkable in it."

"I wouldn't say it was worth four thousand, sir," one of the young officers said.

"What?"

"I was saying, sir, I don't think it could possibly be worth four thousand."

"Four thousand! It's not worth two. There's really nothing to it. Unless, of course, there's something special inside there. . . . Hey, fellow, unfasten this apron."

And before the eyes of the officers appeared Pythagoras Pythagorasovich, sitting, unbelievably contorted, in his dressing gown.

"Ah, there you are . . ." the general said, surprised.

Having said this, the general pushed the calash doors closed, put back the leather apron and rode off with his officers.

The Overcoat

In the department . . . but it's better not to say in which department. There is nothing more touchy than all sorts of departments, regiments, offices, and, in a word, all sorts of official bodies. Nowadays every private individual considers all of society insulted in his person. They say quite recently a petition circulated from a certain police inspector, I don't remember from which town, in which he clearly states that the government institutions are perishing and that his holy name is being pronounced absolutely in vain. And in proof he appended to the petition the hugest volume of some romantic composition, in which, every ten pages, a police inspector appears, in places even in a completely drunken state. And so, to avoid any unpleasantness, we had better call the department in question *a certain department.* And so, in *a certain department* served *a certain clerk,* a clerk one couldn't call very remarkable: of short stature, a little bit pocky, a little bit ruddy, even, to look at, a little bit squinty, with a small bald spot on top, with wrinkles along both sides of his cheeks and with a complexion that is called hemorrhoidal. . . . What can one do! The Petersburg climate is to blame. As regards rank (for among us before everything one must declare one's rank), he was what they call a perpetual titular councillor, about which, as is well known, various writers who have the praiseworthy habit of attacking those who can't bite back have japed and jibed their fill. The clerk's surname was Bashmachkin. By the very name it is already apparent that it at one time came from *bashmak,* shoe; but when, at what time and in what way it came from *bashmak,* nothing is known about this. The father and the grandfather and even the brother-in-law, and absolutely all the Bashmachkins went around in boots, only changing the soles about three times a year. His name and patronymic were Akaky Akakievich. Perhaps it will seem a bit strange and contrived to the reader, but it can be demonstrated that they didn't contrive it at all, but that such circumstances occurred of themselves that made it quite impossible to give him any other name, and it happened precisely like this: Akaky Akakievich was born, if only my memory doesn't deceive me, in the early hours of March 23rd. The late mother, a clerk's wife and a very good woman, arranged as is proper to christen the child. The mother still lay on the bed opposite the doors, while on her right hand stood the godfather, a most excellent person, Ivan Ivanovich Yeroshkin, who served as head clerk in the senate, and the godmother, the wife of a police officer, a woman of rare virtues, Arina Semyonovna Belobryushkova. They presented the mother with the choice of any three that she wanted to choose; Mokkiya, Sossiya, or to call the child after the martyr Khozdazat. "No," thought the late mother, "those are all such names." To satisfy her, they opened the calendar in another place; again three names turned up: Trifily, Dula and Varakhasy. "What an affliction," said the old lady, "what names they all are, I really never heard the like. At least if it were Varadat or Varukh, but Trifily and Varakhasy!" They turned another page—Pavsikaky and Vakhtisy turned up. "Well, I see already," said the old lady, "that clearly such is his fate. If it's like that, better let him be called after his father. The father was Akaky, so let the son be Akaky too." In this way Akaky Akakievich came about. They christened the baby, at which he burst out crying and made such a grimace, as if he foresaw that he would be a titular councillor. And so, that's the way all this came about. We mentioned this so that the reader could see for himself that this happened entirely by necessity and to give any other name was quite impossible. When and at what time he entered the department and who appointed him, this no one could recall. However often directors and all sorts of superiors were changed, he was always seen at one and the same place, in the same position, in the same post, the same copying clerk, so that later they were convinced that he, evidently, was born into this world already entirely finished, in a uniform and with a bald spot on his head. In the department he was shown no respect whatsoever. The porters not only did not get up from their places when he passed by, but didn't even glance at him, as if a simple fly had flown through the reception hall. Superiors treated him somehow coldly and despotically. Some department head's assistant would thrust papers right under his nose, not saying even: "Copy it," or, "Here's a nice little interesting case," or something pleasant, as is done in well-bred offices. And he would take it, looking only at the paper, not noticing who presented it to him and whether he had the right to. He would take it and right away get set to copy it. The young clerks laughed at him and made jokes about him to the degree that clerk wit permitted; right in front of him they told various stories that had been made up about him; about his landlady, a seventy-year-old lady, they said she beat him, asked when their wedding would be, scattered bits of paper on his head, calling it snow. But not one word would Akaky Akakievich answer to this, just as if nobody were in front of him; it didn't even affect his work: among all these annoyances he would not make a single mistake in writing. Only when the joke was too unbearable, when they jogged his elbow, keeping him from doing his work, he would say: "Leave me alone, why do you insult me?" And something strange was contained in the words and in the voice in which they were pronounced. In it resounded something so evoking of pity that one recently appointed young man who, by the example of the others, was on the verge of permitting himself to laugh at Akaky, suddenly stopped as if transfixed, and from that time on it was as if everything had changed for him and appeared in another form. Some preternatural force alienated him from the comrades he had become acquainted with, having taken them for decent, well-bred people. And long after, at the gaiest moments, the short little clerk with the bald spot on top would appear to him with his penetrating words: "Leave me alone, why do you insult me?" And in these penetrating words rang other words: "I am your brother." And the poor young man would cover his face with his hands, and many times later in his life he would shudder, seeing how much inhumanity there is in man, how much fierce coarseness is hidden in refined educated breeding, and, God! even in the very man whom the world deems noble and honorable.

Hardly anywhere could one find a man who so lived for his work. It is too little to say he worked zealously, no, he worked with love. There, in this copying, he saw a certain special varied and pleasant world all his own. Delight was expressed on his face; some letters were his favorites, and when he would come upon them he would be beside himself, chuckle, wink and work them along with his lips, so that on his face, it seemed, one could read every letter his pen produced. If they had rewarded him in proportion to effort, he, to his own amazement, perhaps might have even landed among the state councillors; but he earned, as the wits, his comrades, expressed it, a button in his buttonhole, and netted hemorrhoids in another hole. However, it cannot be said that no attention whatever was paid him. A certain director, being a kind man and wishing to reward him for his long service, ordered that he be given something a little more important than the usual copying; namely, he was told to readdress an already prepared case to another office; it was only a matter of changing the main heading and of here and there changing the verbs from the first person to the third. This gave him such difficulty that he broke into an utter sweat, wiped his brow and at last said: "No, better let me copy something." From then on they left him to copying forever. Outside of this copying, it seemed, nothing existed for him. He didn't think at all about his dress: his uniform was not green, but of some reddish-floury color. The collar on it was narrow and low so that his neck, although it wasn't long, seemed, coming out of the collar, unusually long, like on those plaster kittens with bobbing heads whole dozens of which foreign peddlers carry on their heads in Russia. And something or other was always sticking to his uniform: either a piece of straw or some thread or other;

furthermore he possessed the rare talent, walking along the street, of arriving under a window precisely at the very time when someone was throwing all sorts of rubbish out of it, and therefore he perpetually carried away watermelon and cantaloupe rinds and similar trash on his hat. Not once in his life had he paid attention to what is done and what goes on every day on the street, at which, as is well-known, his brother, the young clerk, will always look, sharpening his alert gaze to such acuity that he will even notice whose trouser strap has come undone on the other side of the pavement, which always summons a sly smile to his face.

But Akaky Akakievich, even if he had looked at something, would have seen over everything his clean lines written out in level handwriting, and only possibly if, coming from who knows where, a horse's muzzle settled on his shoulder and let out a whole blast on his cheek through its nostrils, only then would he notice that he was not in the middle of a line, but rather in the middle of the street. Arriving home, he would at once sit down at the table, quickly gulp his cabbage soup and eat a chunk of beef with onion, not noticing their taste in the least, eat all this with flies and with whatever God would send at the moment. Noticing that his stomach was beginning to swell, he would get up from the table, take out a little pot of ink and would copy papers he had brought home. If there didn't happen to be any, he would deliberately take, for his own enjoyment, a paper to copy for himself, particularly if it were remarkable not for beauty of style but for being addressed to some new or important personage or other.

Even at those hours when the gray Petersburg sky completely darkens and all the clerk folk have eaten their fill and dined, each as he can, according to the salary he receives and his own whim—when everything has already had a rest after the departmental scratching of pens, after rushing about, after their own and others' essential affairs, and after all of that which indefatigable man voluntarily assigns himself even more than is necessary—when the clerks hurry to dedicate the remaining time to pleasure: the more lively one dashes off to the theater; another out onto the street, to devote the

time to the inspection of certain stupid little hats; another to a party to waste the time in complimenting
some comely girl, the star of a small clerk circle; another,
and this happens most frequently, simply goes to his fellow clerk on the third or fourth floor, to two small rooms
with a hall or kitchen and certain modish pretensions, a
lamp or another article which has cost many sacrifices,
goings without dinner or outings; in a word, even at that
time when all the clerks scatter among the little apart-
ments of their friends to play military whist, sipping tea
from glasses with kopek crackers, drawing smoke from
long chibouks, telling during the dealing some gossip
that has drifted down from high society, from which a
Russian can never and under no circumstances desist, or
even, when there's nothing to talk about, retelling the
eternal anecdote about the Commandant who was told
that the tail of the horse on Falconet's monument* had
been chopped off—in a word, even when everyone was
trying to distract himself, Akaky Akakievich wouldn't
yield to any distraction. No one could say that they had
ever seen him at any party. Having written his fill, he
would go to bed, smiling in advance at the thought of
the next day: what would God send him to copy tomorrow? Thus flowed the peaceful life of a man who could
be satisfied with his lot on a salary of four hundred, and
it would perhaps have flowed on into advanced old age
if there weren't various disasters strewn along the path
of life not only of titular but even of privy, actual, court
and all sorts of councillors, even those who don't give
anyone counsel or take it from anyone themselves.

There is in Petersburg a powerful enemy of everyone
receiving four hundred rubles a year or thereabouts in
salary. This enemy is none other than our northern frost,
although, by the way, they do say it's very healthy. From
eight to nine in the morning, precisely at the hour when
the streets are covered with those going to the department, it begins to give such hard and prickly flicks on
all noses indiscriminately that the poor clerks positively
don't know where to put them. At this time, when the

---

*The equestrian statue of Peter the Great, which stands on the
banks of the Neva.

foreheads of even those who occupy higher posts ache
from the frost and tears come to their eyes, the poor
titular councillors are sometimes defenseless. The only
salvation consists in running through five or six streets
as fast as possible in a scraggy little overcoat and then
stamping one's feet thoroughly in the cloakroom until,
in this way, all the frozen abilities and gifts for dis-
patching one's duty thaw out. Akaky Akakievich had for
some time begun to feel that his back and shoulder had
somehow begun to be seared particularly forcibly, despite the fact that he tried to run across the usual space
as fast as possible. He wondered, at last, whether there
weren't certain faults in his overcoat. Having looked it
over thoroughly at home, he discovered that in two or
three places, namely on the back and on the shoulders, it
had become exactly like cheesecloth: the broadcloth was
so worn that it was transparent, and the lining was falling
apart. One should know that Akaky Akakievich's overcoat also served as an object of merriment for the clerks;
they took away even its honorable name of overcoat and
called it a housecoat. Indeed, it had a certain strange
demeanor: its collar diminished more and more with
every year, for it served for patching the other parts.
The patching showed no signs of the tailor's art, and it
all came out quite baggy and unattractive. Seeing what
the matter was, Akaky Akakievich decided that it would
be necessary to take the overcoat over to Petrovich, the
tailor, who lived somewhere on the fourth floor on a
back stairway, who, despite his one eye and the pock-
marks all over his face, engaged rather successfully in
the repair of clerks' and all other sorts of trousers and
tailcoats, of course, when he was in a sober state and
not nourishing some other notion in his head. One ought
not to say much, of course, about this tailor, but since
it is already established that the personality of every
character in a story should be described completely,
there's nothing to be done, let's have Petrovich too. At
first he was called simply Grigory and was a serf of some
landowner; he began to call himself Petrovich when he
received his freedom and began to drink rather heavily
on all the holidays, at first on the big ones and then,
indiscriminately, on all church holidays, wherever there

was a little cross on the calendar. In this respect he was true to the traditions of his grandfathers and, arguing with his wife, would call her a worldly woman and a German. Since we have already let slip something about the wife, it will be necessary to say a couple of words about her too; but, unfortunately, not much was known about her, except that Petrovich had a wife, that she even wore a cap and not a kerchief; but she could not boast, it appears, of her beauty; at least, on meeting her, only soldiers of the guard would peek at her under her cap, twitching a whisker and emitting some peculiar sound.

Making his way up the stairway leading to Petrovich's, which, to do it justice, was all soaked with water and slops and saturated through and through with that ammoniac smell which eats at the eyes and, as is well known, is inevitably present on all the back stairs of Petersburg houses—making his way up the stairway, Akaky Akakievich was already speculating how much Petrovich would ask, and mentally determined not to give him more than two rubles. The door was open, because the mistress, preparing some fish, had filled the kitchen with so much smoke that it was impossible to see even the very cockroaches. Akaky Akakievich went through the kitchen, unnoticed even by the mistress herself, and at last entered the room where he saw Petrovich sitting on a broad wooden unpainted table and crossing his legs under him like a Turkish pasha. His feet, as is the custom of tailors sitting at their work, were bare. And the first thing to strike the eye was his big toe, very well known to Akaky Akakievich, with a sort of deformed nail, thick and strong as the shell on a tortoise. Around Petrovich's neck hung a skein of silk and threads, while on his knees were some sort of rags. Already for about three minutes he had been aiming the thread at the needle's eye, not hitting it, and therefore was very angry at the darkness and even at the thread itself, muttering under his breath "She won't go in, the little barbarian; you've worn me out, you rascal!" Akaky Akakievich was distressed that he had come precisely at a moment when Petrovich was angry: he liked to order things from Petrovich when the latter was already a little under the influence, or, as his wife expressed it, "glutted with rotgut, the one-eyed devil." In this state Petrovich usually very willingly gave in and agreed, he even bowed and thanked one every time. Later, it's true, his wife would come in crying and say that her husband was drunk and therefore had let him off cheap; but usually you added one ten-kopek piece, and the cat was in the bag. Now Petrovich was, it seemed, in a sober state, and therefore curt, intractable and eager to demand the devil knows what prices. Akaky Akakievich sensed this and already was about, as they say, to beat a retreat, but the business had already been begun. Petrovich screwed up his one eye at him very intently, and Akaky Akakievich involuntarily blurted out: "Greetings, Petrovich!"

"I greet you, sir," said Petrovich and squinted his eye at Akaky Akakievich's hands, wanting to make out what manner of booty he carried.

"I just came to you, Petrovich, sort of. . . ." One should know that Akaky Akakievich expressed himself for the most part in prepositions, adverbs, and finally, in such particles as have absolutely no meaning whatever. And if the matter was very difficult, he even had the habit of not finishing the sentence at all, so that quite often, having begun a speech with the words: "That, really, is completely sort of . . ." but then there was nothing, and he himself would forget, thinking he had already said everything.

"What is it?" said Petrovich and at the same time inspected Akaky's whole uniform with his one eye, from the collar to the sleeves, the back, the coattails and the buttonholes, all of which was very familiar to him, because it was his own work. Such is the habit of tailors; that's the first thing they do on meeting one.

"Well I just sort of, Petrovich . . . my overcoat, the broadcloth . . . just look, everywhere in other places it's quite strong, it's gotten a bit dusty and seems old, but it's new, and, see, only in one place it's a little bit sort of . . . in the back, and also here on one shoulder it's a bit worn, and just on this shoulder a bit—see, that's all. Only a little work. . . ."

Petrovich took the housecoat, first laid it out on the table, looked it over for a long time, shook his head and

groped with one hand at the window for a round snuffbox with the portrait of some general, precisely which is
not known, because the place where the face was had
been punched out with a finger and then pasted over
with a square scrap of paper. Having taken some snuff,
Petrovich spread out the housecoat in his hands and examined it against the light and again shook his head.
Then he turned it lining upwards and again shook his
head, again took off the lid with the general pasted over
with paper, and, having stuffed some snuff in his nose,
closed it, put away the snuffbox and finally said:

"No, it's impossible to fix: a rotten garment!"

At these words Akaky Akakievich's heart skipped a
beat.

"Why impossible, Petrovich?" said he, almost in the
pleading voice of a child, "It's really only that it's worn
at the shoulders, you really must have some little scraps
or other. . . ."

"Sure you can find scraps, scraps can be found," said
Petrovich, "but you can't sew 'em on: the thing's completely rotten, touch it with a needle—and it'll fall apart."

"Let it fall apart, and you put a patch on right away."

"But there's nothing to put a patch on, there's nothing
for it to hang on to, it's had an awful lot of wear and
tear. You can call it broadcloth, but just let the wind
blow and it'll fly to pieces."

"Well, so, just reinforce it. How can it be, really,
sort of! . . ."

"No," said Petrovich decisively, "it's impossible to do
anything. A bad business altogether. Better make yourself leg cloths out of it when the winter cold spell comes,
because a sock doesn't keep you warm. The Germans
thought that up to get more money for themselves
(Petrovich liked on occasion to take a poke at the Germans); but obviously you'll have to have a new overcoat made."

At the word "new" Akaky Akakievich's vision grew
foggy, and everything in the room began to jumble before him. The only thing he saw clearly was the general
with the face pasted over with paper on the lid of Petrovich's snuffbox.

"What do you mean, new?" he said, still as if in a dream. "But I really don't have the money for that."

"Yes, new," said Petrovich with barbaric calm.

"Well, if a new one had to . . . how would it sort of. . . ."

"That is, what will it cost?"

"Yes."

"Three fifties plus will have to be got together," said Petrovich, and he compressed his lips at this significantly. He very much liked strong effects. He liked suddenly somehow to perplex one completely and then steal a peek at what kind of face the perplexed one would make after such words.

"One hundred and fifty rubles for an overcoat!" shrieked poor Akaky Akakievich, shrieked, perhaps, for the first time in his life, for he had always been distinguished by the quietness of his voice.

"Yessir," said Petrovich, "and it also depends on what kind of overcoat. If you put marten on the collar, and add a hood with a silk lining, then it might even get up to two hundred."

"Petrovich, please," said Akaky Akakievich in a pleading voice, not hearing and not trying to hear the words Petrovich said and all his effects, "fix it up somehow so that it will do just a little longer."

"No, it'll end up: you both waste the work and spend money for nothing," said Petrovich, and after these words Akaky Akakievich went out completely destroyed. And after his departure Petrovich kept on standing a long time, significantly compressing his lips and not getting to work, satisfied that he had neither lowered himself nor betrayed the tailor's art.

Having gone out onto the street, Akaky Akakievich was as if in a dream. "There's a business there," he said to himself, "I, really, didn't even think that it would turn out sort of . . ."—and then, after a certain silence, he added—"So that's how it is! That's what finally turned out, but I, really, couldn't have even at all supposed that it was like that." After this a long silence again followed, after which he said: "So that's it! What a really completely unexpected sort of . . . wouldn't have at all. . . .

What a situation!" Having said this, he, instead of going home, went in the entirely opposite direction, not suspecting it himself. On the way a chimneysweep brushed him with his whole unclean side and blackened his whole shoulder; an entire hatful of lime spilled down on him from the roof of a house being built. He didn't notice any of this, and only later, when he bumped into a policeman who, standing his halberd next to himself, was shaking some snuff out of a horn onto his calloused fist, only then did he come to a bit, and then because the policeman said: "Whad're you bashing right into my snout for, don't you have the whole sidework?" This made him look around and turn homewards. Only now he began to collect his thoughts, saw his position in a clear and realistic light, began to talk to himself, no longer spasmodically, but reasonably and openly, as with a sensible friend with whom one can discuss the most tender and intimate matter. "Well, no," said Akaky Akakievich, "it's impossible to talk sense with Petrovich now: now he's sort of . . . his wife, clearly, had given him a beating or something. But it's better if I go to see him on Sunday in the morning: after Saturday night he'll be squinting and groggy so he'll need the hair of the dog, but his wife won't give him the money, and then I'll sort of put ten kopeks into his hand, and he'll be more agreeable, and then the overcoat sort of. . . ." Thus Akaky Akakievich reasoned with himself, encouraged himself and awaited the next Sunday, and, seeing from a distance that Petrovich's wife was going out somewhere, went straight to him. After Saturday Petrovich was in fact squinting strongly, holding his head toward the floor, and completely groggy; but despite all this, as soon as he learned what the matter was, it was just as if the devil had given him a shove. "Impossible," he said, "kindly order a new one." Akaky Akakievich here thrust the ten kopeks at him. "I thank you, sir, I'll fortify myself a wee bit to your health," said Petrovich, "but kindly don't distress yourself about the overcoat; it won't serve any service. We'll sew you a glorious new overcoat, I guarantee you that."

Akaky Akakievich was still about to go on about repairing it, but Petrovich didn't hear him out and said,

"I'll sew you a new one without fail, kindly depend on it, we'll make every effort. It could even be in the latest fashion, the collar will fasten with silver appliquéd clasps."

Here Akaky Akakievich saw that it was impossible to get by without a new overcoat, and his spirits fell completely. How indeed, on what, on what money to have it made? Of course, he could depend in part on a future bonus for the holidays, but this money had already long ago been distributed and disbursed in advance. He needed to acquire new pants, to pay the shoemaker an old debt for putting new vamps on his old boot-tops, and he ought to order from the seamstress three shirts and a couple of that article of linen which it is indecent to name in print, in a word: absolutely all the money had to be spent, and even if the director were to be so kind as to designate, instead of a forty-ruble bonus, forty-five or fifty, all the same some utter nonsense would remain which would be a drop in the ocean of the overcoat capital. Although, of course, he knew that Petrovich was subject to the whim of suddenly asking the devil knows what exhorbitant price, so that even his wife herself was unable to keep herself from shrieking: "Have you gone crazy, you fool! Another time he'll take work for nothing, but now the evil spirit's possessed him to ask such a price as he's not worth himself!" Although, of course, he knew that Petrovich would take the work even for eighty rubles, however, all the same where to get these eighty rubles? He could find half of it: a half could be unearthed; perhaps even a little bit more; but where to get the other half? But first the reader should know where the first half came from. Akaky Akakievich had the habit, from every ruble he spent, of putting aside half a kopek in a small box locked with a key, with a little hole cut in the lid for throwing money in. At the end of every half year he would review the accumulating copper sum and replace it with silver change. Thus he continued for a long time, and in this way in the course of some years the accumulated sum turned out to be more than forty rubles. And so, half was in his hands; but where to get the other half? Where to get the other forty rubles? Akaky Akakievich thought and thought and decided that it would be necessary to cut down his usual expenditures, at least for one year; to give up using tea in the evenings, not to light candles in the evenings, and if something had to be done, to go to the landlady's room and work by her candle; when walking along the streets to step as lightly and carefully as possible on the cobblestones and paving stones, almost on tiptoe, in order in this way not to wear out his soles rapidly; to give his linen to the laundress to wash as seldom as possible, and, so that it wouldn't get dirty, to throw it off every time he came home and remain in only his cotton bathrobe, which was very ancient and spared even by time itself. The truth must be told that at first it was somewhat difficult for him to get used to such limitations, but then he somehow got used to it and all went well; he even entirely mastered going hungry in the evening; but on the other hand he was nourished spiritually, carrying in his thoughts the eternal idea of the future overcoat. From this time on it was as if his very existence had become somehow fuller, as if he had gotten married, as if some other person were with him, as if he were not alone, but some pleasant female life companion had agreed to travel life's road together with him—and that companion was none other than that same overcoat with the thick quilting, with the strong lining which wouldn't wear out. He became somehow livelier, even firmer in character, like a man who has already defined and set a goal for himself. Doubt, indecision, in a word, all the vacillating and indefinite traits, disappeared by themselves from his face and actions. At times a fire would show in his eyes, the most daring and audacious thoughts even flashed through his head: shouldn't he actually put marten on the collar? Deliberations about this almost brought him to absentmindedness. Once, copying a paper, he even almost made a mistake, so that he cried, "ookh!" almost out loud and crossed himself. In the course of every month he, at least once, would visit Petrovich to discuss the overcoat, where it was better to buy broadcloth, and what color, and at what price, and although somewhat anxious, he always returned home satisfied, thinking that finally the time would come when all this would be bought and when the overcoat would

be made. The business went even faster than he antici-
pated. Contrary to every expectation, the director
awarded Akaky Akakievich not forty or forty-five but a
whole sixty rubles: whether he had a premonition that
Akaky Akakievich needed an overcoat, or whether it
happened like that by itself, nonetheless through this he
found himself with an extra twenty rubles. This circum-
stance accelerated the pace of the business. Some two
or three months more of slight starvation and Akaky
Akakievich would have actually collected about eighty
rubles. His heart, usually quite calm, began to pound.
On the very first day he set off with Petrovich for the
store. They bought some very good broadcloth—and it
wasn't hard, because they had thought about it half a
year ahead and it was a rare month that they didn't drop
into the stores to compare prices; furthermore Petrovich
himself said that better broadcloth didn't exist. For the
lining they chose calico, but so durable and solid, that
in Petrovich's words, it was even better than silk and
even dressier and glossier in appearance. They didn't
buy marten, because it was really expensive, but instead
they chose cat, the best that could be found in the store,
cat which from a distance one could always take for
marten. Petrovich fussed over the overcoat two weeks
in all, because there was so much quilting, but otherwise
it would have been ready sooner. For labor Petrovich
took twelve rubles—less was quite impossible: everything was solidly sewn with silk, with a fine double seam,
and Petrovich went over every seam with his own teeth,
impressing various configurations with them. It was . . .
it's hard to say on exactly what day, but, probably, on
the most triumphant day of Akaky Akakievich's life,
that Petrovich finally brought him the overcoat. He
brought it in the morning, just before the time when he
had to go to the department. The overcoat could never
have arrived at a more appropriate time, because rather
heavy frosts were already beginning and, it seemed,
threatened to intensify even more. Petrovich appeared
with the overcoat as a good tailor should. On his face
was displayed such a significant expression as Akaky
Akakievich had never yet seen. It seemed he felt in full
measure that he had done no small deed and that he

had suddenly demonstrated to himself the abyss which divides tailors who only put in linings and do repairs from those who sew from scratch. He took the overcoat out of the handkerchief he had brought it in; the handkerchief had just come from the laundress; he then folded it and put it in his pocket to use. Having taken out the overcoat, he looked at it quite proudly, and, holding it in both hands, threw it quite deftly over Akaky Akakievich's shoulders; then he pulled and smoothed it down in the back with his hand; then he draped Akaky Akakievich with it slightly opened. Akaky Akakievich, as a person of a certain age, wanted to try it with the sleeves on: Petrovich helped him to put the sleeves on—it came out handsome with the sleeves on too. In a word, it turned out that the overcoat was a total and perfect fit. Petrovich didn't lose the opportunity of saying at this point that he'd done it only because he lived without a signboard on a small street and besides had known Akaky Akakievich for a long time, that's why he'd taken the work so cheaply; but on Nevsky Prospect they would have charged him seventy-five rubles for the labor alone. Akaky Akakievich didn't want to debate this with Petrovich and even feared all the high prices with which Petrovich liked to throw dust in one's eyes. He paid him, thanked him, and went right out in the new overcoat to the department. Petrovich went out after him and, remaining on the street, kept looking at the overcoat for a long time from a distance and then deliberately went out of his way so that, catching up by a curving side street, he could run out again onto the avenue and take another look at his overcoat from the other side, that is, head on. Meanwhile Akaky Akakievich walked along feeling in a most festive mood. He felt every moment of the minute that his new overcoat was on his shoulders, and several times he even smiled from inner satisfaction. Indeed, there were two benefits: one, that it was warm, and the other, that it was good. He didn't notice the walk at all and suddenly found himself at the department; in the cloakroom he took off the overcoat, inspected it all over and entrusted it to the special care of the porter. It is not known in what way everyone in the department suddenly found out that Akaky Akakievich had a new overcoat and that the housecoat no longer existed. Everyone ran out to the cloakroom at the same moment to look at Akaky Akakievich's new overcoat. They began to congratulate him, to greet him, so that at first he just smiled, but then even became embarrassed. And when everyone, coming up to him, began to say that one should drink to the new overcoat and that he should at least give them all a party, Akaky Akakievich got completely flustered, didn't know what to do, what to answer and how to get himself out of it. After a few minutes he, blushing all over, was even on the verge of insisting rather simply that it was not a new overcoat at all, that that's how it was, that it was his old overcoat. Finally one of the clerks, some assistant, even, of the head clerk, probably in order to show that he wasn't a snob in the least and even associated with those inferior to himself, said "So be it, I will give a party instead of Akaky Akakievich and request everyone to come to my house for tea: today, as if by plan, is my name day." The clerks, naturally, at once congratulated the assistant department head and eagerly accepted the invitation. Akaky Akakievich was about to get himself out of it, but everyone began to say that it was disrespectful, that it was simply shameful, and he was in no way able to refuse. Furthermore, he later grew pleased when he remembered that because of this he would have occasion to go around in his new overcoat even in the evening. This entire day was really the greatest triumphant holiday for Akaky Akakievich. He returned home in a most happy frame of mind, took off the overcoat and hung it carefully on the wall, again admiring the broadcloth and the lining, and then specially dragged out, for comparison, his former housecoat, which had entirely disintegrated. He glanced at it, and even burst out laughing: there was such a vast difference! And still long afterward at dinner he kept smiling as soon as the condition the housecoat was in would come to his mind. He dined gaily and after dinner wrote nothing more, no papers, but just played the sybarite a little on his bed until it got dark. Then, not prolonging the matter, he got dressed, put his overcoat on his shoulders, and went out onto the street. Where exactly the clerk who had invited him lived, unfortunately we cannot say: our memory begins to deceive us greatly, and everything in Petersburg, all the streets and houses, have so merged and mingled in our head that it is quite difficult to get anything out of it in a decent state. However that may be, it is at least true that the clerk lived in the best part of the city, and therefore not very close to Akaky Akakievich. At first Akaky Akakievich had to pass through some deserted streets with feeble lighting, but the streets became livelier, more populous, and brighter lit in proportion to the proximity to the clerk's apartment. Pedestrians began to show up more often, ladies too began to appear, beautifully dressed, beaver collars appeared on the men, Vankas with their wooden sledges studded with little gilded nails were met with less frequently, on the contrary, daredevil cabdrivers in raspberry velvet hats kept appearing with laquered sleighs, with bear rugs, and carriages with decorated boxes flew across the street, squeaking their wheels on the snow. Akaky Akakievich gazed at all this as a novelty. He hadn't gone out on the street in the evenings for several years. He stopped with curiosity in front of the illuminated window of a store to examine a painting where some beautiful woman was depicted taking off her shoe, thus baring her whole foot, not a bad one at all; and behind her back, from the doors of another room, some man with sideburns and a handsome Van Dyck thrust out his head. Akaky Akakievich shook his head and smiled, and then went his way. Why did he smile, because he had encountered a quite unfamiliar object, but one about which, however, everyone nonetheless cherishes some feeling, or did he think, like many other clerks, the following: "Oh these French! There's nothing to be said, if they want something like that, then it's really sort of. . . ." Or perhaps he didn't even think that—after all, it's really impossible to crawl into a man's soul and find out everything he thinks. At last he reached the house in which lodged the assistant department head. The assistant department head lived in great style: a light shone on the stairway, the apartment was on the second floor. Having entered the front hall, Akaky Akakievich saw whole rows of galoshes on the

floor. Among them, in the middle of the room, stood a
samovar, hissing and emitting puffs of steam. On the
walls everywhere hung overcoats and cloaks, among
which some even had beaver collars or velvet lapels. On
the other side of the wall noise and talk was audible,
which suddenly became clear and ringing when the door
opened and a footman came out with a tray filled with
emptied glasses, a creamer, and a basket of crackers. It
was obvious that the clerks had already long ago assembled and drunk a first glass of tea. Akaky Akakievich,
having hung up his overcoat himself, entered the room
and before him all at once flashed candles, clerks, pipes,
card-tables and fluent conversation rising from all sides
and the noise of tables being moved confusedly struck
his ear. He stopped entirely awkwardly in the middle of
the room wondering and trying to think up what he
should do. But they had already noticed him, received
him with a shout, and everyone instantly went into the
front hall and inspected his overcoat afresh. Although
Akaky Akakievich was becoming a bit embarrassed, he,
being a simple-hearted man, could not but rejoice, seeing
how everyone praised his overcoat. Then, of course,
everyone abandoned both him and his overcoat, and
turned, as usual, to the tables set up for whist. All this—
the noise, the talk and the crowd of people—all this was
somehow wondrous for Akaky Akakievich. He simply
didn't know how to behave, where to put his hands, his
feet and his whole body; finally he sat down with the
players, looked at the cards, kept glancing at the faces
of this one and that one and after a while began to yawn,
to feel bored, the more so since the time had already
long since arrived at which he, according to custom, went
to sleep. He wanted to say good-bye to the host, but
they wouldn't let him go, saying that they absolutely had
to drink a glass of champagne in honor of the renova-
tion. After an hour they served dinner, consisting of vin-
aigrette, cold veal, pâté, pastries and champagne. They
made Akaky Akakievich drink two glasses, after which
he felt that it had become gayer in the room, however,
he could simply not forget that it was already twelve
o'clock and that it was long since time to go home. So
that the host couldn't somehow take it into his head to

detain him, he went out of the room on the sly, found his overcoat in the front hall which he, not without regret, saw lying on the floor, shook it out, took every fluff off it, put it on his shoulders, and went down the stairway onto the street. On the street everything was still light. Some scraggy little grocery shops, those continuous clubs of servants and all sorts of people, were open, others which were closed nonetheless let out a long stream of light through the whole crack of the doorway, signifying that they were not yet devoid of society, and, probably, the serving girls or serving men were still finishing their gossip and conversations, plunging their masters into complete bewilderment as to their whereabouts. Akaky Akakievich walked along in a gay state of mind, he was even suddenly, for some unknown reason, about to dart after some lady who passed by like lightning, every part of whose body was filled with extraordinary motion. However, he stopped right away and again set out very quietly as before, even wondering himself at his gallop which came from who knows where. Soon those deserted streets stretched before him which even in the daytime aren't so gay and even less so in the evening. Now they had become still more solitary and isolated: streetlamps began to appear more seldom—less oil, evidently, was distributed here; wooden houses, fences began; not a soul anywhere; only the snow alone gleamed on the streets, and sleeping low little hovels with closed shutters sadly showed black. He approached the place where the streets intersected in an endless square with houses hardly visible on the other side, which looked like a terrible desert.

In the distance, God knows where, a light flashed in some sentry box which seemed to be standing on the edge of the world. Akaky Akakievich's gaiety here somehow significantly diminished. He stepped onto the square not without a certain involuntary fear, exactly as if his heart had a premonition of something evil. He looked backwards and to all sides: just like a sea around him. "No, it's better not to look," he thought, and walked on with closed eyes, and when he opened them to find out if the end of the square were near, he suddenly saw that in front of him stood almost in front of his nose some people with mustachios, what kind exactly he could not even make out. His vision grew foggy and a pounding started in his chest. "But that's my overcoat!" said one of them in a thundering voice, grabbing it by the collar. Akaky Akakievich was about to cry "help," when another put his fist, the size of a clerk's head, right up to his mouth, saying: "Just you give a shout!" Akaky Akakievich felt only how they took the overcoat off him and gave him a kick with a knee before he fell backwards onto the snow and already felt nothing more. After a few minutes he came to and got up onto his feet, but there was already no one there. He felt it was cold in the square, and he'd no overcoat. He began to shout, but his voice, it seemed, had no thought of carrying to the ends of the square. Despairing, not ceasing to shout, he set off at a run across the square straight to the sentry-box next to which stood a policeman who, leaning on his halberd, looked, it seems, with curiosity, wanting to know why the devil a person was running to him from a distance and shouting. Akaky Akakievich, having run up to him, began in a breathless voice to shout that he was asleep and not looking after anything, not seeing how they robbed a man. The policeman answered that he hadn't seen anything, that he saw how some two men stopped him in the middle of the street but thought that these were his friends; but instead of carrying on for nothing, let him drop in tomorrow to the inspector, that way the inspector would find out who took the overcoat. Akaky Akakievich ran home in total disorder, his hair which could still be found in small quantity on his temples and in back was completely disheveled, his side and chest and his entire trousers were covered with snow. The old lady, the landlady of his apartment, hearing a terrifying knock on the door, quickly leapt out of bed and with a shoe on only one foot ran to open the door, holding her nightdress to her bosom, out of modesty, with her hand; but having opened it, stepped back, seeing Akaky Akakievich in such a state. When he explained what the matter was, she threw up her hands and said that he should go straight to the commissioner and that the local inspector would trick him, make promises and start leading him a merry chase; but best of all to go straight to the commissioner, that she even knew him, because Anna, the Finn who used to work for her as a cook, had now found a job at the commissioner's as a nurse, that she often saw him himself as he drove by their house, and that he also goes to church every Sunday, prays, and at the same time looks gaily at everyone, and that, probably, by all appearances, he must be a kind man. Having heard this solution, the sad Akaky Akakievich made his way to his room, and how he spent the night there is presented for judgment to him who can the least bit imagine the position of another. Early in the morning he set out for the commissioner's; but they said he was asleep; he came at 10—they said again: he's asleep; he came at 11 o'clock—they said: but the chief isn't at home; at dinner time—but the clerks in the reception room didn't want to let him in at all and absolutely wanted to know on what business and what duty brought him and what had happened. So that finally Akaky Akakievich for once in his life decided to show character and said flatly that he needed to see the commissioner himself personally, that they wouldn't dare not to let him in, that he came from the department on government business, and that he would just lodge a complaint against them and then they'd see. The clerks didn't dare say anything against this, and one of them went to call the commissioner. The commissioner received the story of the theft of the overcoat somehow extraordinarily strangely. Instead of paying attention to the main point of the matter, he began to question Akaky Akakievich: And why was he returning so late, and hadn't he dropped in and hadn't he been in a certain disreputable house, so that Akaky Akakievich got completely embarrassed and went out, not knowing himself if the case of the overcoat had been set in proper motion or not. This whole day he wasn't in attendance (the only time in his life). The next day he appeared all pale and in his old housecoat, which had become still more lamentable. Despite the fact that there were such clerks as didn't lose the chance to laugh at Akaky Akakievich even now, the tale of the theft of the overcoat moved many. They at once decided to take up a collection for him, but they collected a mere trifle,

because the clerks without this had already spent a lot
subscribing to the director's portrait and to some certain
book, at the suggestion of the division head who was a
friend of the author—and so, the sum turned out most
trifling. Only one of them, moved by sympathy, decided
at least to help Akaky Akakievich with good advice,
saying that he should go not to the local inspector, because it might even happen that the inspector, wanting
to earn the approval of his superiors, would find the
overcoat in some way or other, but the overcoat would
all the same remain at the police, if he didn't present
legal proof that it belonged to him; but best of all, he
should consult a certain Important Personage, that the
Important Personage, corresponding and communicating
with the appropriate people, could make the case go
more successfully. There was nothing to be done, Akaky
Akakievich decided to go to the *important personage*.
What was precisely and in what consisted the duty of
the important personage, that has remained unknown to
this day. One should know that the certain *important
personage* had recently become an *important personage*,
but before that time he was an unimportant personage.
However, his position even now is not considered important in comparison with others still more important. But
such a circle of people will always be found for whom
the unimportant in the eyes of others is still important.
However, he tried to reinforce his importance by many
other means, namely: he ordained that the lower level
clerks would meet him already on the stairway when he
arrived at work, that no one would dare to come to him
directly, but that everything should go in the strictest
order: the collegiate registrar would report to the district
secretary, the district secretary—to the titular or whatever other one he had to, and that in this way the matter
would come to him. Thus in Holy Rus everything is in-
fected by imitation, everyone emulates and simulates his
superior. They even say that some titular councillor,
when they made him the director of some small separate
office, at once fenced himself off a special room, calling
it "the audience room," and put some footmen with red
collars and gold braid by the doors who would take the
door by the handle and open it to every arrival, although

an ordinary desk could hardly fit in the "audience room." The manners and customs of the *important personage* were sedate and majestic, but not complex. The main tenet of his system was strictness. "Strictness, strictness and—strictness," he would usually say, and at the last word would usually look the one he was speaking to very significantly in the face. Although, however, there was no reason for this whatever, because the dozen clerks who comprised the whole administrative mechanism of the office were in constant terror even without this: catching sight of him from a distance, they would leave their work and wait, standing at attention, until the director would pass through the room. His usual conversation with inferiors smacked of strictness and consisted almost entirely of three sentences: "How dare you? Do you know who you're talking to? Do you understand who is standing before you?" However, he was a kind man at heart, good to his friends, obliging; but the rank of general completely knocked the sense out of him. Having received the rank of general, he somehow got confused, lost his way and didn't know how to behave at all. If he happened to be with his equals, he was still a decent man, a very respectable man, in many respects even not a stupid man; but as soon as he happened to be in a group where there were people even one rank lower than he, there he was simply beyond everything: he would be silent, and his situation aroused pity all the more since he himself even felt that he might spend the time incomparably better. A strong desire to join some interesting conversation and circle was sometimes visible in his eyes, but the thought would stop him: wouldn't it be awfully much on his part, wouldn't it be familiar, and wouldn't he lower his importance by this? And in consequence of such deliberations he remained perpetually in one and the same silent state, only occasionally emitting some monosyllabic sounds, and in this way he acquired the title of a most boring man. To such an *important personage* appeared our Akaky Akakievich, and appeared at the most inauspicious time, quite inopportune for himself, although, however, opportune for the important personage. The important personage was in his office and was conversing very very gaily with a certain recently arrived old acquaintance and child-hood friend whom he hadn't seen for several years. At this time they informed him that some Bashmachkin had come to see him. He asked abruptly: "Who's he?" They answered: "Some clerk." "Ah! he can wait, now's not the time," said the important personage. Here it must be said that the important personage completely lied: it was the time, he and his friend had already long since talked over everything and had already long since been interspersing the conversation with quite long silences, only slapping each other lightly on the thigh and saying "So, that's it, Ivan Abramovich!"—"That's it, Stepan Varlamovich!" But despite all that, however, he ordered the clerk to wait, in order to show his friend, a man long since not working and living out his days at home in the country, how much time clerks spend waiting in his reception room. Finally they, having had their fill of talk and having had a still greater fill of silences, and having smoked a cigar in thoroughly restful armchairs with re-clining backs, he, finally, seemingly suddenly remem-bered and said to the secretary who had stopped by the doors with papers for a report: "Oh yes, there's a clerk, it seems, standing out there; tell him that he may come in." Seeing Akaky Akakievich's meek appearance and his decrepit uniform, he turned to him suddenly and said: "What do you want?"—in an abrupt and hard voice which he had specially practiced previously in his room in private and in front of the mirror, still a week before receiving his present position and a general's rank. Akaky Akakievich already felt the requisite timid-ity in advance, was somewhat embarrassed and, as best he could, to the degree that freedom of tongue would permit him, explained with the even more frequent addi-tion than ever of the particles "sort of," that there was, you see, an absolutely new overcoat, and now he'd been robbed in an inhuman way, and that he was appealing to him so that through his intercession he could some-how sort of correspond with Mr. Head Police Commis-sioner or with another someone, and find the overcoat. Such manners, for unknown reasons, seemed familiar to the general.

"What do you mean, my dear sir," he continued

abruptly, "don't you know the protocol? Where have
you come to? Don't you know how business is conducted? You should have submitted a petition to the
office about this; it would have gone to the department
head, to the head of the division, then it would have
been transferred to the secretary, and the secretary
would then have delivered it to me. . . ."

"But, your Excellency," said Akaky Akakievich, trying to collect the entire small handful of presence of
mind that he had in him, and feeling at the same time
that he was sweating in a terrible way, "I, your Excellency, dared to trouble you because the secretaries are
sort of . . . an undependable bunch. . . ."

"What what what?" said the important personage.
"Where did you get such nerve? Where did you get such
thoughts? What rebellion has spread among young people against their chiefs and superiors!" The important
personage, it seems, didn't notice that Akaky Akakievich had already passed fifty. Probably, if he could be
called a young man, then perhaps only relatively, that is
in relation to one who is already seventy. "Do you know
who you're saying that to? Do you understand who is
standing before you? Do you understand that, do you?
I ask you." Here he stamped his foot, raising his voice
to such a loud pitch that even a better man than Akaky
Akakievich would have been terrified. Akaky Akakievich froze, staggered, his whole body shaking, and
couldn't stand up at all: if the doormen hadn't at once
run up to support him, he would have flopped onto the
floor: they carried him out almost immobile. But the
important personage was satisfied that the effect had exceeded even his expectations, and completely intoxicated
by the thought that his word could even deprive a man
of consciousness, stole a glance at his friend to see how
he viewed it, and not without satisfaction saw that his
friend was in the most indefinite state and was even for
his part beginning to feel terror himself.

How he went down the stairs, how he went out onto
the street, nothing of this did Akaky Akakievich remember. He felt neither his arms nor his legs. In his life he
had never yet been so badly raked over the coals by a
general, and by someone else's yet. He went through the

storm which whistled in the streets, with his mouth agape, losing the sidewalks; the wind, according to Petersburg custom, blew on him from all four sides and from all the side streets. In an instant it blew a quinsy down his throat, and he got home not having the strength to say a single word; he swelled all up and went to bed. A proper raking over the coals is sometimes that bad! The next day it was discovered that he had a high fever. Thanks to the generous aid of the Petersburg climate, the illness progressed faster than might have been expected, and when the doctor appeared, he, having felt his pulse, found there was nothing to be done except to prescribe a poultice, if only so that the patient should not remain without the beneficent aid of medicine; he, however, immediately pronounced him a definite *kaput* in a day and a half. After which he turned to the landlady and said: "And you, my good woman, don't waste any time, order him a pine coffin at once, because an oak one would be expensive for him." Whether Akaky Akakievich heard these fateful words, and if he did hear, whether they produced a shocking effect on him, whether he regretted his miserable life—nothing of this is known, because he was delirious and feverish the whole time. Visions, one stranger than the other, came to him incessantly: now he saw Petrovich and was ordering him to make an overcoat with some kind of traps to catch the thieves which he incessantly imagined to be under his bed, and he kept calling the landlady every minute to pull one thief out even from under his blanket; now he was asking why his old housecoat was hanging before him, that he had a new overcoat; now it seemed to him that he was standing before the general listening to the proper raking over the coals and saying: "Excuse me, your Excellency"; now, finally, he was even foulmouthing, saying the most terrible words, so that the old lady, the landlady, even crossed herself, never having heard anything of the sort from him in her life, all the more since these words followed directly after the words "your Excellency." From then on he uttered absolute nonsense, so that it was impossible to understand anything; one could only see that his disordered words and thoughts revolved around one and the same overcoat.

At last poor Akaky Akakievich gave up the ghost. They sealed neither his room nor his things, because, first of all, there were no heirs, and second of all, very little inheritance remained, namely: a bunch of goose quills, a quire of white government paper, three pairs of socks, two or three buttons which had come off his trousers, and the housecoat already known to the reader. Who got all this, God knows: even the narrator of this tale, I admit, wasn't interested in this. They took Akaky Akakievich down and buried him. And Petersburg remained without Akaky Akakievich as if he had never been in it. There had vanished and disappeared a being defended by no one, dear to no one, interesting to no one, not even calling himself to the attention of a naturalist who doesn't neglect to mount an ordinary fly on a pin and examine it under a microscope—a being who had submissively borne the office jokes and gone to the grave without any extraordinary fuss, but for whom all the same, albeit before the very end of his life, there had flashed a radiant guest in the form of an overcoat, which had enlivened his poor life for an instant, and on whom disaster had then crashed down just as unbearably as it has crashed down on the tsars and the sovereigns of the world. . . . Several days after his death a doorman from the department was sent to his apartment with an order to appear immediately and to say the chief demands it; but the doorman had to return with nothing, reporting that Akaky couldn't come anymore, and to the query: "Why?" expressed himself with the words: "He just can't, he's dead, they buried him four days ago." In this way they learned about Akaky Akakievich's death in the department, and already the next day a new clerk sat in his place, much taller and turning out the letters not in such level handwriting, but much more slanted and sloping.

But who could imagine that this is still not all about Akaky Akakievich, that he was fated to live on noisily for several days after his death, as if in reward for a life unnoticed by anyone? But that's what happened, and our poor history unexpectedly acquires a fantastic ending. Suddenly rumors spread around Petersburg that by the Kalinkin Bridge and far further a corpse in the guise of a clerk had begun to appear by night, searching for some pilfered overcoat and, on account of the purloined overcoat, pulling off of all shoulders, without regard to rank or profession, all overcoats: with cat, with beaver, with cotton; raccoon, fox, bear coats, in a word, coats of every sort of fur and hide as people have invented for covering their own. One of the department clerks saw the corpse with his own eyes and instantly recognized Akaky Akakievich; but this instilled in him, however, such fear, that he ran off at top speed and therefore couldn't get a good look, but saw only how he shook his finger at him from a distance. Complaints came incessantly from all sides that backs and shoulders, if it were only of titular, but even of the most privy councillors, were subjected to absolute chills because of the nightly pulling-off of overcoats. An order was given to the police to catch the corpse, no matter what, dead or alive, and to punish him, as an example to others, in the cruelest manner, and they even almost succeeded in this. More precisely, the policeman of some block on Kiryushkin Street was already about to seize the corpse completely by the collar on the very scene of the crime, in the act of pulling a frieze overcoat off of some retired musician who in his time had tooted the flute. Having seized him by the collar, he summoned with his shout two other comrades whom he commanded to hold him, while he burrowed just for a minute in his boot to pull a birch-bark snuffbox out of it to temporarily refresh his nose, frostbitten six times in his life; but the snuff was probably of the sort which even a corpse couldn't bear. The policeman had hardly managed, having covered his right nostril with his finger, to inhale half a handful with his left, when the corpse sneezed so violently that he completely splattered all three of them right in the eye. While they were lifting their fists to wipe them, the trail of the corpse was lost, so that they didn't even know whether he had actually been in their hands. From that time on, policemen conceived such a terror of the dead that they were even afraid to seize the living, and would only shout from a distance: "Hey you, on your way!"—and the clerk-corpse began to appear even beyond the Kalinkin bridge, causing no small terror to all timid people. But we, however, completely abandoned the *certain important personage* who, in reality, was all but the *cause of the fantastic direction, incidentally, of a perfectly true story.* Before everything justice demands it be said that the certain important personage, soon after the passing of poor Akaky Akakievich, who had been raked over the coals into a fluff, felt something akin to regret. Sympathy was not unknown to him; his heart was capable of many kind impulses despite the fact that his rank quite often prevented their discovery. As soon as the visiting friend had left his office, he even got to thinking about poor Akaky Akakievich. And from then on almost every day pale Akaky Akakievich appeared to him, who had not withstood the official raking-over the coals. The thought of Akaky distressed him to such a degree that, a week later, he even decided to send a clerk to him to find out what had happened, how he was, and whether it was in fact possible to help him with something; and when they reported to him that Akaky Akakievich had suddenly died in a fever, he was even left stunned, feeling pangs of conscience, and was out of sorts all day. Wishing to distract himself somewhat and to forget the unpleasant impression, he set off for a party to one of his friends at whose place he found a sizable gathering, and best of all, everyone there was of almost one and the same rank, so that he would be restricted by absolutely nothing. This had a surprising effect on his emotional disposition. He opened up, became pleasant in conversation, amiable, in a word, spent the evening very pleasantly. At supper he drank a couple of glasses of champagne—a means, as is well known, not ineffective in disposing one to gaiety. The champagne imparted to him an inclination for various extravagances, namely: he decided not to go home yet, but to drop in on a certain lady of his acquaintance, Karolina Ivanovna, a lady, it seems, of German extraction, with whom he had perfectly friendly relations. It is necessary to say that the Important Personage was already not a young person, a good spouse, a respected *pater familias.* Two sons, of whom one already served in the office, and a pretty sixteen-year-old daughter with a slightly hooked, but attractive little nose, came to kiss his hand every day, saying, "Bonjour, Papa." His wife, a woman still fresh and not at all bad, first gave him her hand to kiss and then, turning it over on the other side, kissed his hand. But the important personage, perfectly, incidentally, satisfied with domestic family tenderness, found it becoming to have a lady friend for friendly relations in another part of town. This lady friend was not a bit better or younger than his wife; but such puzzles exist in the world, and to judge them is not our affair. So, the important personage went down the stairs, got into a sled and told the coachman: "To Karolina Ivanovna's," and he, having wrapped himself quite luxuriously in a warm overcoat, remained in that pleasant state better than which you won't conceive for a Russian, that is, when you aren't thinking about anything, but meanwhile thoughts creep into your head of themselves, one more pleasant than the other, not even giving one the trouble of chasing after them and looking for them. Full of contentment, he lightly recalled all the gay moments of the evening he'd spent, all the words that had made a small circle guffaw; he even repeated many of them under his breath and found that they were all as funny as before, and therefore it's not surprising that he himself laughed wholeheartedly. Occasionally, he was bothered, however, by a gusty wind which, having suddenly sprung up from God knows where or for who knows what reason, so cut into his face, hurling clumps of snow into it, blowing out his overcoat collar like a sail, or suddenly with unnatural force throwing it onto his head and in this way necessitating perpetual fussing to extricate himself from it. Suddenly the important personage felt that someone had seized him quite firmly by the collar. Turning around, he noticed a man of short stature, in a worn uniform, and not without terror recognized Akaky Akakievich. The face of the clerk was as pale as the snow and he looked like an absolute corpse. But the terror of the important personage exceeded all bounds when he saw that the corpse's mouth twisted and, breathing the terrible smell of the grave on him, uttered these words: "Ah! So here you are at last! At last I've sort of got you by the collar! It's your overcoat I need! You didn't take any pains about mine, and raked me over to boot—

now give me yours!" The poor *important personage* almost died. However much character he had in the office and in general before his inferiors, and although, looking only at his manly appearance and figure, everyone would say: "Ooh, what character!" here he, like quite many who have a heroic exterior, felt such terror, that not without reason he even began to fear some kind of morbid attack. He even quickly took off his overcoat from his shoulders himself and cried to the coachman in a voice not his own: "Drive home as fast as you can!" The coachman, hearing a voice which was usually used at critical moments and would even be accompanied by something much the most effective, hid his head in his shoulders just in case, waved the whip and shot off like an arrow. In a little more than about six minutes, the Important Personage was already in front of the entrance to his house. Pale, panic-stricken and minus his overcoat, instead of going to Karolina Ivanovna's, he went home, dragged himself somehow to his room and spent one night in quite great confusion, so that the next day in the morning at tea his daughter said to him directly: "You're quite pale today, Papa." But Papa was silent and said not a word to anyone about what had happened to him, and where he had been, and where he had wanted to go. This event made a strong impression on him. He even began to say much less often to his subordinates: "How dare you, do you understand who is standing before you?" If he did say it, then not before first having heard what the matter was. But still more remarkable was that from that time on the appearances of the clerk-corpse entirely ceased; obviously, the general's overcoat turned out to fit him perfectly; at least, such incidents in which someone had his overcoat pulled off were no longer heard of anywhere. However, many active and careful people wouldn't calm down at all and kept saying that in distant parts of town the clerk-corpse was still appearing. And actually, a certain policeman in Kolomna saw with his own eyes how a ghost appeared from out of a certain house; but, being by nature somewhat feeble, so that one time an ordinary adult suckling pig rushing out of some private house had knocked him off his feet, to the enormous amusement of the coach-

men standing around, from whom he demanded ten kopeks each for snuff for such mockery—so, being feeble,
he didn't dare to stop him, but just walked behind him
in the darkness until finally the ghost suddenly glanced
around and, stopping, asked: "Whaddaya want?" and
showed him such a fist as you won't find even among
the living. The policeman said "Nothing," and at once
turned back. The ghost, however, was much taller, wore
huge mustachios, and, directing his steps, as it seemed,
to the Obukhov Bridge, vanished completely in the darkness of the night.

Taras Bulba

1

"Come on, boy, turn around. What a sight! What's that—a cassock or something? They all wear those in your seminary?"

This was old Bulba's welcome to his two sons, back home from the Kiev Seminary, where they had just completed their studies.

The sons dismounted. They were big and strong and they hung their heads and looked up from under their brows as befits seminary students. Their healthy faces were covered with down still untouched by a razor. Their father's reception took them aback and they stood staring at their feet.

"Fine, you just stand there. Let's have a good look at you," Bulba said, swinging the lads around, first one, then the other. "Well, your coats certainly aren't too short. Some coats! Never seen the like in my whole life. Come, I'd like to see one of you run in that garb. Come on, get going! I bet you get tangled up in your skirts and fall flat on your face."

"Stop it, Pa. Don't laugh at me, I tell you," the older of the two said finally.

"Look at that! Sensitive, eh? Why shouldn't I laugh?"

"Why? . . . because you may be my pa, but if you keep on baiting us, I'll take a poke at you, by God."

"What! At your father? Are you mad?" Bulba said, surprised, and retreated a few steps.

"Father or no father, I don't take that from anyone."

"So how shall we fight? Fists?"

"Anything'll do."

"So fists it is," Taras Bulba said, rolling up his sleeves. "Let's see what kind of a man you are with 'em."

And, instead of hugging one another after their long separation, father and son began to aim heavy blows at the other's ribs, belly and chest, side-stepping, moving back, attacking again, their eyes glued on each other.

"People should see it! The old man's gone right out of his head!" Taras's wife wailed. Thin, pale, and kindly looking, the boys' mother had come out onto the doorstep to kiss her precious sons. "The children come home after a whole year and he can think of nothing better than a fistfight!"

"Well, I swear, this one can fight," Bulba said, dropping his hands. "I'll say that for him." He was panting heavily. "Yes," he said, "I can tell right off he'll make a good Cossack. All right, son, let me kiss you."

And father and son embraced.

"Good boy! Just keep on swinging like you swung at me. Don't let anyone get away with anything! But I still say that's some getup you have on. What's this string? And you, you big lout, you still standing there with your arms hanging down?" Bulba said to his younger son. "Want to have a go at me too, you son of a dog?"

"Anything else?" the mother said, putting her arms around the boy. "What an idea! For a child to hit his own father! And what a time to pick, when he's traveled so far and is tired . . ." The child in question was almost twenty and well over six feet tall. "He ought to rest and eat something and you want to make him fight!"

"Don't listen to your mother, boy," Bulba said. "She's a woman. She doesn't know a thing. You don't need her coddling. The only coddling you need is from the open steppe and a good horse. See this saber? That's your mother. All the rest is garbage, all the things they stuff your heads with at the seminary—all those books, dictionaries and philosophies. I wouldn't give a good goddamn for all that——" Here, Bulba uttered an unprintable word. "Tell you what I'll do for you. Next week, I'll send you to Zaporozhe. There you'll learn something. That's a school for you. They'll ram some sense into your heads there."

"So they'll only have a week at home?" the mother

said, standing there, frail and pitiful, with tears in her eyes. "The poor dears won't have a proper rest or a chance to enjoy their home, and I'll never see enough of them."

"Come on, come on—stop whimpering! A Cossack's not made to spend his time with women. You'd like to hide them under your skirts and sit on 'em like a hen on her eggs. You'd better go and put everything we have in the house on the table. And that doesn't mean honey buns and poppy-seed cakes and puddings; give us a whole sheep, or maybe a goat, and our own old home-brew to go with it, and vodka, but not with raisins and stuff like that in it—real vodka to scorch our throats."

Bulba led his sons into the living room of the house. As they entered, two pretty servant girls wearing coin necklaces darted out of the room. They had been tidying up and apparently the arrival of the two young masters had frightened them, or else they were simply bowing to the feminine custom, upon seeing a man, of letting out a little shriek, rushing away, and then, for a while, bashfully keeping the face covered with a sleeve.

The living room was furnished in the taste of the time. Only suggestions of that style have come down to us through the old songs, songs that used to be sung in the Ukraine by blind minstrels, to the strumming of the lute. In the style of those troubled times, of skirmishes and battles for union of the Ukraine with Russia, the walls of the room were covered with smooth colored clay and hung with sabers, knouts, bird and fishing nets, guns, an elaborately carved powder horn, gilded horse bits and tether ropes adorned with silver plates. The windows were small, with round, opaque panes, such as can only be seen today in old churches. Painted red bands ran around the windows and doors. On shelves in the corners there were jugs, bottles, and green and blue glass flasks, engraved silver mugs, and gilded drinking cups. They were of varied origin, the handiwork of Venetian, Circassian, and Turkish workmen that had reached Bulba's living room by roundabout ways, changing hands frequently, often violently, as was usual in those restless times. Against the walls stood birch-bark benches. In the center, a large table. The icons hung in their special corner and on the other side of the room stood a huge, tiled stove which provided many comfortable nooks and cozy corners.

It was all familiar to the two lads. They had come home for their summer vacations each year—walking the whole way since, seminary students not being allowed to ride horseback, they couldn't keep mounts there. All that marked them as Cossacks was the tuft of hair left on their cropped heads, by which any arms-bearing Cossack had the right to pull them. It was only now that they'd completed their studies that Bulba had sent a couple of young stallions from his herd.

Bulba had invited all the local Cossack chiefs under him to celebrate the return of his sons. When his second-in-command, Dmitro Tovkach, an old friend, arrived with several others, he pointed to his sons and said:

"Look at 'em! Some lads, eh? Soon I'm going to send them to Camp Zaporozhe."

The guests congratulated father and sons, telling them it was the best thing they could do, that there was no better place to train young men than Camp Zaporozhe.

"Well, brothers, sit down anywhere you like. Sons—let's start with a good strong drink! God bless you! Your health, sons! To you, Ostap, and to you too, Andrei. God send you success in war. May you beat all comers—Turks, Tartars, and, if the Poles start scheming against the faith again, let 'em have it too. By the way, how do you say vodka in Latin? You see, boy, how stupid those Latins were? They didn't even know that there was such a thing as vodka. What was he called—the one who wrote those Latin verses—what's his name? I don't know, I'm not much of a scholar myself. Horace or something?"

"That's Pa for you," Ostap, the older son, thought, "the old dog knows it all and he still keeps playing the fool."

"I bet your Archimandrite wouldn't let you get even a sniff of this stuff," Taras went on. "And tell me the truth, boys, they gave you some good thrashings with those birch switches, on your backs and everything else a Cossack has? And when you got too smart, I'll bet they gave you the whip too. And I'll wager they not only beat you on Saturdays, but on Wednesdays and Thursdays too—right?"

"Forget it, Pa," Ostap said composedly, "all that's past."

"Let 'em try it now," Andrei said. "Let anybody try. Just let some Tartar turn up and I'll show him what a Cossack saber can do."

"Right, son, right! Come to think of it, I'll go to Zaporozhe with you. Why, yes, I'll come. What the devil have I got to gain by staying around here? Grow buckwheat, run the house, look after the pigs and sheep, get fussed over by the wife? The hell with it! I'm a Cossack! And what if there isn't a war just now? I'll come to Zaporozhe with you just for a change. By God, I will!"

And getting more and more excited, old Bulba rose from the table, thrust out his chest and stamped his foot.

"We'll ride out tomorrow! Why postpone it? What enemy can we stalk here? What do we need this house for? What can we do with all this? What are all these jars for?" And he started grabbing pots and jars and flasks, hurling them around and smashing them.

His poor wife was accustomed to this sort of thing and looked at him sadly without getting up from her seat. She did not dare object when she heard Taras's decision, but she could not suppress her tears. And when she glanced at her sons an indescribably deep, speechless sorrow fluttered in her eyes and over her convulsively compressed lips.

Taras Bulba was terribly stubborn. The cruel fifteenth century gave birth to such characters in that seminomadic corner of Europe. Russia, abandoned by her princes, had been devastated, burned to the ground, by the irresistible raids of the Mongolian predators. A man who lost his shelter became daring; he became used to facing fire, restless neighbors, and unending perils, and forgot the meaning of fear.

It was in that era, when the peaceful Slav was fired with a warlike flame, that the Cossacks made their appearance. They were like an explosion in which the free, exuberant Russian character found an outlet. Soon valleys, river crossings, sheltered spots, teemed with Cossacks. No one knew how many of them there were, and when the Sultan asked they answered in good faith:

"Who can tell? We are scattered over the entire steppe and wherever there's a hillock, there's a Cossack."

It was the ordeals they had gone through that had torn this strange manifestation of Russian vigor out of the breast of the Russian people. The erstwhile towns and princely domains, with their feuding and trading, had disappeared and their place had been taken by warlike settlements linked by the common danger and by the hatred of the heathen predators. The unbreakable resistance of this people saved Europe from the merciless hordes from the East. The Polish kings had replaced the petty princes and become the official, although weak and distant, rulers of these vast lands. They had early realized the advantage of having the plains inhabited by a warlike, free-roving race and they tried to encourage and preserve the Cossacks' wild way of life. Under their remote guidance, the Cossacks elected headmen and divided the territory into military districts. They had no visible, regular army but, when a war or an uprising broke out, each man rode in, fully equipped, to report, and receive his gold piece from the King. Within a week's time a force assembled which could never have been recruited. And when the emergency was over, the trooper went back to his field or his river, traded, brewed beer—in a word, became once more a free Cossack.

There were few things, in fact, that a Cossack could not do. He knew the arts of blacksmithing and gunsmithing, how to distill vodka, build a wagon, prepare powder, and, above all, he knew how to drink and carouse as only a Russian can.

Moreover, besides the registered Cossacks, those who were paid to appear fully equipped in time of emergency, it was possible to recruit a whole army of volunteers. All that was needed was for Cossack chiefs to appear at various marketplaces and village squares, mount a cart and call out:

"Hey, you beer brewers! Enough! You've lain around on your stoves too long, feeding the flies with your

bacon! What about seeking a little glory! Hey, you plow-
men, shepherds, skirt-lovers! Stop muddying your yellow
boots and wasting your vigor on women! Time to act
like Cossacks!"

And these words were like sparks on dried wood. The
plowman broke his plow, the brewers threw away their
casks and destroyed their barrels, the merchants let their
stores go to ruin, broke pots and pans and everything
else in their houses, mounted horses and were off. In a
word, the Russian soul found its outlet in the Cossack
and his powerful physique.

The Bulbas were an old Cossack family and Taras
was one of their oldest and most respected colonels. He
seemed to have been born especially for danger and war.
He was blunt and straightforward. At that time, Polish
influence was beginning to be felt among the Russian
aristocracy. Many adopted Polish customs, wallowed in
luxury, went in for large retinues, for falconry and for
all sorts of amusements. Taras had never approved. He
liked the simple Cossack life and quarreled with those of
his friends who leaned toward Warsaw. He called them
flunkies of the Polish gentry. Always on the alert, he
regarded himself as a champion of the Russian Orthodox
Church. He took justice into his own hands and rode
into villages when people complained of being perse-
cuted by landlords or of being forced to pay unbearable
taxes. Bulba meted out his own justice. He had set himself a rule—he would always use his saber in the following three instances: when government officials failed to
remove their caps before Cossack elders or to show
them proper respect; when the Orthodox faith was
slighted and ancestral customs were neglected; and finally when he had to deal with pagans or Turks, against
whom he always considered it commendable to take up
arms in the name of Christendom.

Now he was enjoying the thought of his arrival at the
camp with his sons, when he would say:

"See what a pair of lads I've brought you."

He mused about how he was going to introduce them
to his old, battle-tested brothers-in-arms; how he'd witness their first exploits in fighting and in drinking, which
he also considered a major attribute for a warrior.

He had planned to send his sons by themselves. But when he saw how young and tall, how strong and handsome they were, the warlike spirit stirred in him and he decided to go along, although there was no reason for it outside of his own stubborn desire.

Right away, he began giving orders. He selected horses and their trappings for his sons, inspected the stables and the storehouses, designated the men who were to leave with him the next morning. He handed over his command to Dmitro Tovkach with firm instructions to rally immediately to the camp with the whole regiment if Bulba sent him a signal. And although he was feeling the effects of the drinks he had had, he forgot nothing. He even saw to it that the horses were watered and given the best grain. By the time he had completed these rounds, he was tired.

"All right, children," he said, "time to sleep now. Tomorrow we'll get off to an early start. No," he said to his wife, "don't bother to make our beds. We don't need 'em. We'll sleep outside."

Darkness had only just fallen but Bulba always liked to go to bed early. He sprawled out on a rug and covered himself with his sheepskin coat both because the night air was fresh and because he liked to cover himself warmly. Before long he began to snore and the rest of the household were soon following his example. They all snored and whistled; the watchman snored the loudest of all because he had drunk more than anyone else to celebrate the homecoming of the young masters.

Only the mother did not sleep. She sat by the heads of her two sons, who were sleeping side by side, combed their tousled locks and wet them with her tears. She gazed at them with all her being. All of her turned into vision and she could not get her fill of looking. She had breastfed both. She loved them, and now she was to be allowed to see them for a brief moment only.

"My sons, my dear sons, what will happen to you? What's in store for you?" she murmured, and her tears were caught in the wrinkles which had so changed her once-pretty face. She was indeed pathetic, as was any woman in that troubled time. She had had but a brief moment of love, during the first heat of passion, in the first flush of youth, and then her rough conqueror had deserted her for his saber, for his comrades, for revelry. She would see her husband for two or three days and then he would disappear for several years. And when she did see him, when he was home, what kind of a life was it? She put up with insults, even blows, and tenderness was hardly ever shown her at all. She was a strange being among all these wifeless warriors on whom Zaporozhe had left its grim imprint. Her youth flashed by without joy and her fresh cheeks withered unkissed before their time. All her love, all her feelings, all that is passionate in a woman, turned into a mother's tenderness. She wheeled above her children with anxiety and passion—like a gull over the steppe. And now they were taking her darlings away from her, this time possibly for good. Who knew—perhaps in the very first encounter their heads would fall, severed by the slash of a Tartar saber. And she wouldn't even know where their bodies lay, abandoned to be torn asunder by scavenging birds. She felt she would gladly have given all of herself for each drop of their blood. Crying, she had looked into their eyes until sleep had overcome them and thought:

"Perhaps after all Bulba will put off their departure for a couple of days, perhaps he decided to go off in such a hurry because he had a bit too much to drink."

The crescent moon, high in the sky, lighted the courtyard with its crowd of sleepers, the thick clump of pussy willows and the tall steppe grass which washed over the fence. The mother sat by her sons' heads, never taking her eyes off them, not thinking of sleep. Already the horses, sensing the approaching dawn, had stopped grazing and had lain down in the grass; the top leaves of the willow began to whisper and little by little the rustling current worked its way down to the lowest branches. And she sat there until daybreak, wishing that the night would last forever. The ringing whinny of a foal came from the steppe. Red stripes appeared clearly in the sky.

Bulba awakened suddenly and jumped to his feet. And he was well aware of what he had decided the evening before.

"All right, lads, you've slept enough—get up! Water your horses. And where's the old woman? Hey, old woman, fix us something to eat, we've a long way to go today."

The mother, sad and stooping, deprived of her last hope, went into the house. And while she was preparing their breakfast, Bulba tossed out orders, went to the stables and personally selected the best equipment for his sons.

The seminary students were suddenly transformed into quite different men. Soft red leather boots with silver studs replaced their old, muddy ones; their trousers were as wide as the Black Sea, had hundreds of pleats in them, and were belted with golden cords from which hung straps with tassels, tinkling charms, and pipes. Their scarlet cloth coats were girt with sashes in which Turkish pistols were stuck, and their sabers clanked at their heels. Their faces, not yet weatherbeaten, looked even handsomer, and their young black mustachios further emphasized the whiteness of their skin and their youthful freshness. They looked so good to their wretched mother, under their sheepskin hats with golden tops, that she simply stood speechless and even her tears stopped streaming.

"All right, children, we're all set. No use wasting time!" Bulba said finally. "And now, let's all sit down before leaving as is the Christian custom."

And everybody sat down, even the stableboys who had been standing respectfully by the door.

"Go on, Mother, bless your children," Bulba said. "Pray God that they may fight bravely, always stand up for their honor and for the true Church of Christ, and that, if they fail, they may disappear so that not one speck remains in God's world! Go to your mother, boys. A mother's prayer will help you on land and sea."

The mother embraced them, weak as she was and, tears pouring down her cheeks, put two small icons on cords around their necks.

"May the Mother of God preserve you . . . don't forget me, sons . . . send me news when you can . . . ." She could not continue.

"All right, children, we're off," Bulba said.

Their saddle horses stood by the porch. Bulba jumped on his Devil, who reared crazily, feeling the three-hundred-pound load on his back. Bulba was heavyset and fat besides.

The mother watched her sons mount their horses too, then she rushed toward the younger, in whose features there was somehow more gentleness. She grasped the stirrup and the back of his saddle and clung on to them with a desperate look in her eyes. Two big Cossacks pulled her gently away and carried her into the house. But when the cavalcade had already ridden out of the gates, she darted out behind them like a wild goat, with an agility quite unexpected in a brittle old woman. With surprising strength, she stopped the horse and, with a strange, uncontrolled violence, put her arms around her son's waist. They led her off again.

The two young Cossacks rode forward, confusedly fighting back their tears, afraid that their father might see them. But he too was unsure and was also trying not to show it.

It was one of those gray days which lend a strange glitter to the green of the grass and cause the birds to twitter somehow discordantly. After a short while, they looked back. Their house seemed to have sunk into the earth. All they could see above the steppe were the two chimneys and the tops of the trees in whose branches they used to leap around like a couple of squirrels. Before them there still stretched the meadow with which the story of their lives was so closely intertwined, from the time they had rolled in the dewy grass to the time they had waited there for a dark-browed Cossack girl, timidly approaching on her quick, young legs. And now there was nothing to be seen on the horizon except the pole over the well with a cartwheel nailed to it, erect and lonely against the sky. And the terrain, which had seemed flat as they crossed it, loomed up behind as a hill, hiding everything that lay beyond.

And so it was the end of childhood, of games, of all such things.

2

They rode in silence. Taras thought of the past, of his bygone youth, wishing sadly that he could have been always young. Then he thought of the old comrades he was going to meet in the camp. He tried to recollect which ones had died and which should still be around. A tear was slowly trying to find its way out of his eye, and his gray head was bowed.

The sons' thoughts were different. But first, more should be known about them. As each reached the age of twelve, he was sent to the Kiev Seminary. In that day, people of consequence considered it proper to give their children an education, although they expected them to forget everything they had learned soon after. Having been brought up in unrestrained freedom, such children arrived at the seminary quite wild. And they received a certain polish there which gave them all something in common.

Ostap, the elder, began his scholastic career by trying to run away. He was caught, given a terrible whipping and sent back to his books. Four times he tried to get rid of his primer by burying it and four times they gave him a sound thrashing and bought him a new one. There's no doubt that he would have buried it a fifth time had it not been for his father's solemn promise that he would put him in a monastery as a lay brother for twenty years and that he would never see Zaporozhe again unless he learned everything they had to teach him at the seminary. That threat must have sounded strange coming from Taras, who professed to despise all learning.

From that day on, Ostap began to work with extraordinary diligence. He would spend hours studying some dull book and soon become one of the best pupils. At that time, there was little connection between actual life and what was taught. The scholastic, rhetorical, grammatical and logical refinements had no application in real life. Even men of learning were ignoramuses because they were completely lacking in experience. Moreover, the democratic organization of the seminary and the great number of healthy young lads attending it resulted in all sorts of extracurricular pursuits. The poor fare, the frequent deprivation of food as a punishment, the drive to satisfy the many urges of a vigorous youth— all this combined—produced in the students that spirit of adventure which would be further developed later in Zaporozhe. Hungry seminary students, roving the streets of Kiev, put everyone on his guard. At the sight of a passing student, stallkeepers covered pies and cakes with their hands like she-eagles spreading their wings over their young. The monitor, who was supposed to keep his fellow students in line, had such awesome pockets in his trousers that he could have stuffed them with all the goods displayed on the stall of a not-too-alert merchant. Even the military governor, Adam Kisel, although he was a patron of the seminary, kept the students out of Kiev society and insisted that an eye should be kept on them at all times. This recommendation was, of course, quite superfluous because neither the rector nor the monk-professors spared rod or whip, and, on their orders, the lictors often lashed the monitors so severely that they went around patting their trousers for weeks afterward. Many students took this quite nonchalantly; they considered it to have just a bit more bite than a good swig of vodka with pepper; others, tired of ceaseless whippings, escaped to Zaporozhe, if not caught and brought back. And Ostap Bulba, despite his zeal in studying logic and even theology, never managed to stay away from the merciless rod. Of course, all this went to harden him and develop in him the ruthlessness characteristic of many Cossacks. He was always considered the most reliable friend. Seldom did he initiate or lead a raid on an orchard or vegetable garden, but he was always one of the first to rally to an adventurous gang and, if caught, would never betray a comrade, despite incarceration, beatings, and all the rest. He seemed immune to all temptation except the temptation to fight and drink—at least he gave no thought to the others. He was straightforward with his equals. He was as kind as it was possible to be with his sort of character living at that particular time. And now, riding, he was deeply touched by his mother's tears; it was the only thing that disturbed him, causing him to lower his head thoughtfully.

His younger brother, Andrei, was experiencing feelings which were more vivid and somehow more complex. He had studied more willingly and his studies had not required so much effort that his willpower was put to a

test. He was more inventive than his brother and was
often the leader of some risky venture. But he managed
to avoid punishment by using his imagination at times
when his brother would resignedly take off his coat and
lie down on the floor without arguing or begging for
mercy. Like his brother, he spoiled for adventure, but
he had room for other feelings too. By the time he was
eighteen, the need for love had flared up in him. The
picture of a woman had begun to haunt his arid dreams.
During the philosophical debates at the seminary, she
was constantly before him, blooming, black-eyed, and
tender. Her firm bosom, her wonderfully soft, bare arms,
and even her dress, under which he could guess at her
strong but feminine limbs, filled his dreams with a sort
of unexpressed sensuousness. He saw to it that these
stirrings of youthful passion remained secret from his
comrades, because at that time it was considered shameful for a Cossack to think of women and love before he
had seen battle. In his final years at the seminary, he
had less often taken part in adventurous expeditions at
the head of a band of students. Instead, he wandered
alone through the quieter parts of Kiev, where the little
cottages peeped out onto the streets from among the
cherry orchards. Sometimes he would walk through the
quarter where the Ukrainian and Polish gentry lived,
where the houses had pretensions to elegance. Once,
when he was meandering along absorbed in his dreams,
he was almost run down by the carriage of some Polish
gentleman and a terrifyingly mustachioed coachman
slashed at him rather accurately with his whip. The
young student was furious. Recklessly, he grabbed a
spoke of the rear wheel of the carriage and brought it
to a stop. But the coachman, fearing reprisals, whipped
up the horses and they tore away. Andrei, lucky enough
to get his hands away from the wheel, crashed to the
ground, his face in the dirt. Ringing, musical laughter
sounded above him. He looked up—the most beautiful
girl he had ever seen was standing at a window. Her
eyes were black and her complexion made him think of
snow lit by the glow of the morning sun. She was laughing with abandon and her laughter added a sparkling
power to her uncanny beauty. He was dumbfounded. He

stared at her, no longer knowing where he was, absent-mindedly rubbing dirt all over his face. Who was she? He tried to find out from the richly liveried servants who were gathered by the gates, listening to a strolling lute player. But they just laughed at his mud-caked face and wouldn't tell him. Still, in the end, he learned that she was the daughter of the Polish military governor of Kovno, who was in Kiev temporarily. The very next night, with schoolboyish brashness, he squeezed himself through the palings of the fence into the garden and climbed a tree whose branches spread over the very roof of the house. From the tree, he jumped onto the roof, hoisted himself up into the chimney and let himself down it, straight into the beautiful Polish girl's bedroom. She was sitting near a lighted candle taking off a pair of expensive earrings. The sudden appearance of a stranger so frightened her that she was unable to utter a sound. But when she saw him standing there with eyes downcast, too shy even to move an arm, she recognized the seminary student she had seen lying in the mud and burst out laughing again, her fright completely gone. Indeed, there was nothing frightening in Andrei's appearance—as a matter of fact, she thought he looked very handsome. She kept laughing and teasing him for quite a while. This beautiful girl, like many of her compatriots, was something of a scatterbrain, but her enchantingly clear, piercing eyes looked steadily at Andrei. And he could not stir a limb, as though he had been sewn up in a sack. The daughter of the Polish governor stepped up to him, put her sparkling diadem on his head, hung her earrings from his lips, threw her transparent muslin chemisette with its gold-embroidered frills round his shoulders. She adorned him thus and did a thousand other silly things, with the childish naughtiness so typical of pretty Polish girls. All this embarrassed the poor student more and more. He presented a laughable sight, standing there with his mouth open, gazing into her dazzling eyes. Then there was a knock at the door and she became frightened again. She bade him hide under the bed and as soon as the danger was past, called her maid, a Tartar prisoner, and told her to lead him cautiously out into the garden and from there to see him over the fence.

But this time he was less lucky in getting over the fence. The awakened guard grabbed him by a foot and he had to take a beating from the servants, who kept hitting him even when he was out on the street, where only his speed of foot saved him. After that, it was dangerous even to walk past the house, because the governor had many servants. He met her once more in the Catholic church. She noticed him and smiled pleasantly, as if he were an old acquaintance. He saw her in passing yet once again. And soon after that the governor of Kovno left Kiev and, instead of the beautiful, black-eyed Polish girl, a fat face appeared in her window. That's what Andrei was thinking of, his eyes lowered to his horse's mane.

And meanwhile the steppe had taken them all into her green embrace, and the high grass, closing around them, hid them from view, so that only their black Cossack caps flashed among its green tips.

"Why so quiet, lads?" Bulba said finally, coming out of his own reverie. "You're like a lot of monks! Come on, all together, the hell with thinking! Take your pipes in your mouths and let's light up, let's spur on our horses, let's fly so fast that the birds won't be able to overtake us!"

And the Cossacks, bending over their horses' necks, disappeared completely into the grass. Now not even their black caps could be seen and only a ribbon of parted grass marked their swift passage.

The sun had long been up in the clear sky and was pouring its warm, life-giving light out over the steppe. Everything that was dim and gloomy in the Cossacks vanished and their hearts stirred like waking birds.

The farther they went the more beautiful grew the steppe. In those years, the entire southern part of Russia, all the way to the Black Sea, was a green, virgin wilderness. Never had a plow driven through the long waves of wild growth and only the horses, hidden in it as if among the trees of the forest, trampled the tall grass. There could be nothing more beautiful in the world: the visible surface of the earth looked like a golden green ocean, its waves topped by multicolored spume. Through the tall, slender stems of the grass showed sky-blue, marine, and purple star thistles; yellow broom thrust up its pyramidal head; the white parasols of Queen Anne's lace gleamed near an ear of wheat that had appeared there God knows how and was now growing heavy. Partridges scurried among the thin stalks of the steppe plants, their necks outstretched, and in the sky hawks hung immobile on their outspread wings, eyes glued on the ground; and from the grass rose a steppe gull and bathed herself luxuriously in the blue waves of the air. Now she dissolved in the soaring heights; now she reappeared like a little comma; now, as she turned, her wings reflected a ray of sunlight.

They stopped for only a few minutes to eat. The ten Cossacks who were accompanying them dismounted, got out the wooden casks of brandy and the pumpkin shells that they used as drinking vessels. They had nothing but bread and fat and dry biscuits to eat and had only one round of brandy—just enough to sustain themselves, because Taras Bulba allowed no one to get drunk while traveling. After that they kept riding until nightfall.

In the evening, the steppe was completely transformed: the whole multicolored area caught the last bright reflection of the sun and then began to darken. They could see the shadows invading it and turning it dark green. Fragrance from the plants increased—every flower, every blade of grass released its incense and the whole steppe was bathed in a wild, noble aroma. Right across the steadily darkening azure of the sky, bright pink and golden stripes appeared as if from under the brush of some Titan. Here and there whitish transparent cloudlets floated, pushed along a fresh little breeze that tenderly rippled the tops of the grass and almost imperceptibly tickled the cheeks of the riders. The daytime music was replaced by a different one: spotted marmots crept out of their holes, rose on their hindlegs and filled the steppe with their whistling. The whirr of grasshoppers gradually dominated the other sounds. Sometimes, like a silver trumpet, the cry of a swan reached them from some distant lake.

They stopped in the middle of the steppe and selected a spot to spend the night. They lit a fire and hung a pot over it in which they cooked their supper. The steam rose into the air in a slanting column. When they had eaten, the Cossacks hobbled their horses and left them loose to graze, and then lay down themselves. They slept on their coats with the stars staring into their eyes. Their ears took in an infinity of little noises made by the insects teeming in the grass: buzzing, whirring, chirping, clicking, humming—they resounded, purified by the fresh air, and lulled them to sleep. And when one of them got up in the night he had in front of him a steppe sparkling with the gleaming dots of fireflies. Here and there the night sky would be dimly lit by the faraway glow of dry reeds burning in the fields and along the riverbanks and then a dark flight of northbound geese would suddenly appear in the reddish silver light and they became pink handkerchiefs flying in a dark sky.

They continued their journey without incident. They did not come across a single tree. All the way there was the same boundless, free, beautiful steppe. Only from time to time, could they make out the faraway roof of a forest that framed the banks of the Dnieper. Only once did Taras point out to his sons a black spot bobbing up and down in the grass and say:

"Look, boys, see over there? That's a Tartar and he's galloping."

The Tartar stopped at a good distance, turned his small head so that they could see his drooping mustachio, and looked straight at them out of his slanting narrow eyes. Then he sniffed the air like a greyhound, and, seeing that there were thirteen of the Cossacks he had stumbled on, disappeared in the grass.

"Try to catch him, boys! No, better not even try. You'll never make it, his horse is even faster than my Devil."

After that Bulba took certain precautions, fearing a Tartar ambush. They changed direction and rode toward a tributary of the Dnieper called the Tatarka. When they reached it, they entered the water, horses and all, and swam downstream for quite a while before climbing out onto the bank again and turning directly toward their destination.

And three days later, they were almost there. The air suddenly became cooler and they felt the proximity of the Dnieper. Soon the big river appeared in the distance, a black ribbon against the horizon. It breathed on them its cold, damp, watery breath, and, as they drew still nearer, it suddenly filled half the earth's surface. This was the part of the river's course where it finally escapes the narrow-banked confines of the rapids and broadens out freely like a sea, the spot where the islands scattered in it push its waters far over the low banks, which have neither rocks nor steep places to contain them. The Cossacks dismounted, embarked on the ferry and three hours later reached the shores of the island of Khortitsy, where at that time the constantly shifting Camp Zaporozhe was situated.

A group of people on shore were arguing with the ferryman. The Cossacks tightened their saddle girths and straightened their horses' bridles. Taras stood straight, hitched his belt, and swaggeringly smoothed his long mustachio. His sons also gave their appearance a once-over, feeling a strange sort of joy mixed with fear. Then they all rode off toward the camp.

Within about half a mile of it, they came to a settlement. They were deafened by the clang of fifty black-smith's hammers banging against twenty-five anvils sunk into the earth. Strong tanners sat under awnings soften-ing oxhides with their big hands; merchants sat in booths with piles of flint and powder before them; an Armenian displayed expensive kerchiefs; a Tartar turned pieces of mutton on spits around a fire; a Jew, his head thrust forward, slowly poured liquor out of a cask. Then they came across the first Zaporozhe Cossack. He was sleep-ing in the middle of the road, his arms and legs out-stretched. Taras stopped to admire him.

"Just look at him lying there! A stout lad, by God!"

The sight was quite impressive. The man lay there like a lion, the long tuft of hair above his forehead was thrown back like a lion's mane, his trousers, of expen-sive, blood-red cloth, were bespattered with tar, a mark of their wearer's utter disdain for them. Having admired the Cossack to their hearts' content, the Bulba party passed on through the narrow streets filled with crafts-men practicing their trades on the spot, people of all nationalities who lived on the fairlike outskirts of the camp, outskirts which dressed, fed, and equipped the camp-dwellers who knew only how to carouse and to shoot.

At last they left this behind and came upon a few scattered barracks covered with turf or, in Tartar fashion, with felt. Some of these were surrounded by cannon. Here there were none of the small houses with awnings in front of them, like those they had seen in the outskirts. A low wall and a ditch without sentries attested to an incredible recklessness. A few Zaporozhe Cossacks, lying in the very middle of the street with their pipes between their teeth, looked at them indifferently without budging. The Bulba party carefully made their way among the reclining bodies and Taras kept saying, "Greetings, gentlemen," and they replied, "Greetings to you, too."

They found groups of brightly clad men scattered all over the central square. By their sunburned faces it could be seen that these were battle-hardened veterans who had been exposed to all sorts of weather during raids and campaigns. This was Camp Zaporozhe, the nest from which the strong, bold Cossacks took off and rode all over the Ukraine.

On the square where the Council of the Camp usually assembled, a Cossack, stripped to the waist, sat on a barrel sewing up holes in his shirt. Further, their path was barred by a group of musicians in the middle of which a young fellow, his hat clinging somehow to the very back of his head, was doing a wild Cossack dance and shouting:

"Faster! Faster! Go on, Thomas, give more vodka to these Orthodox Christians! Faster!"

And Thomas, a Cossack with a blackened eye, complied, pouring out a huge tot of vodka for everyone upon request. Around the young dancer four older Cossacks who had been jigging their feet in short, brisk steps suddenly leaped into the air, landing almost on the heads of the musicians and making the firm soil ring resoundingly under their silver-shod heels.

But the young Cossack shouted the loudest and jumped the highest. His tuft streamed through the air, his bare muscular chest, covered with sweat, was completely exposed, his thick jacket flung wide open.

"At least take your jacket off," Taras said finally, "it's fairly steaming."

"I can't," the Cossack shouted without stopping. "What I take off, I drink!"

The lad had already lost his hat. His belt was gone too and so was his neckerchief. All had gone the way of vodka.

The crowd was growing around him. More and more people joined in the dance and it was fascinating to see how the men succumbed to the beat of this free, wild Cossack dance which bears the name of its inventors.

"If it weren't for these damned horses, I'd have joined them," Taras explained.

Meanwhile, he had begun to recognize in the gathering venerable gray heads who had been prominent chiefs and were respected by one and all. Ostap and Andrei heard nothing but greetings:

"How're you making out, Pesherits? Hello, Kozolup!"

"God! Where've you been, Taras?"

"And you, what are you doing here, Doloto?"

And these adventurers, gathered from all the corners of the free Cossack world, embraced one another fondly and Taras kept firing questions about common friends:

"Heard anything of Pidsishok? What about Borodavka? What happened to Koloper?"

And the answers Taras obtained were to the effect that Borodavka had been hanged in Tolopan, that they had torn Koloper's hide off him at Kizkir, that Pidsishok's head had been sent to Constantinople in a barrel of brine. And the old Bulba lowered his own mournfully and kept repeating sadly:

"A great Cossack, what a great Cossack he was. . . ."

3

Taras Bulba and his sons had been at the camp for almost a week. Ostap and Andrei spent little time on military exercises. The Cossacks of that era did not bother with them much, believing that experience in action was sufficient training for a young man. And, indeed, the fighting was almost uninterrupted. It bored the Cossacks to exercise their warlike skills during the quiet intervals. They did some target shooting, perhaps, or held horse races, or pursued some animal across the steppe. And the rest of their time was devoted to revelry, which was considered a mark of manliness and generosity. The camp presented an incredible sight: an endless noisy party. A few Cossacks ran small shops, some others practiced certain crafts, but the overwhelming majority caroused from morning to night, as long as there was an opportunity and as long as the wealth they had acquired had not passed into other hands. This permanent party had something bewitching about it. This was no gathering of people drinking to forget their misery—it was the simple release of an exuberant gaiety. Everyone entering the camp shed all his erstwhile preoccupations. In fact, one might say, he spat on his past and gave himself unstintingly to the brotherhood of reckless revelers who, like himself, were quite unconcerned about home, family, relatives, in fact about anything except the open sky and eternal gaiety. This was what produced the insane exhilaration that otherwise would have been impossible. The stories which circulated among the gathering, lazily sprawled out on the ground, were often so comical and told so vividly that it required a great deal of self-control to maintain the expressionless composure, without so much as twitching the mustachio, that has become characteristic of the southern Russian, distinguishing him from his northern brethren. And with all this, it was not the gloomy drinking of a man trying to forget himself among gloomy companions; it was rather like a bunch of schoolboys having a wildly good time. The only difference was that instead of sitting with a textbook and listening to some teacher's boring explanations, they went out on five thousand horses to raid the outside world, and, instead of playing ball in a closed field, they had playing fields with unguarded boundaries near which they might catch sight of a rapidly vanishing Tartar head and from which the Turk frowned grimly at them from under his green turban. Another difference was that while they had been forced to share the community of school, to come here they had left their fathers and mothers of their own free will, sometimes had even fled their homes. Some of these men had already felt the rope round their necks and then, instead of pale death, they had found life here in its full flow. Some of them, following a noble tradition, could never keep a kopek in their pockets; to some, before coming here, a ruble had seemed a fortune and you could have turned their pockets inside out without ever hearing anything fall. In the camp were to be found former seminary students who had been unable to stand the academic switch and had never learned one letter of the alphabet and others who knew Horace and Cicero and what the Roman republic was all about. There were many officers here who were later to distinguish themselves in the army of the King, many who felt that it made no difference whom and where they fought as long as they had a chance to fight. Some had come to the camp just so that later they would be able to say that they had been there and were therefore hardened warriors. But, as a matter of fact, who wasn't there? The strange republic was a product of the century, a place where those who sought gold coins, rich brocades, golden cups, and precious jewels could always find employment. Only worshippers of women found nothing there for them—no woman was allowed even in the vicinity of the camp.

Osfap and Andrei found it strange that people kept pouring into the camp without anyone ever asking where they had come from or even what they were called. It was as though they were returning to a home they'd left an hour before. The newcomer simply reported to the headman, who usually said:

"Welcome. Do you believe in Christ?"

"I do."

"And in the Holy Trinity?"

"I do."

"And you attend church, don't you?"

"I do."

"Cross yourself then!"

And when the newcomer had crossed himself, the headman would tell him:

"Fine. Go and pick yourself a unit, whichever you prefer."

And that was that.

The whole camp attended the same church and was ready to defend it to the last breath, although none of them wanted to hear anything about fasting or abstinence.

Typical of the Zaporozhe Cossacks was their refusal to bargain. They would thrust a hand into a pocket and whatever it happened to grab was paid to the merchant. That is why, prompted by the prospect of gain, Jews, Armenians, and Tartars accepted the risks involved in living on the fringe of the camp. And the life of these merchants was quite precarious. They were like people living at the foot of Vesuvius, because whenever the Cossacks were short of cash they tore the shops apart and took the goods for nothing.

The camp consisted of more than sixty military units—troops—each with its own barracks, which were somewhat like independent republics and even more like boarding schools where the children could find a bed ready and meals. No one acquired or kept anything for his personal use; everything was handed over to the troop chief. He was entrusted with everyone's money, clothes, provisions, and even firewood. Often there were quarrels between troops which usually turned into free-for-alls. The inhabitants of two barracks would pour out into the square, belabor one another with their fists until one side gained the upper hand. Then the drinking bouts took over. This was the life the camp had to offer young men.

Ostap and Andrei flung themselves into it headlong, with all the enthusiasm of youth, and soon forgot their home, the seminary, and all that had touched them before. Everything fascinated them: the revelry that went on around them and the uncomplicated traditions of self-government which at times seemed to them rather severe for such a free republic. When, for instance, a Cossack stole something, even a thing of little value, it was considered a disgrace to the whole Cossack community. The culprit was tied to the pillar of shame and a club was placed at his feet. Each passer-by was obliged to strike him one blow until he was beaten to death. A debtor who did not pay up was shackled to a cannon and had to sit there until one of his comrades decided to buy him out by settling his debt. But what produced the grimmest impression upon Andrei was the horrible execution of a man for murder. They dug a pit in front of the condemned man, then lowered him into it and on top of him placed the coffin containing the body of his victim. Then both were covered with earth. For a long time afterward, the youth relived the grim ceremony and saw the face of the man buried alive with the terrible coffin.

Soon the two brothers gained good standing among the Cossacks. They rode out into the steppe with their troops to shoot deer, wild goats, and the infinite variety of steppe birds. At other times they went to the lakes, rivers, and streams to lay nets and to pull in a rich catch on which the whole troop would feast. And although there was no way to test the value of a Cossack directly, they soon stood out among the young men because of their reckless daring as well as their all-around achievements. They could shoot fast and straight and swim across the Dnieper in a strong current—the sort of things that made a newcomer acceptable in Cossack society.

But the old Taras had other plans for them. This idleness was not to his taste. He was spoiling for action and kept thinking up ways to draw the camp into the sort of daring venture in which a man could really show his mettle. Finally, one day, he went to the headman and said:

"Say, headman, isn't it time for our Cossacks to set out and enjoy a bit of fighting?"

"Nowhere to set out for," the headman said, taking his short pipe out of his mouth and spitting sideways.

"What d'you mean nowhere? We could go for the Turks or have a poke at the Tartars."

"Turks, Tartars—can't be done," the headman said coldly, and pushed his short pipe back into his mouth.

"Why can't be done?"

"Just so. We've promised the Sultan peace."

"But he's an infidel, isn't he? Remember, God Himself, in His Holy Scriptures, ordered us to fight the infidels. You know that."

"We've no right. Perhaps we could've if we hadn't sworn by our faith. But now it's impossible. Can't be done."

"How can you say impossible? I've got two sons, two young men, see. Neither of them has seen war yet, and you try to tell me that we've no right. Then there's no need for Cossacks, is that it?"

"Well, we mustn't attack."

"Does that mean that our young Cossack manpower is to be wasted? That a man should die like a dog without having done his duty to his motherland and to Christendom, and, in general, without having been of any use? What are we on this earth for? What do we live for?"

The headman did not answer. He was a stubborn Cossack. For a short while he remained silent altogether, then he said:

"And I still say—no war."

"No war?" Taras insisted.

"Right."

"Not even a hope?"

"Not even a hope."

Taras thought, "I'll show you yet, you scrawny old cockerel," and decided to teach the headman a lesson.

He took a few men into his confidence and organized a drinking bout, after which several drunken Cossacks rushed to the square where the kettledrums stood that were used to beat out the general assembly. Not finding the drumsticks, which were in the custody of the official drummer, they grabbed pieces of wood and started banging on the kettledrums. The first to arrive was the tall, one-eyed drummer. He came running, rubbing his single eye, which looked very sleepy.

"Who the hell dared to beat the kettledrums?" he wanted to know.

"Shut up. Go get your goddamn drumsticks and start beating when you're told!" the drunks told him.

The drummer produced the sticks from his pocket, knowing only too well where this sort of thing was likely to lead him. The drums sounded and soon black groups of Cossacks were pouring into the square like bumblebees. A circle was formed and, after the third roll of the drums, the elders made their appearance. The headman, his mace, the symbol of his office, in his hand, the judge with the seal, the scribe with an inkpot, and the senior troop chief with his staff. The headman and the elders removed their fur hats and bowed in all four directions to the assembled Cossacks, who stood proudly, their arms akimbo.

"What does this assembly mean? What do you want, gentlemen?" the headman said. Shouts and curses drowned him out.

"Put down your mace! Put it down, you son of a toad, put it down immediately! We don't want you any longer!" some voices shouted from the crowd. Some of the Cossacks from troops that happened to be sober objected and soon everything was a fistfight between drunk and sober troops.

The headman was on the point of saying something, but, knowing that the crazed mob might beat him to death, as almost always happened if resistance was shown, bowed low, put down his mace and disappeared in the crowd.

"And do you wish, gentlemen, that we too should give up our symbols of office?" the judge asked, and he, the scribe, and the senior troop chief made as if to lay down seal, inkpot, and staff.

"No, no, you stay. We only wanted to get rid of the headman—he's an old woman and we need a man for the job."

"Who, then, is to be the new headman?" one of the elders inquired.

"We want Kukubenko!" some shouted.

"No, no! Not Kukubenko! It's too early for him yet! His mother's milk is still dribbling from his mouth."

"Shilo! Let Shilo be headman!"

"Take your Shilo and get out of here! What kind of a Cossack is he? Remember, he was caught red-handed, stealing like a Tartar!"

"Stuff that no-good Shilo in a bag and drown him!"

"Borodaty, what about Borodaty?"

"No Borodaty for me! Off with him to the accursed mother of hell!"

Taras Bulba was elbowing his way through the crowd whispering into many ears: "Kirdiaga, Kirdiaga, demand Kirdiaga . . ." and the crowd shouted:

"Kirdiaga! Kirdiaga! Borodaty-Borodaty-Borodaty! Kirdiaga! Shilo! To hell with Shilo! Kirdiaga. . . ."

When they heard their names shouted, the candidates immediately left the crowd lest people should suspect that they were taking a direct part in promoting their own election.

"Kirdiaga—Kirdiaga!" The name seemed to resound the loudest.

"Borodaty!"

The fistfight that ensued brought Kirdiaga the head-manship.

"Go and fetch Kirdiaga!"

A dozen men detached themselves from the crowd. They could hardly stand on their feet, having managed to take on an enormous load. They went to announce his election to Kirdiaga.

Kirdiaga, an elderly man who still nevertheless had a firm grip on things, was sitting in his barracks as though completely unaware of what had happened.

"What, gentlemen, can I do for you?"

"Come. You've been elected headman."

"Oh no, no! I don't deserve the honor. I lack the wisdom for such a post. Is it possible that, in the whole camp, they couldn't find anyone better qualified?"

"Go on. Do as you're told," the Cossacks shouted, grabbing him under the arms. He tried to backpedal with his feet but was finally dragged to the assembly square to the accompaniment of curses, pushes, and kicks.

"Don't try to get out of it, son of a toad; accept the honor when it's offered, you dog."

When he was in the middle of the circle, those who had brought him addressed the crowd:

"What do you say, gentlemen, are you willing to accept Kirdiaga as your headman?"

"We are willing! We are willing, all of us!" the crowd howled and their shouts thundered for a long time over the square.

One of the elders picked up the mace and handed it to the newly elected headman. According to custom,

Kirdiaga refused it. Offered it a second time, he again refused, only accepting it at the third offering. A roar of approval came from the crowd and again their shouts resounded all over the square. Then four of the oldest Cossacks in the camp, the four men with the whitest mustachios and the whitest tufts, stepped out of the crowd. They weren't really all that old but there were none older in the camp—the Zaporozhe Cossacks never died of old age and these four were the oldest available. Each of them bent down, took a handful of earth, which, since it had rained that day, had turned to mud, and placed it on Kirdiaga's head. The wet earth ran off his head, down his cheeks and his mustachio and muddied his whole face. But Kirdiaga stood there without budging and thanked the Cossacks for the honor shown him.

Thus the rowdy election was completed, and if anyone was pleased with the result it was Taras Bulba. To start with he had taught a lesson to the former headman. Then, Kirdiaga was an old friend. They had shared many land and sea campaigns, and had past dangers and hardships in common. The crowd scattered and proceeded forthwith to celebrate the election of the new headman. This celebration exceeded anything that Ostap and Andrei had witnessed thus far. Liquor stores were taken to pieces and vodka, beer, and mead were seized without payment, the owners considering themselves lucky if they got away with their hides intact. The whole night was spent in shouting, singing and rejoicing, and the crescent moon looked down for a long time on bands of musicians parading in the streets with balalaikas, guitars, flutes, and tambourines, along with the church choir kept in the camp to sing songs glorifying the exploits of the Cossacks, in addition to their church singing.

In the end, alcohol and fatigue began to overcome their stubborn heads. Now here, now there, a Cossack would collapse on the ground, and a friend, deeply touched and with tears in his eyes, would embrace him as a brother and fall beside him. Here, a whole group would lie down in a heap; there, a provident man would carefully pick out a log to put under his head. The last of them, the one who had the strongest head, still went on giving a disconnected speech. But in the end the spirits got him too. He fell and moved no more. The entire camp was now asleep.

4

The very next day, Taras Bulba conferred with the new headman about stirring up the Cossacks for some venture or other. The headman was shrewd and knew Cossacks through and through. At first he said:

"An oath cannot be violated. It's out of the question."

Then, after a pause, he added:

"Never mind. We'll manage something without violating our oath. Assemble the people . . . I mean, not on my order, just by themselves, you understand. . . . You can arrange it, I'm sure. Then the elders and I, we'll happen to come along, as if we knew nothing about it."

And within an hour the kettledrums rolled. All at once, hundreds upon hundreds of Cossack caps poured out onto the square. Some of the Cossacks were drunk, of course, and others unreasonable. A murmur arose:

"Who sounded the assembly? Who ordered it?"

There was no reply. But from various corners, voices were raised:

"Cossack energy is wasted without war! The elders have grown sluggish lying around! Their eyes are buried in fat! There's no justice in the world!"

At first the other Cossacks listened. Then they began to repeat:

"True enough—no justice in the world!"

The elders appeared to be thunderstruck at such remarks. Finally the headman came forward and said:

"Cossacks! Allow me to speak."

"Speak!"

"Probably, gentlemen, you know better than anyone else that many of our Cossacks have got into debt to the tavernkeepers, to the Jews, as well as to their brother Cossacks, so that now not even the devil will give them credit. Then, we have among us many lads who have never seen war. And you know, gentlemen, a young man cannot be brought up without war. How can he become a Cossack if he has never fought the heathen?"

"He puts it just right," Bulba thought.

"Don't imagine for a moment, gentlemen, that I am saying this because I intend to break the truce. God forbid! I'm just stating facts. Now, let's take our church. It's in a disgraceful state. Look how many years, by the Grace of God, the camp has stood here, and, to this day, not only the church but even the icons themselves have been left undecorated. If at least someone had wrought a silver frame for them. But all the church receives is what Cossacks leave in their wills. And you know yourselves that that's not much, because they mostly drink up just about everything they have while they're still alive. So I'm not saying this because I want to make war on the infidels. We have sworn by our faith that we won't start a fight against the Sultan, and it'd be a great sin on our part to break our oath."

"What's he getting it all mixed up for?" Bulba muttered under his breath.

"So you see, gentlemen, while our code of honor prevents us from starting a new war, in my humble opinion our young men could still go out in the boats and pay a little visit to the coast of Asia Minor. Now what would you think of that, gentlemen?"

"Lead us, lead us all!" they shouted from all over the square. "We're ready to lay down our lives for the Faith!"

The headman was alarmed. He did not at all want to arouse the whole of Camp Zaporozhe. To break the peace in that way seemed wrong to him.

"Gentlemen! Allow me to speak once more!" he cried.

"We've heard enough," shouted the Cossacks, "you couldn't put it any better."

"Well, if that's it—so be it. You're giving the orders. And it says in the Scriptures that the voice of the people is the voice of God. No one is wiser than the people. I must only warn you, gentlemen, that the Sultan won't let the pleasures our young lads will indulge in go unanswered. But by then we would be prepared, our forces would be fresh and afraid of no one. But if we all went, the Tartars might attack in our absence. They're just the Turks' dogs and they wouldn't attack openly; they won't dare come when the master is home, but they'll bite at his heels from behind, and painfully too. And if it comes to that, to tell the truth we haven't enough boats or powder for everyone to go. But I'll gladly go, nevertheless—I'm at your service."

The shrewd headman fell silent. The Cossacks split into little groups and began to talk the matter over. The troop chiefs conferred. Fortunately, not too many of them were drunk and so they decided to abide by the headman's sensible advice.

Right away, several men crossed to the opposite bank of the Dnieper, where the army's stores were kept in inaccessible hiding places, under the water and in the reeds. This was where the treasury chest and a part of the captured arms were secreted. The others all rushed to inspect the boats and fit them out for the trip. In no time, a crowd of people thronged the bank. Carpenters appeared carrying axes. Weather-beaten, broad-shouldered, sturdy old Cossacks, some with black mustachios, others already turning gray, stood in the water with their trousers rolled up to their knees and pulled the boats down from the bank into the water. Others collected lumber and all sorts of wood. They planked the boats, and, turning them bottom up, caulked and tarred them. They lashed long-stemmed reeds to them, Cossack fashion, so that they would not be sunk by sea waves. Farther along the shore they built fires and boiled pitch in copper caldrons to pour over the boats. The old and the experienced guided the young. Banging, hammering, and shouting filled the air and the whole bank seemed to sway and move, as though it had come alive.

At that moment, a large ferryboat came alongside. The knot of people standing on it had been waving at the shore even while quite a distance away. Now one could make out that they were Cossacks. Their coats were torn and their disheveled appearance—many of them had nothing but their shirts and the short pipes between their teeth—indicated that they had just escaped from some disaster or that they had been on a real binge and had squandered even the clothes on their backs. A broad-shouldered, stocky Cossack of about fifty stepped forward and started shouting and waving his hands, but his words could not be heard over the din ashore.

"What happened to you?" the headman asked when the ferry pulled in. All the workers, stopping and raising their axes and chisels, looked up expectantly.

"Disaster!" the stocky Cossack shouted from the ferry.

"What disaster?"

"Cossacks—gentlemen—may I speak?"

"Speak!"

"But perhaps you'd rather call your assembly."

"Speak! We're all here."

They all crowded closely together.

"Have you really heard nothing of what's going on around us?"

"What do you mean?"

"What do I mean? The Tartars must have stuffed your ears with mud."

"Go on, speak, man. What's been happening?"

"Things are going on the like of which no living Christian has ever seen before."

"Tell us what's happening, you dog!" shouted someone in the crowd, fast losing patience.

"The time has come upon us when our churches are no longer our own."

"What do you mean by that?"

"They've been mortgaged to the Jews. Nowadays, if you don't pay up, you just can't say mass in 'em."

"What are you babbling about?"

"And if some dog of a Jew doesn't first make his sign with his dirty hand on the holy Easter cake, then it can't be blessed."

"He's lying, brothers—it can't be that an unclean Jew could be allowed to put his sign on the holy Easter cake."

"Listen! That's not the half of it. The Catholic priests are riding all over the Ukraine in carriages. And it's not the fact that they travel in carriages that's so terrible but that they're drawn not by horses but by Orthodox Christians! And even that's not all. They say that Jewish women are making themselves skirts out of our priests' vestments. That's what's going on in the Ukraine, gentlemen! And you sit here in Camp Zaporozhe and have yourselves a good time. It looks like the Tartars have scared you so much that you've neither eyes nor ears—nothing—and you just don't know what's going on in the world!"

"Stop, stop!" the headman interrupted him. Up till then, he had been standing with his eyes lowered to the ground, as indeed had all the Cossacks. In important matters, they never gave way to their first impulses, but kept silent. But their anger was growing.

"And now, tell me, what—may the devil boil you alive—what have you been doing yourselves over there? Surely you must have had your sabers? How did you allow such lawlessness?"

"How did we allow it? I'd like to see you try to take care of fifty thousand Poles alone. And then, let's face it, there were treacherous dogs among our own people who switched to the Roman faith."

"And what about your headman and your chiefs—what about them?"

"What about them? Well, God preserve us from such a fate!"

"What do you mean by that?"

"I mean that by now our headman, roasted in a copper pot, lies in Warsaw, while the hands and the heads of our chiefs are being exhibited in all the fairs. That's what about our chiefs!"

The crowd froze. Over all its length the bank became dead-quiet. Then suddenly it came violently alive. It seemed as if the whole bank had burst out talking.

"What! Jews renting our own churches to us!"

"Whoever heard of papist priests harnessing Orthodox Christians!"

"Incredible! How can such things be tolerated from filthy unbelievers!"

"You realize what they did to the headman and the chiefs?"

"No, no, no! We won't stand for it! And on Russian soil! We won't, we won't, we won't!"

The words flew over the heads of the Cossacks and they were not an expression of superficial agitation. Their tempers were becoming heated now, slowly and thoroughly, and they were going to retain their heat for a long time.

"String up the Jews!" a shout came from the crowd. "That'll teach 'em to sew skirts from the cassocks of our priests! That'll stop 'em from tracing signs on the Easter cakes! Let's drown the whole bunch of unbelievers in the Dnieper!"

This little harangue made by somebody in the crowd had the effect of lightning striking dry wood. The throng stirred, then rushed toward the outskirts of the camp with the intent of slaughtering all Jews.

The wretched sons of Israel tried to hide in empty vodka barrels, under stoves, and some even crawled under the skirts of their women, but the Cossacks always found them.

"Gentlemen, gentlemen!" shouted a tall, thin, sticklike Jew whose fear-distorted features stuck up above the heads of his comrades. "Give us a chance to speak and you'll learn something important, something you don't even suspect. . . ."

"Let him have his say," Bulba said. He always liked to hear out the accused.

"Thank you, gentlemen," the Jew said, "you are extremely fair and generous—how could we possibly have a bad word to say about Zaporozhe Cossacks? Those who are renting churches in the Ukraine have nothing to do with us. They are no Jews, I assure you. God knows what they are. Here, ask them. I'm telling the truth, am I not, Isaac? You tell him, Shmul."

"He's telling the truth—he's right," Isaac and Shmul confirmed with bloodless lips.

"We've never had any contact whatsoever with your enemies, and as for the Catholics—we don't want anything to do with them, may they see the devil in their dreams! And the Zaporozhe Cossacks—we treat them like our own brothers—"

"What? What's he saying? Brothers, did you say? . . . Damn you, Jew! Into the Dnieper with the lot of 'em, let's drown the unbelieving dogs!"

These words, shouted by someone in the crowd, were like a signal and Jews were seized and hurled into the choppy river. Frightened wails came from the water, but the grim Cossacks just laughed at the sight of legs encased in shoes and stockings kicking in the air.

The tall thin Jew who had spoken tore free from those holding him by slipping out of his coat, and rushed up to Taras Bulba.

"Sir," he said imploringly, "I used to know your brother, the late Dorosh. There was a warrior for you! I gave eight hundred sequins to pay his ransom when he was captured by the Turks. . . ."

"You knew my brother? What's your name?"

"Yankel."

"All right," Taras said. "Listen," he said to the Cossacks, "you'll have plenty of time to hang him. Let me have him for the moment."

Taras led Yankel to his wagons, by which his Cossacks were standing.

"All right, climb under that cart and stay there, and you, brothers, see that he stays there."

After which Taras went to the assembly square into which the crowd was now flowing.

The preparation and equipping of the boats were abandoned because the Cossacks were now faced with a land campaign rather than a sea venture and what they needed was not boats but horses and wagons.

Now there was unanimity. Everyone wanted to go, old and young. The headman, the council of the elders, and the barrack chiefs—all agreed, and with popular approval, that they would drive straight for Poland to avenge the insults to the faith and to Cossack honor, to capture a lot of booty, to set fire to the Polish cities, villages and wheat fields, to spread the renown of the Cossack army far and wide.

Everyone began to prepare arms and equipment. The headman grew by a whole foot. He was no longer the subtle interpreter of the unreasonable whims of an exuberant bunch of people—he had become an absolute, despotic ruler who only gave orders. When he spoke even the hottest-tempered Cossacks stood quietly with lowered heads, not daring to lift their eyes, and the headman spoke unhurriedly, as an experienced Cossack who knew how to carry out his own well-devised plans.

"Inspect your gear thoroughly," he said. "See that your wagons are in good order, the axles properly greased. Do not take too many clothes with you: one extra shirt, two pairs of trousers. Bring two cooking pots of cereal. No more. We'll carry the necessary provisions in the wagons. Each man is to have two horses. We'll also take with us two hundred oxen—we'll need them at the fords and in the marshes. And, above all, gentlemen, I want you to maintain discipline. I know that some of you are greedy enough to stuff silk or velvet into your boots rather than leave such things behind. Well, you're not going to. You'll throw away all those skirts and things and take only good weapons and gold and silver coins as well, because they occupy little space in proportion to their usefulness. And now I warn you—if one of you gets drunk, there'll be no trial; he'll have his head put in a noose and be dragged like a dog behind a baggage wagon no matter if his past record is the most glorious imaginable. Then he'll get a bullet through his head and be left without burial to be eaten by scavengers, because a man who drinks on the march doesn't deserve a Christian burial. Young men, you'll obey your seniors. Now, if a ball grazes you, if you get nicked by a saber slash, in the head or anywhere else, don't let it stop you. Mix a little gunpowder in a cup of brandy, swallow it down, and you'll be all right—you won't even have a fever. As to the wound, if it's not too deep, just pick up a handful of earth, mix it with some spit and then the bandage won't stick to it. All right, get to work, lads. Don't rush though—do things thoroughly. Get moving."

And when the headman had finished, the Cossacks immediately became busy. The whole camp grew sober. It seemed impossible to believe that drunkards had ever been found among its inhabitants. Some repaired the hoops on wagon wheels, others changed axles, still others carried bags with food supplies. From every side could be heard horses' hoofbeats, shots fired in practice, swords clanging, oxen mooing, wagons creaking as they were turned over, the businesslike exchange of words, and sharp cries urging on the beasts.

And soon the Cossack caravan was spread out over

the plain; anyone wishing to race all the way from its head to its tail would have been out of breath before he reached his goal.

In the small wooden church the priest conducted the services, and, as each in turn kissed the cross, he sprinkled holy water on him. As the caravan moved out, Cossacks turned to look back at the camp and many muttered:

"Good-bye, Mother, may God keep you from all harm."

Passing through the outskirts, Taras saw that his protégé Yankel had already managed to erect a stall with an awning for himself and was selling flints, handfuls of gunpowder in paper cones, and other military items—even bread rolls and dumplings.

"What the hell's he waiting here for?" Taras thought, and riding up to him, he said:

"Fool, do you want to be shot?"

Yankel made him a sign with his hands that he wanted to tell him some secret, and, coming very close, said:

"Please keep it to yourself, sir, but among the wagons there's one of mine with all sorts of supplies that'll be needed during the campaign, and I'll supply you at lower prices than you'll be able to find anywhere else. I swear it, sir."

Taras shrugged, marveling at this sample of Jewish enterprise, and rode on toward his wagons.

5

Soon all southwest Poland was a prey to fear. Everywhere the alarm went out: "Cossacks! The Cossacks are coming!" Everyone who could fled. In those unsettled years, people just picked themselves up and scattered. At that time, men built neither fortresses nor castles. Each man set up a flimsy hut for himself, figuring to use it for a short time only, thinking to himself:

"Why should I waste time and money building myself a real house? The Tartars'll raze it in their next raid anyway."

Everyone took fright at the news of the Cossack advance. Some swapped oxen and plows for a horse and a gun and set out to join the armies; others fled, driving off their cattle and taking along everything that could be carried. There were some who resisted the invaders, weapons in hand, but mostly people fled even before they arrived. They all knew that it was almost impossible to get along with the violent crowd known as the Zaporozhe Band, a force which for all its apparent wild disorderliness was actually very thoughtfully organized and well disciplined in time of war. The mounted Cossacks rode without burdening or straining their horses; those afoot calmly followed the wagons. They moved only at night, resting during the daytime in a concealed spot or in the forest. The main body was preceded by reconnaissance patrols sent out to find out what was what and who was where.

Often the army would appear in places where it was least expected. They would appear from nowhere and then everything around was doomed. Fire devoured whole villages, the cattle and the horses that were not driven off with the army were slaughtered on the spot. They seemed to be at a wild party rather than on a military expedition. Today one's hair would stand on end at the horrible marks of bestiality that the Zaporozhe Cossacks of that wild century left in their wake. Babes with broken skulls, women with breasts cut off, the skin from the soles of the feet to the knees flayed from the legs of those who were left alive. In brief, the Cossacks paid back with interest the horrors they had suffered themselves. The abbot of a monastery sent a couple of monks to them with a reminder that there was an agreement between the Zaporozhe Cossacks and the King of Poland and that they were breaking it and at the same time violating the rights of innocent people.

"Assure your abbot," the headman told these messengers, "that he's seen nothing yet. We're just lighting our pipes."

And soon afterward the imposing Gothic abbey was blazing wildly, its huge carved windows looking grimly out at the world through the fiery flames.

Monks, Jews, and women crowded into towns where some hope could be placed in the garrison and the city ramparts. The belated rescue forces dispatched by the

Polish government either never found the Cossack troops or, when they did, beat hasty retreats after brief encounters, fleeing on their swift horses. But sometimes it happened that officers of the King who had previous triumphs over the Zaporozhe Cossacks to their credit joined forces and made a firm stand against the invaders. And it was in such battles that the young Cossacks were eager to try out their skill. They were not interested in looting and were reluctant to massacre those who were in no position to fight back. They wanted to pit their strength against the boastful Poles on their prancing horses, with plumes on their helmets and their wide sleeves thrown back and floating in the wind.

They acquired experience in these battles and, along with it, expensive trappings and valuable weapons. Within a month, the young cubs became men, and their faces, which until then had retained some of the softness of youth, now became strong and stern. Old Taras saw with joy that his two sons were among the very best of this young brood.

It seemed as though Ostap had been especially picked by fate to perform the most difficult warlike exploits. Never at a loss whatever the contingency, with a cold calculation uncanny in a twenty-two-year-old, he could appraise a situation at a glance, find a way to avoid a blow in order to place his own final counterblow. In no time his movements became self-assured and it was obvious that he was of the stuff of which leaders are made. His physical strength was exceptional and he had the noble comportment of a lion.

"By God, he'll be a terrific colonel, that boy," Taras mused, "a colonel who'll make his pa look like nothing."

Andrei was completely immersed in the music of bullets and sabers, and it enchanted him. He never stopped to weigh their own or the enemy's strength, to calculate their chances. He found a mad delight in battle. He was filled with a sort of holiday feeling, when his face felt as if afire, when everything flashed brightly before his eyes, when slashed-off heads rolled around him, when horses collapsed with thunderous thuds, while he flew through it all as if drunk, to the whistle of the bullets and the lightning of the saber blades, hitting out right and left, not believing in the blows of the enemy. Often Taras wondered at Andrei, watching him perform feats, guided by sheer ardor and by instinct, that would never have been tried by a cold-blooded, thinking warrior. At times the sheer madness of his attack performed miracles that left the old Cossacks gaping. And Taras would murmur:

"And this one, too, is a good one. I just hope he won't get killed with the things he's doing. A good fighter. Not the same as Ostap, but a good one."

It was decided that the army should push directly on to Dubno, where, it was rumored, there was a considerable quantity of stored gold and there were also many rich citizens. The inhabitants decided to fight to the last, preferring to die on their streets, squares, and doorsteps rather than allow the enemy to break into their homes. A high earth rampart surrounded the city and, in places where it was low, a stone barrier, the wall of a house, or an oak fence jutted out above it. The garrison was strong and fully aware of the terrible stakes.

First the Cossacks tried a frontal assault against the rampart, but the garrison met them with grapeshot. And the townsmen apparently did not intend to stand idly by; they crowded onto the rampart. Desperate determination could be read in their eyes. Even the women joined the defenders. Stones, barrels, pots, and boiling water flew down onto the Cossacks' heads and their eyes were blinded by bagfuls of sand. The Cossacks did not like to deal with fortresses. Siege warfare was not their forte. The headman ordered them to draw back.

"Never mind, brothers," he told them, "we'll withdraw. But I'm a heathen Tartar and no Christian if we let a single one of these dogs out of the city! They'll all die of hunger!"

The Cossack force drew up in a vast ring around the city. And, having nothing better to do while they were waiting, they laid waste the surrounding countryside, setting fire to the villages and to the stacks of grain standing in the fields and letting their horses loose to feed on unharvested grain, of which, as luck would have it, the crop was exceptionally good that year. From the city walls people watched horrified as their very means of existence was destroyed. In the meantime, the Cossacks had taken up their positions, divided, as in the camp, into troops, with a sector assigned to each. And they smoked their pipes, swapped loot and weapons, played games, gambled, and watched the town with murderous calm. At night they lit fires. The cooks boiled supper for each troop in huge copper soup kettles; by each fire, a sentinel was posted. But the Cossacks soon grew bored with having nothing to do while sober. Although the headman had doubled the wine ration, as was usual when not on a forced march or in continuous action, this was not enough. The young men, the Bulba brothers in particular, didn't care for this kind of life and Andrei in particular chafed.

"You young goat," Taras said to him, "patience is the mother of virtue. To be a good soldier takes more than bravery in battle; a soldier must endure inactivity and whatever else may come. Only then will he achieve what he's after."

But youth and old age see things differently and cannot communicate.

In the meantime, Taras's troop, led by Tovkach, had managed to join them before the city. There were more than four thousand in the troop, including the volunteers who had joined as soon as they heard the news. The boys' mother had sent them her blessings with a captain and a medallion for each from the Mezhigorsky Monastery in Kiev. Being reminded of their mother somehow made them sad. Perhaps they felt that their mother's blessing carried an omen. Would it bring victory over the enemy and a happy homecoming with spoils and glory to be sung of forever by the lute players? Or was it . . . ? But the future is unknown and it stands before a man like the autumn mist rising from a marsh. The birds fly frantically up and down in it, flapping their wings, unable to make one another out, the dove not seeing the hawk and the hawk not seeing the dove, and neither knows how far he is from his own death. . . .

Ostap returned to his daily preoccupations first, but Andrei remained where he was, strangely depressed for a long time. The Cossacks had already finished their supper. The evening light had long disappeared from the sky and the gorgeous July night saturated the air. But instead of rejoining his troop, instead of trying to sleep, he stood gazing at the scene around him. In the sky numberless stars shone with a sharp, fine glitter. Scattered far over the field were wagons with their grease pots hanging beneath them and carts piled high with provisions and loot taken from the enemy. And under, on top, and around the vehicles, the Cossacks lay sleeping. They lay in picturesque poses, one with a sack beneath his head, another, with his cap, another simply using his comrade's side. Beside each Cossack lay his saber, his gun, his short pipe with its copper-mounted stem, his tinderbox. The heavy oxen lay with their feet doubled under them, looming huge and whitish-looking from a distance, like pale rocks scattered across the sloping plain. From every side snores rose from the grass, intertwined with the indignant neighing of the horses protesting at their hobbled feet. But something awesome and threatening had also crept into the warm July night. The reflections of remote fires shivered in various parts of the sky. Somewhere on the outskirts of the town, buildings were aflame. In one section, the fire was outlined against the summer sky in calm, subdued tones; in another, the flames, having reached something highly combustible, suddenly burst into a whirling flash and soared hissing upward toward the stars. Then incandescent, shapeless fragments, dying, fell down from the heights. Here a burned-out monastery, grim as a black Catholic monk, displayed its bleak magnificence at every flash. Next to it burned the monastery orchard. It seemed as though one could hear each tree hiss as it disappeared in its wreath of smoke. Succumbing to the fire, the ripe plums stepped out of the darkness and appeared in a lilac-colored phosphorescence, while the pears gleamed like yellow gold. Not far off, the blackened bodies of several monks and Jews dangled from the building's wall and from the branch of a tree. And above it all hovered a flock of birds looking like little black crosses against the reddish, fiery background.

One would have thought that the besieged city was quietly breathing in its sleep. Its spires, its towers, the roofs and the walls of its tallest buildings quietly reflected the flashes of the distant conflagrations.

Andrei walked along the Cossack lines. The campfires, beside which sat the men on watch, were nearly out. As to the watchmen, they were asleep, digesting the good meals they had devoured with carefree appetites. He was somewhat surprised at such dereliction of duty and thought how lucky it was that the enemy they were facing here was not really dangerous. Finally, he went over to one of the wagons, climbed on top of it and lay down on his back, his hands clasped under his head. But he could not fall asleep and stayed there staring upward. The sky was completely open above him, the air was transparent and the stars of the Milky Way, which crossed the firmament at a slant, were all immersed in its whitish light. After a while little waves of sleep started to wash over Andrei and the light mist of his dreams would veil the stars for a brief moment, but then it would clear and the outlines of things stood out sharp and precise again.

During one of these veiled moments he had the impression that a strange human face had flashed close by him. Deciding that it was a shadow in his dream that would vanish with it, he forced his eyes open completely and saw that a real, strange, exhausted-looking face was bent over him looking straight at him. Long, coal-black, tangled hair escaped from under a dark shawl thrown over the head and the sharp-featured, deathly sallow face, with its eerily gleaming eyes, made him think that he was facing a ghost. His hand instinctively grasped his pistol and he said, gasping a little:

"Who are you? If you are an evil spirit, vanish! If you are a live man, I don't like such jokes and I'll blow your head off with the first bullet!"

The apparition answered by placing a finger to its lips, apparently imploring him to be quiet. He looked closer at it, lowering his hand. By the long hair, by the shape of the neck, and by the crescents formed by the top of breasts over a dress, he saw that it was a woman. And he saw too that she was not a native of that land. Her exhausted face was dark, the prominent cheekbones stood out above her sunken cheeks, the narrow eyes arched upward. The longer he looked at her face, the more it seemed familiar. Finally he said:

"Who are you? It seems to me I used to know you or that I've seen you somewhere."

"You did. Two years ago in Kiev."

"Two years ago in Kiev," Andrei repeated slowly, trying to muster what was left in his memory of student life at the seminary. He looked at her intently again and suddenly exclaimed aloud:

"Yes—yes, you're the Tartar maid of the young Polish lady, the daughter of the military governor of Kovno! . . ."

"Sh-sh-sh!" the Tartar said, folding her hands in an imploring gesture. She was trembling terribly and turned her head to see whether Andrei's exclamation had awakened anyone near them.

"Tell me, tell me, how did you come here . . ." Andrei whispered, almost breathless from the wave of emotion that had passed over him. "Where is she, where is the Polish girl? She's alive, is she? . . ."

"She's here, in the city."

"In the city?" he exclaimed, again almost shouting, feeling the blood rush to his heart. "Why is she in the city?"

"Because her father is here. . . . He was transferred here. . . . He's been the military governor of Dubno for eighteen months now."

"Is she married? Come on, speak up, why are you so strange? . . . What is she now . . ."

"She hasn't eaten all day."

"What?"

"None of the inhabitants of the city have had any bread for days, some have been eating earth. . . ."

Andrei was like one paralyzed.

"My lady recognized you among the Cossacks from the city wall. She told me, 'Go and tell him that if he remembers me, he should come to me and, if he won't come, to send me a piece of bread for my old mother because I do not wish to see her die, I'd rather die myself first. Beg if you have to, because he too must have an old mother. Let him give you some bread for her sake.'"

Myriads of diverse feelings awoke and began burning in the young Cossack's chest.

"But how did you manage to get here? How did you come over?"

"Through an underground passage."

"Is there one?"

"Yes."

"Where?"

"You won't give me away?"

"I swear by the holy cross I won't."

"You reach it through the creek over there, you cross the brook and go through the reeds. . . ."

"And it takes you inside the city?"

"Straight into the chapel of the monastery."

"Let's go then! Let's go right now!"

"But in the name of Jesus Christ and the Virgin Mary, a piece of bread. . . ."

"Yes, yes, of course. Wait here, by the wagon . . . no, better lie down. No one will find you here, they are all asleep, anyway. I'll be back in no time."

And he walked over to the wagons where his troop's stores were kept. His heart was beating wildly. The past, superseded by the absorbing dangers and excitements of war, came violently back to the surface, in its turn blotting out the present. Again, as if emerging from the dark depths of the sea, he saw in front of him the proud, laughing girl; his memory brought back in a flash the shape of her arms, the curve of her laughing lips, the thick, hazelnut waves of her hair, streaming down her neck and shoulders as she bent forward. He remembered her firm young breasts, the feminine curves of her beautifully proportioned limbs. . . . No, these visions had never been completely extinguished, they had simply been pushed under to make room for other powerful impressions and emotions. And often they had haunted the deep, deep dreams of the young Cossack who, when he was torn awake, would lie sleepless and restless without understanding why.

As he walked, his heart beat faster at the thought that he would see her again. His knees shook. When he reached the provision wagon, he had forgotten what he had come for. He put his hand to his brow and rubbed it, trying to remember what he had to do. Then he suddenly shuddered, filled with fear at the thought that she might die of starvation. He jumped up on the wagon, grabbed several loaves of black bread and was about to rush off with them under his arm when he stopped short. It had occurred to him that, while black bread was all right for a crude Zaporozhe Cossack, it must be quite unsuitable for a graceful, delicate girl. He remembered that the previous evening the headman had reproached the cooks for using up all the buckwheat at once when there was enough of it for three meals. He inspected all the kettles of his father's troop. They were empty—even the huge caldron that held at least ten bucketfuls and under which ashes were still glowing. He was vaguely astounded at the voracity of the Cossacks and was not too hopeful of finding anything left in the kettles of the other troops, since they all received an equal amount of food and Bulba's troop had somewhat fewer men than the others. Automatically the Cossack saying flashed into his mind: "If offered too little—we'll eat it; if offered too much—we'll eat it." Then he decided that there must be a bag of white bread somewhere in their wagon. The bag was not there. Then he saw it: it was under Ostap's head. His brother lay stretched out on the ground, breathing loudly. Andrei seized the bag and gave it a jerk so that Ostap's head banged against the ground. He sat up and, his eyes still closed, shouted so that his voice seemed to fill the whole night:

"Hold him, hold him, the damn Polish bastard! Hold his horse! His horse!"

"Shut up or I'll kill you," Andrei hissed in a panic, swinging at his brother with the sack.

But he did not have to worry—Ostap did not pursue his appeal. Instead, letting out a tremendous snore, he sank down again, breathing so hard that the grass around his nose swayed in rhythm.

Andrei looked gingerly around to see whether Ostap's ravings had awakened anybody. He saw a tufted head rise at some distance, stare for a moment and then fall down again. He waited a couple of minutes, then grabbed the sack of white bread and went back to the Tartar girl, who lay on the wagon scarcely breathing.

"Come," he said, "let's get going. They're all asleep, you've really nothing to fear. Do you think," he asked her, "that you could carry these loaves? I'd like to take some more. . . ."

He put his bag on his shoulder, grabbed another one with millet in it, and at the last second himself took the loaves he had asked the Tartar girl to carry. Then, bending somewhat under his load, he walked boldly among the outstretched Cossacks.

"Andrei!" he heard his father's voice ring out suddenly, as he was passing near the emplacement of their troop. His heart died. He halted, shivering, and asked softly:

"What?"

"There's a woman with you. Wait until I get up, I'll show you! Women will lead you to no good." As he said this, he raised himself, leaning on an elbow, and, resting his cheek on his hand, scrutinized the draped silhouette of the Tartar girl intently.

Andrei stood half-alive, half-dead, unable to look into his father's face. But when finally he did, he realized that the old Bulba had gone back to sleep in the same position, his cheek on his hand.

Andrei crossed himself. Suddenly fear left him completely. He turned back and looked at the Tartar girl. She appeared to him like a granite statue wrapped in her shawl, and when her figure was lighted up by the remote flaring of a fire he could make out only the flash of her eyes in her face, a wooden brilliance, like the eyes of someone dead. He pulled her by the sleeve and they moved on, constantly looking back. Finally they came to the creek and went down its bank. Andrei saw that the slope rising behind him was higher than a man and he could make out some tall blades of grass and behind them the sky with the moon in an oblique crescent— they were completely out of sight of the Cossack camp.

The stir of a small steppe breeze announced the approach of dawn. But not a single cock crowed. For a long time now all the chickens in the entire district had been exterminated. They went across the stream on a plank. The bank on the city side was higher. At this point the city's defenses were apparently considered quite safe and the earth wall was not even manned, because immediately beyond it rose the thick wall of a monastery.

The steep bank was covered with coarse grass and between it and the creek bed grew reeds as tall as a man. Along the top of the bank ran a broken wattle fence which must formerly have surrounded a garden. In front of it grew burdock with blackthorn and sunflowers lifting their heads from among its leaves. Here, the Tartar threw off her slippers and pulled up her skirts because the soil was marshy and full of water. They worked their way among the reeds and stopped before a pile of dry wood. She pushed some logs aside and uncovered an opening like the mouth of a large oven. The girl bent her head and went in. Andrei squeezed himself in behind her, pulling the bags along. They found themselves in total darkness.

6

Andrei, loaded down as he was, had difficulty following the Tartar girl along the dark, narrow earthen tunnel.

"We'll soon be able to see," she said. "We're nearly at the spot where I left a lamp."

Soon the dark walls grew lighter. The passage widened and they came to what might have been an underground chapel: there was a sort of altar by one wall with a very faded Catholic Madonna hanging above it, dimly lit by a small silver lamp. There was also a larger brass lamp on a long thin stand with snuffers, a pin for adjusting the flame, and an extinguisher dangling on little chains. The Tartar girl picked it up from the floor and lit it from the altar lamp. They moved on. And now the swaying lamp made their coal-black silhouettes jump on the walls, which were almost dazzling in the light. It was like a painting by a Spanish master come alive. The handsome, strong features of the young warrior, overflowing with exuberant health, presented a sharp contrast to the thin, exhausted face of his companion. Gradually there was more headroom and Andrei could straighten his shoulders. He examined the underground passage curiously. It reminded him of the Kiev catacombs. As in

Kiev, there were recesses in the walls, holding coffins. And here and there he stumbled on loose human bones which had turned soft and crumbled into powder. Apparently here, too, pious people had taken refuge from the world's storms, griefs and temptations. The tunnel was quite damp and from time to time they found themselves walking in water. Again and again Andrei had to stop to let his companion rest, but, even so, her tiredness returned almost immediately. A small piece of bread she had swallowed caused sharp cramps in a stomach unaccustomed to food and forced her to remain motionless for several minutes at a time.

At last, they saw a small iron door ahead of them.

"Well, thank heaven—we've arrived," the Tartar girl said in a weak voice, trying to lift her hand and knock on the door but finding that she lacked the strength. Andrei banged on it for her. His knock reverberated, indicating that there was a space on the other side of the door. Then the sound of the reverberation changed as if it were now ringing in a high vault. A few moments later there was a clinking of keys; someone, it seemed, was coming down some steps. Finally the door was unlocked and opened by a monk. He stood at the bottom of a narrow staircase holding the keys and a candle. Instinctively Andrei drew back. The sight of a Catholic monk aroused in the Cossacks even greater hatred and disdain than the sight of a Jew. The monk too stepped back when he saw the Zaporozhe Cossack, but a whispered word from the Tartar girl reassured him. He held up the light for them, locked the door behind them, and led them up the staircase. They came out under the high, somber arches of the monastery church. Near one of the altars, on which candles burned in tall candlesticks, a kneeling priest was quietly praying. On either side of him, also kneeling, were two altar boys in lilac cassocks under white lace stoles, with censers in their hands. He was praying for a miracle to save the town, to lift up their fallen spirits; he was praying that the people might be given the strength to endure their hardships, praying for the banishment of the Tempter who brought self-pity and tearful moaning over the ordeals of the flesh.

People were kneeling all around—women, as pale as

ghosts, allowed their heads to rest on the backs of chairs and dark wooden benches in front of them, and men leaned against the pillars and columns. The stained-glass window above the altar was lighted up by the pink glow of the dawn, and circles of blue, yellow and other colors fell from it to the floor. Suddenly, deep in its recess, the altar appeared in a halo of light and the smoke from the censers hung in the air in an iridescent cloud. As Andrei gazed in wonder at the extraordinary effect of the light, a majestic chord from the organ filled the whole church. It swelled and swelled, spread out, changed to heavy peals of thunder, and then, without warning, it turned into heavenly music and floated high up under the arches in sounds reminiscent of girlish voices; then once again it became a mighty roar of thunder and fell silent. For a long time the peals of thunder shook under the arches and, his mouth half-open, Andrei marveled at the majestic music. Then he felt someone pulling at his coat.

"We must go," the Tartar girl said.

They crossed the church without anyone noticing them and came out onto the square in front of it. Now the dawn sky was reddish. The sun was about to rise. The square was completely deserted. In its center stood wooden tables, suggesting that perhaps not more than a week ago this had been a market where food could be bought. The square, which was unpaved (they did not pave streets in those days), was simply a mass of dried mud and was surrounded by one-story stone and mud houses with wooden posts running the whole height of their walls and joined by carved crossbeams, in the style of houses of those days, some of which can still be found in Lithuania and Poland today. They all had very high roofs, with many dormer windows and ventilating holes. On one side of the square, not far from the church, a tall house stood apart from the others. It looked like a town hall or other government building. It had two stories and was topped by an arched belvedere where a soldier stood on watch. Under the roof there was a big clock face.

Although the square seemed dead, Andrei thought he heard a weak moan. He looked all around and saw several bodies lying almost motionless on the ground in a corner. He was trying to make out whether they were dying or just waking up, when he stumbled against something. It was a dead body, a woman, probably Jewish. Something about her suggested that she was still young, although this could not have been told from her distorted, emaciated face. On her head she wore a red silk kerchief and, where it covered her ears, it was decorated with two rows of some sort of pearls or beads. Two or three long, curly locks had escaped from her kerchief and lay on her shriveled neck with its distended veins. Beside her lay an infant, its hand grasping spasmodically at her gaunt breast and twisting at it with an innocent ferocity because it yielded no milk. Now the infant no longer cried nor yelled and only the slight rise and fall of its stomach showed that it was not yet dead, or at least that it still had a few more breaths to draw.

They turned into a side street and were abruptly brought to a stop by a madman who, seeing Andrei's precious load, threw himself on him like a tiger, clinging to him and yelling: "Bread!" But his strength was not equal to his madness and, when Andrei pushed him off, he collapsed on the ground. Moved by pity, Andrei tossed him a loaf. The man threw himself on it like a mad dog, sinking his teeth into it and tearing at it, and died then and there in the street in terrible agony, having become completely unaccustomed to food. At almost every step, they came upon the horrible victims of starvation. It seemed as if many of them had run out onto the street because they were unable to bear their sufferings indoors, almost as if they hoped to find some nourishment in the air. They passed an old woman sitting at her door and it was impossible to tell whether she had fallen asleep, was dead, or was simply deep in thought. In any case, she no longer heard or saw anything and only sat immobile, her head drooping. From the roof of another house hung a rope from which dangled the limp, wasted body of a man. The wretch had been unable to endure the sufferings of hunger and had decided it was better to hasten his end by suicide.

At the sight of this awful starvation, Andrei could no longer restrain himself and asked the Tartar girl:

"Is it possible that these people couldn't find anything—

just to stay alive? In dire circumstances, men eat things
that would disgust them normally, that are forbidden by
religion, everything is made use of. . . ."

"We've eaten everything, every animal; you won't find
a horse, a dog, a cat, or even a mouse alive in this city.
Besides, we never kept any supplies here, everything was
brought in from the countryside."

"But if you're going through this terrible death agony,
how can you hope to save the city?"

"Well," the Tartar girl said, "perhaps the military governor might even have surrendered if he hadn't received
word yesterday, flown in by a hawk. The colonel, the
one in Budzany, asks him to hold out a little longer. He
is coming to our rescue. He's only waiting for another
colonel to join forces with him . . . but here we are."

Andrei had noticed the house quite a while before. It
was not like the others. It was two stories high, built of
fine brick, probably by an Italian architect. The windows
of the ground floor had very prominent high granite cor-
nices; the upper story looked like a gallery with its
arches and lattices covered with coats of arms. Coats of
arms could also be seen on the corners of the house. An
outside staircase led onto the square itself and at its
foot two sentries stood, picturesquely symmetrical, each
holding a halberd in one hand while the other supported
a bowed head. They were not asleep, not even dozing,
but seemed somehow insensitive to the outside world
and they paid no attention to anyone passing on the
stairs. At the top of the staircase, Andrei saw a warrior,
richly attired and equipped, holding a missal in his hand.
He lifted his eyes to them, but the Tartar whispered
something in his ear and he lowered them again to the
pages of his book. They went through into a vast hall
that may have been a reception room. It was filled with
a throng of people sitting along the walls in every
imaginable position: soldiers, maids, valets, kennelmen,
cellarmen—all the domestics a Polish nobleman needs
to maintain his title or his military rank. There was the
smell of a just-extinguished lamp, and two other lamps
on stands as tall as a man were still burning, although
daylight was already evident beyond the latticed window.
Andrei was on the point of going straight through to a

heavy oak door adorned with coats of arms and other carvings, but the Tartar caught his sleeve and pointed to a small side door to one side. Through it they entered a corridor and from there a room which Andrei could not make out too well. Light through a crack in the blind allowed him to see only a raspberry-colored curtain, a gilded cornice and an oil painting on the wall.

The Tartar signaled to him to remain where he was and opened another door through which he saw the gleam of a fire. He heard a whisper and a low voice which made him forget everything else. He saw through the open door the flash of a supple feminine form with a luxurious braid caught on a raised arm. The Tartar girl returned and asked him to come in. He was unaware of following her and of the door shutting behind them. Two candles burned in the room. A lamp smoked under a statue of the Virgin. Before it stood a tall *prie-dieu* such as Catholics use to pray. But he took all this in only vaguely and turned around. He saw a woman who seemed frozen in the middle of some quick movement. It looked as if her whole body had been about to throw itself toward him when it had suddenly become petrified. And looking at her, he felt turned to stone.

He had never expected to find her like this. She was not the one he remembered. She was completely altered, more marvelous, more extraordinary. Before, there had been something unfinished about her. Now she was a work of art to which the artist had put the very last stroke of the brush. The other, the one of the past, had been an enchanting, light-hearted girl; this was a finished woman. Her wide-open eyes radiated full-blooded emotion—not a little emotion, nor a hint of emotion, but a full, total emotion—and the bright traces of tears still stood in her eyes. Her breasts, her neck and her shoulders fell exactly within the narrow boundaries assigned to perfect beauty, her hazelnut hair, which once scattered in soft waves over her face, was gathered in a magnificent heavy braid. It seemed to him that every one of her features had changed. In vain he tried to recognize at least one from his memory of her.

She was terribly pale but this did not mar her incredible beauty. On the contrary, it seemed to add something irresistible, something supernatural, to it. Awe filled Andrei's soul as he stood immobile, staring at her.

And she too was impressed by the looks of the young Cossack. He was strikingly handsome and manly and even in his immobility one could guess at the freedom and grace of his movements. His eyes sparkled under velvety, firmly arched eyebrows, the youthful freshness of his cheeks showed through his deep tan, his thin black mustachio looked soft and silky.

"No, I cannot—it is beyond my power to thank you, generous knight," she said finally and the silvery sound of her voice vibrated tenderly. "God alone can reward you, not a weak woman like me. . . ." She dropped her eyes, lowering the hemispheres of her heavy lids with their arrowlike, silky black lashes. As her head bent forward, a delicate blush, rising from her neck, colored her face.

Andrei could find nothing to say. He would have liked to tell her all that he felt but he could not. Something locked his mouth. He knew he would not be able to find the right words. How could he, educated in the seminary, raised in the steppe, leading a nomadic, restless life, answer her? At that moment, he deeply despised his Cossack nature.

The Tartar girl returned to the room. She had already sliced some of the bread which Andrei had brought and carried the slices on a golden dish which she placed before her mistress, who glanced at the bread and then looked up at Andrei. There were many things in that long look—tenderness, exhaustion and also her feeling that she could not convey to him what she felt, and it touched him directly, even more than her words, and suddenly he felt free and easy. His heavy shackles were broken and an inexhaustible flow of words was about to pour out of him.

At that moment, she suddenly turned toward the Tartar girl and asked:

"And what about Mother? Have you taken some to her?"

"She's asleep, ma'am."

"And Father?"

"Yes, ma'am. The master said he would come and thank the knight personally."

The beauty then took a slice of bread and brought it to her mouth. Andrei, hardly breathing, watched her slender white fingers break off small pieces of bread and put them into her mouth. Suddenly he remembered the man who had died in front of his eyes after swallowing a piece of bread. He turned pale and grasped her hand.

"Enough," he shouted, "no more! You haven't eaten for so long. . . . It can be like poison."

She immediately dropped her hand and replaced the slice in the golden dish with a childlike obedience, looking into his eyes with . . .

But neither chisel nor brush nor the mighty word can express what may be found sometimes in the eyes of a woman, any more than they can convey the storm of tenderness which sweeps over the one those eyes are looking upon.

"My tsarina, my empress!" Andrei muttered, overwhelmed. "Tell me what you want me to do. Order me to accomplish the most impossible things and I'll obey you. If you want me to do what no man alive can do, I'll do it or die trying. And I swear to you by the holy cross that dying thus would be sweet for me, I cannot tell you how sweet. . . . I have three farms, and half of my father's herds of horses belong to me; also, all that my mother had when she married my father, much of which she has concealed from him . . . all that must go to me, to me alone. None of our Cossacks own weapons such as I do: for the hilt of my saber alone they would give me their best drove of horses and three hundred sheep. And all this I would gladly give up, discard, flood, scorch, lay waste, if you were to say one word, if you simply made a sign with your curved black eyebrow. . . . But I know I must seem stupid and uncouth—I've spent my life in the seminary and in the Zaporozhe steppes and I'm not fit to speak in a house where kings, princes, and the flower of knighthood are received. I see that you are a creature altogether different from us—the wives and daughters of our boyars are unworthy of you.

We, we are unworthy even to serve you—only the heavenly angels are good enough for that."

The young woman listened to him with growing amazement, without uttering a word. She felt that his speech reflected his young, violent spirit like a mirror. And each simple sound, coming straight from the depths of his heart, had in it a singular force. Her beautiful face was turned toward him, her unruly hair was pushed impatiently back, her lips parted and for a long time remained parted while her eyes were fixed on his. She began to say something, but stopped. . . .

It had struck her suddenly that the Cossack was destined for different things. His father, his brothers, his entire country, loomed behind him as grim avengers. She remembered that the terror-instilling Zaporozhe Cossacks were besieging the city, that they had doomed everybody in the city to a horrible death. . . . Her eyes suddenly filled with tears. She seized a silk kerchief and covered her face with it. He saw the damp marks of her tears darkening it. For a long time she remained in that position, biting her lip with her white, even teeth, feeling as though she had been bitten by a viper. Her head was pushed back and she kept her face covered to conceal her heartbreaking grief from him.

"Say just one word," Andrei said, taking her satin-smooth hand.

A sparkling flame shot through his entire body as he squeezed her inert hand in his.

But she did not speak, did not uncover her face and remained immobile.

"Why are you so sad? Tell me, why are you so sad?"

She tore the kerchief from her face, threw back the long tresses of hair that fell over her eyes and spoke in a very quiet, sad tone reminiscent of the breeze that rises suddenly on a calm evening and whispers through a thicket of reeds on a riverbank with a mournfully tender sound—that brings the traveler to a halt, filled with an unaccountable nostalgia, and makes him forget the approach of night, the songs of the laborers returning from the fields and the rattling of the wheels of a passing cart.

"Am I not to be eternally pitied, just like the mother

who brought me into this world? Is not fate crueler than a hangman or a torturer? Oh, life threw at my feet the scions of the nobility, the wealthiest lords and counts, foreign barons and the very flower of our Polish knighthood. Many of them loved me and I had only to wave my hand and any one of them, the handsomest and the noblest, would have considered it a supreme happiness, and an honor too, to become my husband. But, as cruel fate would have it, none of them ever touched my heart—it had to let pass the finest knights in my own world and go out to a stranger, to the enemy. Why, Holy Mother, why do you torture me so cruelly? What horrible sins have I committed? My days once flowed by in luxury and abundance; the most delicate foods and the oldest wines were my fare. And what was it all for? Was it all so that I might end up dying a death more miserable than that of any beggar in the kingdom? And, as if it were not enough to be doomed to such a cruel end, as if it were not enough to have to watch my mother and father, for whom I would have given my life twenty times, die in unbearable agony, before I die myself; as if all this were not enough, I have been sentenced before this end to meet, to hear and to feel the words and the love I have never known. He had to come now, to tear my heart to shreds, to make my destiny even more bitter, to make me cry even more despairingly over my young life, to make my impending death even more terrifying and force me to curse you even more angrily, you, my fate, and you, too, Mother of God, may I be forgiven for it. . . ."

Her voice died and an infinite hopelessness covered her face. Every one of her features, the pale lowered brow, the downcast eyes, her cheeks with the traces of her tears on them, seemed to cry out that this beautiful girl was not destined for happiness.

"That's unheard of, impossible—it won't happen," Andrei said. "The most beautiful of all women could only be born to be worshipped by all that is best in the world. No, you shall not die. Dying is not for you, I swear to it by my birth, by everything that is dear to me in life. But, should it happen that neither strength, nor prayer, nor daring, nor anything, can change that bitter fate, then we shall die together and I will be the first. And only when I am dead, if then, will they be able to take you away from me."

"Don't deceive yourself, Cossack, and do not deceive me," she said, slowly shaking her finely shaped head. "I realize—oh, I realize it to my great sorrow—but, alas only too well, that you *must* not love me. I know your place and your duty: your father, your comrades, and your native land call out to you—and we, we are your enemies."

"And what's my father to me, what are my comrades and my native land?" Andrei said. He threw his head back, straightened himself up, standing there strong as an oak. "Well, if it comes to that, I have no one in the world. No one, no one, no one!" he repeated and stressed his words with a happen-what-may gesture of his hand. "And who says that the Ukraine is my country? Who made her my country? A man's country is something sought by the heart, the thing that is dearest to him. . . . My country . . . you are my country! And I shall carry that country in my heart as long as I live. Let any Cossack try to tear it out! Everything I have, I'll sell, give away, destroy, for that country!"

For one second she was again a magnificent stone statue gazing into his eyes. Then suddenly she burst into a torrent of tears, and as only a great-hearted, noble woman could do, she threw herself toward him, put her arms around his neck, sobbing. And, although at that very moment shouts and the sound of drums and trumpets came from the street, Andrei heard nothing. He felt only her warm, pure breath, her tears wetting his face, and her perfumed silky tresses.

Suddenly the Tartar maid rushed into the room shouting:

"We're saved, we're saved! Our troops have broken through and entered the city, bringing bound Cossacks with them."

But neither he nor she understood who were these "our" troops who had brought in the captured Cossacks. Andrei turned his face and, feeling something unlike anything he could imagine existed on earth, he kissed her soft lips. She responded and they were united in a way people can be but once in their lives.

And that was the end of the Cossack. He was lost to the great Cossack brotherhood! Never again would he see his native Zaporozhe, his father's farms, his Orthodox churches. And never again would the Ukraine see one of her boldest children, pledged to defend her. And old Taras would tear a handful of hair from his gray Cossack tuft and curse the hour when, to his disgrace, he had conceived this son.

7

The Cossack camp was in an uproar. At first, no one could explain how the Polish force had managed to make its way into the city. Only later did it turn out that every last man of the Pereyaslav troop, which had been stationed before the side gate of the city, had been dead drunk and that it was no wonder that half of them had been killed and the other half captured before they knew what had hit them. And by the time the nearest detachments, awakened by the noise, had grabbed their arms, the Polish relief force was already entering the gates with the rear guard firing at the sleepy and only half-sober Cossacks pursuing them.

The headman ordered a general assembly and when they all stood around him with heads uncovered, he spoke:

"So you know what happened last night, my very dear friends. You see now what drunkenness can do. That's quite a slap we got from the enemy. Apparently a few too many glasses of vodka make you so blind that the enemy of Christ's army can not only pull the trousers off you but can sneeze in your faces without your knowing it!"

The Cossacks stood with lowered heads, abashed. Only Kukubenko, the chief of the Nezamaikovsky troop, protested:

"Wait, headman," he said, "I know it's not usual to object when the headman speaks to the assembled force, but I must tell you it didn't happen that way. It's not fair to blame the entire Christian force. The Cossacks would be guilty, they would deserve death, if they had drunk themselves into such a state while on the march or in action or doing strenuous work. But we've been sitting around with nothing to do in front of this city. And there's been no fast day or any other Christian reason for abstinence. Now, how can a man not get drunk when he's idle? There's nothing wrong with that. What we'd better do is to teach the Poles a lesson for their cowardly attack. We've walloped them before and now we'll give them such a walloping that they won't get home standing up."

The Cossacks liked Kukubenko's speech. Many raised their lowered heads and nodded their approval. They began to shout:

"Well said, Kukubenko! Well put!"

And Taras Bulba, who was standing near the headman, said:

"Well, headman, looks like Kukubenko has a point there—what d'you say to that?"

"What do I say? Well, I say lucky is the father who begot a son who'll say a word which, instead of knocking a man down when he is in trouble, will spur him on and give him courage. That takes more wisdom than is needed to reproach him. I was going to say a word of comfort myself, after my reproaches, but Kukubenko beat me to it."

"Well said, headman!" voices were heard from the crowd. "The headman speaks well!"

And the elders, who stood there puffed up like gray-headed pigeons, nodded, and, stroking their mustachios, agreed:

"He certainly knows how to put it, this headman."

"Now listen, friends," the headman said, "I don't believe in taking a fortress by climbing and digging as the Germans do. I leave that to the enemy. It's not a fitting occupation for a man and a Cossack. Well, the way things look, the enemy have entered the city without many supplies. They brought only a few carts along. Now, the people in there must be hungry, so the chances are they'll gulp everything down. Then, horses must have hay . . . unless, of course, one of their saints tosses some down from the sky—although these Catholics are better at words than at miracles. So for one reason or another, they'll come out of the gates. Therefore, we'll break up into three detachments, one stationed on each of the roads facing the three city gates. The detachment before the main gate will consist of five troops, the two others of three each. The Diadkiv and the Korsun troops will wait in ambush. The Bulba troop also in ambush. The Tytarev and Tymashov troops will be held in reserve on the right flank, behind the wagons, Sherbinov and Stablikiv—on the left flank. Now I want those of you who have the sharpest tongues to step forward: you'll taunt and tease the enemy. The Poles are empty-headed, they can't stand abuse and possibly we'll be able to lure the lot of them out no later than today. I want every troop chief to inspect his troop thoroughly. If you are short of men, fill up your ranks from what is left of the Pereyaslav troop. Check everything carefully. And to keep the men going, have them each issued a loaf of bread and a glass of vodka, although they should still be full from yesterday—they put away so much that it's a sheer miracle they haven't burst. And now, one more thing: if any Jewish merchant sells a Cossack even one single jug of vodka, I'll have a sow's ear nailed to the bastard's forehead and then I'll have him hung by his feet. Now, get on with it—get going!"

The Cossacks bowed to him and dispersed toward their troops and wagons, only putting their hats back on when they were quite a distance away. Then they proceeded to prepare for action, testing their sabers and broadswords, filling their powder flasks, rolling their wagons into position and choosing themselves horses.

Walking toward his troop's emplacement, Taras was worrying about Andrei. Could he have been bound up in his sleep and taken prisoner with the others? "No," he thought, "that's unlikely, he'd never let them capture him alive." But then, Andrei's body had not been found among the Cossacks killed. Taras was deep in thought and for quite a while did not hear his name being called.

"Who wants me?" flashed through his mind when awareness of the world returned to him. It was Yankel, the Jew.

"Colonel Bulba, sir," he was saying in a hurried, gasping voice, sounding as though he had something urgent to tell, "I have come straight from inside the city, sir . . ."

"How the hell did you manage to get in there?" Taras asked, bewildered.

"You see, Colonel Bulba, sir, when I heard the shooting at dawn, I grabbed my coat and rushed off without even bothering to put my arms through the sleeves, for I had to find out what the uproar was all about and why the Cossacks were firing so early in the morning. So I found myself by the gates at the very moment when the last Polish troops were pouring through them. And whom do you think I recognized among them but Pan Galiandovich, an old acquaintance of mine, who happens to have owed me a hundred gold pieces for about three years. So I decided to claim the debt and followed him into the city."

"You mean you entered the city and started claiming the debt? What was there to stop him from having you strung up like a dog?"

"Well, he almost did have me hanged. His servants had already got hold of me and put a noose round my neck but I begged the Polish gentleman to let me loose. I said he didn't have to pay me until he felt like it, on the contrary, I'd lend him more money if he'd help me to collect some other debts from the other Polish gentlemen . . . for it must be said that Galiandovich doesn't have a gold coin in his pocket, although he has estates and farms and four castles and grazing land right near Shklov. Still, for pocket money he's no better off than a Cossack—his pockets are just as empty. . . . And had it not been for the Breslau Jews, he couldn't have bought his arms and then he wouldn't have been able to fight in this war. And that's why he doesn't attend the Sejm any more————"

"So what did you do in the city? See any of our people?"

"Our people, sir? Of course, sir, Isaac, Haim, the Jewish contractor————"

"Goddam you, I'm asking about Cossacks—did you see any Cossacks?"

"No, sir, I didn't see any Cossacks, but I saw the young gentleman, Andrei Bulba, your son, Colonel, sir."

"You saw Andrei? Well, tell me, tell me, where?

Where did you see him? In a dungeon? Tied up in a pit? Beaten up? Bound?"

"Oh no, sir, there's no one who could lay a hand on Knight Andrei Bulba. He is a very important knight, sir. I hardly recognized him myself: his shoulderpieces are gold, his arm guards are gold, his breastplate is gold, his helmet is gold, and there's plenty of gold on his belt. In fact there's gold all over him. He's like the sun in spring when all the little birds twitter and sing and every blade of grass is fragrant and radiates light—he's all radiant too, all flooded with golden glitter! And the military governor gave him the best horse. . . . I'd say the horse by itself would fetch a couple of hundred . . ."

Bulba was dumbfounded. He muttered woodenly:

"Why . . . why did he put on . . . their attire? . . ."

"He put it on because it's most costly. And now he's riding all over the place with them and he instructs them and they instruct him and he's like one of the wealthiest Polish noblemen."

"But how did they make him do it?"

"But I didn't say that anybody forced him. Don't you know, sir, he went over to the other side of his own free will?"

"Who did?"

"Knight Andrei."

"Went over where?"

"To the other side, sir. Now he is completely one of them."

"You're lying, you swine!"

"How could I lie? Do you think I'm mad or something? Do you think I'm asking to be hanged? I know that it'd cost me my life if I lied. . . ."

"So you're trying to tell me that he's sold his country and his faith, is that it?"

"But I never said he'd sold anything. I simply said he'd gone over to them."

"You're lying, you damned Jew. Such a thing couldn't happen to an Orthodox Christian. Unless you're mixing something up, you muddleheaded fool. . . ."

"Let the grass grow over the doorstep of my home if I'm lying. Let every passer-by spit on the grave of my father, my mother, and my mother's father if I have it all confused. And, if you want to know, sir, I can even tell you why he's gone over to them."

"Why?"

"The military governor has a beautiful daughter. By the God of my fathers, an incredibly beautiful daughter, sir."

At this point, Yankel tried to convey the beauty of the Polish lady. He spread out his arms, screwed up his eyes, twisted his mouth to one side as though he had tasted something delicious.

"Well, what's that got to do with it?"

"So he did it all for her. When a man falls in love, he becomes like a boot sole soaked in water, it can be bent any way you like."

Bulba was plunged deep in thought. He remembered how powerful a weak woman can be, how many strong men she has sent to perdition. He also thought of Andrei's vulnerability to women and he remained standing there for a long time like a post.

"Listen, sir, and I'll tell you everything," Yankel said. "As soon as I heard the uproar and saw the Poles pouring through the gates, I grabbed a string of pearls, reckoning that there were beauties in the town and noblewomen and as long as there are beauties and noblewomen around, even if they have nothing to eat, they'll still buy pearls. And as soon as the servants of Galiandovich let me go, I dashed to the military governor's place to sell my pearls. I found out everything from a Tartar maid. She told me: 'The wedding will be celebrated as soon as the siege is lifted. Sir Andrei has promised to chase the Cossacks away.' "

"And you didn't kill the son-of-a-bitch on the spot?"

"Why should I kill him? He acted of his own free will. What wrong has he done? He was happier over there, so he went over."

"And . . . and did you see his face?"

"Of course I did, sir. What a glorious figure of a warrior! The handsomest of them all! May God preserve him! He recognized me at once and when I came up to him, he said———"

"Go on, go on, what did he say?"

"First he made me a sign with his hand and then he

said: 'Hello, Yankel.' 'Pan Andrei,' I said to him. 'Yankel,' he says, 'tell my father, tell my brother, tell the Cossacks, the lot of them, that my father is my father no longer, my brother, no brother, my comrades, no comrades to me. That I'll fight them all, I'll fight the lot of them.' "

"You're lying, you damn Judas," Taras howled, losing all control of himself. "You're lying, you swine! You crucified Christ, you God-accursed bastard! I'd like to kill you, Satan! Go on, run, run as fast as you can, if you don't want to die on the spot!"

Taras unsheathed his saber and Yankel took to his heels and ran as fast as his puny calves would carry him. And he kept running for a long time without looking back, between the Cossack wagons and then further, clear across the field, although Taras did not even try to pursue him—he had realized that it was unreasonable to take out his rage on the first person who happened to be at hand.

Now it came back to him that he had seen Andrei walking past their wagons with a woman, and his gray head sank onto his chest. But he still refused to believe that such ignominy could have befallen him, that his own son could have sold his faith and his soul.

Finally he snapped out of it and deployed his troop in ambush behind a wood, the only one that hadn't been scorched by the Cossacks. In the meantime, the Cossacks, on foot and on horseback, advanced along the three roads toward the gates. One after the other, the troops advanced: the Uman, the Popovich, the Kanev, the Steblikiv, the Nezamaikovsky, the Guguziv, the Tytarev, and the Timashev. Only the Pereyaslav was missing. The men of the troop had drunk well and they had drunk away their lives. Some had awakened bound and in enemy hands, others had never awakened at all and had passed in their sleep into the damp earth; Khlib, their chief, had found himself a Polish prisoner with neither weapons nor trousers.

The city became aware of the Cossacks' movements. They all hastened to the ramparts and the Cossacks saw a painting come alive: Polish knights, each more magnificent than the next, profiled against the skyline. Their

copper helmets shone like suns and were topped by
feathers as white as swans. Some wore light blue and
pink caps cocked on the sides of their heads, their dou-
blets had wide, loose sleeves and were embroidered with
gold or adorned with several rows of braid. Their swords
and other weapons had sumptuous settings which must
have cost a great deal. There was a great variety of dazzling apparel. At their head was the colonel from Budzany wearing a red, gold-spangled headgear. The colonel
was heavy, taller and bigger than the others, and his
expensive doublet was tight on him. On the opposite
side, almost above a side gate, stood another colonel, a
smallish, dried-up man with sharp little eyes looking
brightly out from under his thick eyebrows. He kept
turning from one side to the other and pointing with his
thin, dry hand, giving orders, and it was obvious that
despite his small stature, he knew much about the art of
war. Not far from him stood Galiandovich, extremely
tall and thin, with a thick mustachio and a face that was
certainly not lacking in color. It was obvious that this
Polish knight liked good food and strong liquor. Behind
them stood many of the nobility, some equipped by their
own gold, some by courtesy of the king's treasurer, others on funds obtained from the Jews, by pledging everything that they could lay hands on in their grandfathers'
castles. Among them also were plenty of parasites who
buzzed around the senate, whom the senators invited to
feasts because of their illustrious names, and who stole
silver cups from the table and from the cupboards and
then, after the day's glory, were to be found on a coach-
box, employed as coachman by some gentleman. There
were all sorts of men up there and some of them could
not even have afforded a drink. But to go to war, all
had managed to turn out elegantly.

Before the walls, the Cossacks stood in silence. There
was no gold on them—only here and there precious
metal flashed on the hilt of a saber or the inlaid stock
of a gun. The Cossacks did not dress up for battle. They
wore dark clothes and plain coats of mail and their uniform red-topped, black sheepskin hats dotted the plain
in a black-and-red crescent.

Two Cossacks rode out from the ranks. One of them

still very young, the other older, but both known for their sharp tongues and both quite good in action too. They were Okhrim Nash and Mykyta Golokopytenko and behind them rode Demid Popovich, a thickset man who had seen much. He had taken part in the siege of Adrianople, was nearly burned alive, and had returned to the camp with his head all blackened and singed and his mustachio scorched. But Popovich grew himself a new tuft long enough to reach his ear, and a new mustachio as thick and black as tar. This Popovich was no amateur at the taunting, acid word.

"Beautiful those red coats you people have. But I'd like to know if there's any red blood under them?"

"I'll show you!" the big colonel shouted. "I'll have the lot of you bound up! You'd better hand over your guns and your horses, you bunch of peasants! You serfs! You see how I bound up your men? Hey!" he shouted, turning back, "bring the prisoners out onto the rampart!"

And they brought the bound Cossacks out onto the rampart. At their head was Troop Chief Khlib, with neither trousers nor coat, just as he had been when they had captured him drunk. The Cossack chief hung his head, ashamed before his comrades because of his nakedness and because he had let himself be captured, like a pig, while asleep. His hair had turned gray overnight.

"Cheer up, Khlib! We'll rescue you!" the Cossacks shouted from below.

"Cheer up, friend," Troop Chief Borodaty called out, "it's not your fault they took you naked, anyone can have bad luck. The shame is theirs for bringing you out here without decently covering your nakedness."

"I can see you're all very brave men when it comes to fighting sleeping men!" said Golokopytenko, looking up at the ramparts.

"Just wait, we'll be cutting off your tufts!" the Poles shouted from above.

"I'd like to see that! I'd like to see 'em cut off our tufts!" Popovich said, twisting and turning in front of them on his horse. Then turning to look at his own men, he shouted:

"Who knows? Maybe the Poles are right, especially if

big-belly there leads them out. That'll give 'em good cover."

"How will it give 'em cover?" asked the Cossacks, knowing that Popovich had the answer all prepared.

"You blind? The whole army can hide behind him and you won't get to more'n a couple of the dogs with your spears."

The Cossacks burst out laughing, and, for a long time, many of them continued to shake their heads, saying:

"That Popovich! If you need someone to turn a phrase, well just . . ."

But well just what, they did not say.

"Back! Get out from under the wall!" the headman shouted suddenly. It looked as if the Poles could not stand even this much taunting. The colonel made a signal with his hand.

The Cossacks got out of the way just in time. A hail of grapeshot rattled from the rampart. There was a commotion and the old military governor in person appeared on horseback. The gates flew open and out marched the Poles.

First came the embroidered hussars, riding in even columns. They were followed by the mailed foot soldiers. Behind these came the lancers in armor, then a column of men, all of them in brass helmets. And finally the noblemen appeared, separately, each outfitted to his own taste. The proud noblemen did not like to mix with the others and those without a command rode surrounded by personal retinues. Then several columns marched out with the mounted standard-bearer, Galiandovich, between them and more infantry columns, followed by the stout colonel. And, finally, after all the rest, the short little colonel.

"Don't wait! Don't give them a chance to deploy themselves!" the headman shouted. "Everybody at 'em! Every troop! Forget the other gates! Tytarev troop, get onto their left flank! Diadkiv, on the right! Press on the rear, Kukubenko and Palyvoda! Harass them, harass them. Stop them from forming ranks!"

And the Cossacks fell on them from all sides, toppled them, and, breaking their own ranks, wrought havoc in the Polish formation. They didn't even give them a chance to fire but closed in and fought at close quarters with sabers and spears. They fought in a tight mass and each man had only himself to rely on.

Demid Popovich ran his spear through three foot soldiers and then unhorsed two of the noblemen.

"Those are good horses!" he said. "I've been after something like them for a long time!"

And he drove the horses far out into the field, calling out to the Cossacks standing there to catch them. Then he fought his way back into the knot of fighters again and once more fell upon the noblemen he had unhorsed. He killed one and flung a noose around the neck of the other, tying it to his saddle and dragging him right across the field, having first taken his saber, which had a valuable hilt, and untied a bag of gold coins from his belt.

Kobita, a young Cossack but already a good one, also picked out one of the finest-looking Poles, and they battled a long time. They fought hand to hand. The Cossack won: he stabbed his foe in the chest with a sharp Turkish dagger. But he did not escape himself—as he struck, a scorching bullet hit him in the temple. He had been slain by an illustrious and handsome Polish knight who came from an ancient princely family. He sat astride his dun-colored horse like a shapely poplar. And he had already displayed his daring by cleaving two Cossacks from shoulder to hip. Then he'd toppled over Fedor Korzha, horse and all, shot the horse and dug the good Cossack from under with his lance. He'd slashed off many more Cossack heads and arms and now he slew Kobita with a bullet through the temple.

"There's one I'd like to tangle with!" Kukubenko, the chief of the Nezamaikovsky troop, said. He spurred his horse and hit the Pole from behind with his horse's chest, letting out such an inhuman cry that those standing near shuddered. The Pole tried desperately to turn his horse and face Kukubenko, but his mount did not answer to the rein. Frightened by the terrible cry, it shied to one side and Kukubenko's bullet struck the rider between the shoulder blades, knocking him from his horse. The Pole still managed to get his blade out of its sheath and lift it to strike, but his strength was leaving him fast and his saber hand fell limply to his side. Then

Kukubenko took his heavy broadsword in both hands and smote him right across his bloodless lips. The sword knocked out a couple of the Pole's teeth, split his tongue in two, broke his spinal cord and bit deep into the ground. And so he remained nailed to the damp earth forever. His bright red blood gushed upward in a jet, staining the yellow gold-embroidered coat. Kukubenko left him there, and, followed by his Nezamaikovsky troop, pushed his way into another knot of fighters.

"Well, well! He left him without taking his things!" Borodaty, the chief of the Uman troop, exclaimed.

He left his men and rushed toward Kukubenko's dead nobleman.

"I've killed noblemen myself but none of them had trappings nearly this rich."

Borodaty's greed overcame him. He bent to strip the Pole of his expensive armor—he took his Turkish dagger, set with precious stones, unfastened from his belt a purse full of gold, and took from his breast a pouch containing fine linen, valuable silver and a lock of a girl's hair. And he was so absorbed in what he was doing that he failed to hear the red-nosed Galiandovich bearing down on him—Galiandovich whom he had knocked from his saddle once earlier and given a gold slash to remember him by. The red-nosed Pole swung his saber from the shoulder and struck Borodaty's bent neck. The Cossack's greed had brought him no good. His fearsome head flew off and the headless body fell, drenching the ground far around it. His stern Cossack soul rose, puzzled and angry, surprised to be parted so early from the strong, young body. Galiandovich did not have time to grab the troop chief's head by its tuft to tie it to his saddle before a stern avenger appeared. As a hovering hawk, after describing many circles on smooth-flying wings, suddenly stretches out and hurls himself like an arrow upon a calling quail cock, Ostap Bulba, Taras's son, came down upon Galiandovich. He swung his rope and threw it around the Pole's neck and his already red face grew crimson as the cruel noose tightened. He tried to use his pistol, but his twitching hand could not aim and the bullet flew far afield. Ostap unwound from Galiandovich's saddle the silk cord the Poles carry to tie up their prisoners, bound him with his own cord, and dragged him across the field, calling loudly for all Cossacks of the Uman troop to have a look at the one who had slain Borodaty and to come and pay their last respects to their troop chief.

When the Uman troop heard that their chief was no longer alive, they left the battle and ran to pick up his body and then went into a huddle to discuss whom they should choose to be their new chief. They quickly agreed.

"What's there to discuss?" one of them said. "Where would we find a better chief than Bulba's Ostap? Although he's younger than any of us, he's as smart as an older man."

Ostap Bulba, removing his cap, thanked all his Cossack comrades for the honor and without stopping to plead either his youth or his inexperience, knowing that in an emergency there is no time for such things, he led them all straight back into the fray and proceeded to show them that they hadn't picked him as chief for nothing. The Poles began to feel that things were getting too hot. They disengaged, withdrew, and tried to re-form their lines. The little colonel waved toward the gate, where a reserve of four hundred men was waiting. These men opened up with grapeshot. The shot hit only very few men; most of it landed instead among the Cossacks' oxen, who were staring at the battle. The oxen bellowed in fright, turned, and were about to stampede the Cossack wagons. But, at that moment, Taras Bulba and his men tore out of their ambush and with frightful shrieks rushed to intercept the beasts. The crazed herd, frightened by the shrieks, turned back again, and, in a wild stampede, cut into the Polish regiments, creating havoc among the cavalry and toppling and scattering the lot of them.

"Well done, oxen, thank you, brothers! Thank you!" the Cossacks cheered all around. "You've been auxiliaries for a long time and now you've seen real combat duty!"

And they followed up by attacking the Poles with redoubled fury. Many of the enemy were slaughtered that day. Many Cossacks distinguished themselves. Finally,

the Poles saw that things didn't look too good for them.
So they lowered their standards and shouted for the
gates to be opened. The iron-studded gates drew back
with a screech and received the exhausted, dust-covered
riders like sheep into the fold. Many Cossacks wanted
to rush after them but Ostap stopped his Uman troop,
admonishing them:

"Keep back from those walls, brothers—it could be
dangerous to get too close."

And he was right, because all sorts of things came
flying from the walls and many who were underneath
were hit. At that moment, the headman rode up to
Ostap. He was full of praise and said:

"Here's a new chief and he leads his troops like a
veteran!"

Old Taras Bulba heard this and turned his head to find
out what new chief the headman was talking about and
saw his Ostap at the head of the Uman troop, his sheepskin hat pushed jauntily to one side and a commander's
staff in his hand. And Taras muttered to himself, "Well,
I'll be damned," and rode over to thank all the men of
the Uman troop for the honor they had shown his son.

The Cossacks withdrew again toward their encamp-
ment and the Poles reappeared on the city rampart, but
now their bright garments were torn, there was dried
blood on their expensive coats, and their beautiful copper helmets were covered with dust.

"Well, why didn't you tie us up?" the Cossacks
taunted them from below.

"We'll show you yet!" the big fat colonel shouted
from the wall, brandishing a rope at them. And the exhausted, dusty men kept exchanging threats and some
even managed to find biting words to hurl at one another.

Finally, however, they all dispersed. Some lay down
to recuperate from the battle, others poured loose earth
on their wounds and bandaged them with scarves and
expensive linens taken from the enemy, and those who
were less tired went to attend to the dead. They used
swords and spears to dig graves and scooped out the
earth in their hats and the skirts of their coats. Then
they laid the Cossack bodies neatly in the graves and
covered them with fresh earth, to save their eyes from

being pecked out by ravens and eagles. As to the Polish bodies, they tied them by the dozen to horses' tails. Then they set the horses loose and pursued them for a long time, whipping them across their flanks. The frenzied animals galloped over ridges and hills, over ditches and streams, and the blood-covered, dusty bodies of the Poles were battered against the ground.

Then they sat in circles and discussed at length the exploits and deeds performed that day, which would be retold many a time to their descendants and to strangers. It was a long time before they began to lie down to sleep.

And, as he sat up, old Taras kept wondering why he hadn't seen Andrei among the enemy force. Had the Judas been conscience-stricken at the idea of coming out against his own people? Or had Yankel lied—had he simply been taken prisoner? But then he remembered how vulnerable was Andrei's heart to a woman's ardent word, and anguish swept over him. He cursed the beautiful young Pole who had bewitched his son. And he swore that without even a glance at her beautiful face, he would grab her by her thick, luxuriant braid and drag her behind his horse across the field in full sight of all the Cossacks. He imagined her splendid, magnificent body torn asunder, limb from limb. But Bulba could not know what God was preparing for the morrow. He began dozing, off and on, and finally fell asleep. And some Cossacks still talked among themselves and, all night long, the guards stood by the fires, gazing fixedly all around without once closing their eyes.

8

Before the sun had run even half its course, the Cossacks had gathered in groups. News had arrived from the camp: during their absence, Tartars had stormed it, looted everything they had found there, dug up the buried treasure, murdered half of those who had been left behind and driven the rest into captivity along with the herds of cattle and horses. And from there, it seemed, the Tartars had ridden directly to Perekop. Only one of the captured Cossacks, one Maxim Golodukha, had managed to escape. He had stabbed a Tartar chieftain, untied the bag of gold coins from his saddle, stolen his Tartar garments, and, disguised in them, had galloped for thirty-six hours without stopping, riding one horse to death, finding another, riding him to death too—only on the third horse had he reached a Cossack village where they had told him that the Zaporozhe army was besieging Dubno. This was all that Golodukha had said; he did not have time to explain how the disaster had happened, whether those left behind to guard the camp had been drunk and had been captured in that state, or how the Tartars had managed to find out where the treasure was buried. None of this did Golodukha mention. He was completely exhausted, his face swollen from exposure to sun and wind. He collapsed into a deep sleep.

Usually, in such circumstances, the Cossacks would have set out immediately after the raiders and tried to overtake them on their way, because otherwise the prisoners would find themselves in the marketplaces of Asia Minor, Smyrna, Crete—and God knows where else their tufted Cossack heads would pop up. And that was why the Cossacks had assembled. All kept their hats on because they had not gathered to hear orders from their headman but to discuss the matter as equals.

"Let's hear what the elders have to say," one suggested.

"Let the headman have his say first," another said.

And the headman, taking off his hat, and, not as chief but just as one of them, thanked the Cossacks for the honor and said:

"There are many among us who are senior to me in years and in wisdom, but since you have honored me by asking my advice, here it is. Let us waste no time. Let's go after the Tartars. For you know yourselves what kind of man a Tartar is: he won't wait to squander the goods he has plundered from us. We won't find so much as a trace of our treasure. So, I say, let's go. We've had enough of a good time here. We have shown these Poles what Cossacks are. We have vindicated our faith as far as possible under the circumstances. And then, there's not much to take in this starved city. So my advice is— go after the Tartars."

"Let's go! Let's go!" loud voices rose from various troops.

But Taras Bulba did not like it. And he knitted tighter than ever his iron-and-coal brows which were like bushes growing on the slope of a hill, their tops covered with white frost. And he spoke next:

"No, headman, I don't agree. You seem to be forgetting our people imprisoned by those damn Poles. Do you suggest that we break the sacred vow of brotherhood, that we leave our brothers behind to be flayed alive, to have their Cossack bodies quartered and their limbs exhibited in Polish towns and villages, as they did with our headman and the best Russian warriors of the Ukraine? Don't you think they have already insulted enough the things we hold sacred? No, I ask you, friends, what sort of people are we, to abandon our comrades in their misfortune, to leave them behind like dogs to die on alien soil? If that's the way you feel, if your honor is nothing to you, if some of you wish to allow people to spit into your gray mustachios, then let no one blame me if I don't go along. I'll stay here alone if necessary."

There was hesitation in the ranks, then the headman spoke again:

"You've perhaps forgotten, gallant colonel, that the Tartars have some of our comrades too. If we do not save them now, they'll be doomed for the rest of their lives to be the slaves of all sorts of pagans—and that's worse than the cruelest death. And perhaps you've forgotten too that they have our treasure, paid for with Christian blood?"

The Cossacks did not know what to think. None of them wanted shamefully to abandon their comrades. Then from their ranks stepped Kasia Bovdug, the oldest man in the entire army. He was much respected by all the Cossacks; he had twice been elected headman and had been a great fighting Cossack in his day. But for some time now he had been too old for such things and he did not even like to give advice anymore. All the old warrior liked now was to lie on his side in a group of Cossacks and listen to them talking about all sorts of things that had happened in past and present campaigns.

He never interfered in their conversation. Pressing the ashes into a very short pipe which was never out of his mouth, he would lie in the same position for a long time with eyes half-closed so that those around him could never tell for certain whether he was asleep or still listening. For some time now he had stayed behind during campaigns, but on this last expedition something had roused the old man. He'd made a gesture with his hand as though pushing everything around him out of his way and decided to come along. Maybe, he thought, I can somehow still be of some service to the Cossack brotherhood.

The Cossacks fell silent now when he came forward, for they hadn't heard a word from him for a long time. One and all wanted to know what Bovdug had to say.

"I guess my turn has come to say a word, gentlemen and brothers," he began. "Listen to an old man, children. What the headman has said is wise. Being our headman, his duty is to look out for our interests and to worry about our treasure. No one could give you wiser advice. Well, let that be my first speech! And now, listen to my second. Colonel Bulba told a great truth too, may God grant him long life and may there be more such colonels in the Ukraine! The first duty of a Cossack is to respect the laws of comradeship. I have lived a long time, gentlemen, and I have yet to hear of a Cossack abandoning or selling a comrade. Now, both those in the hands of the Tartars and those in the hands of the Poles are our comrades and it does not matter whether there are more of them here or there: all our comrades are dear to us. So here's what I propose: let those whose closest comrades have been captured by the Tartars go, and those whose dearest ones are in the city stay. Let the headman lead those who go after the Tartars and let those who stay here, if they want to listen to a white head, elect as their acting headman Taras Bulba and no one else, because no one is superior to him in bravery."

Bovdug had said what he had to say and the Cossacks seemed relieved. They threw their hats into the air and shouted:

"Thank you, Father Bovdug! You've kept silent so long and now that you have spoken at last, you've been of great service to all the Cossacks, as you felt you'd be when you decided to come with us this time!"

"You all agree to this?" the headman asked.

"Yes, yes, yes!"

"Can we end the discussion?"

"End it, end it!"

"Now, listen to instructions," the headman said, putting on his hat while all the Cossacks took theirs off and bowed their heads, looking down as they were supposed to do when their headman spoke in his official capacity. "Those," he said, "of you gentlemen who wish to go after the Tartars, step to the right, those who elect to stay here, to the left. Each troop chief must follow the majority of his troop, while the minority will join another troop."

And they all started moving, some to the right, others to the left, and finally there were about an equal number of men on each side. Among those who elected to continue the siege were the entire Nezamaikovsky troop, most of the Popovich and Uman troops, the whole of the Kanev troop, and more than half of the Stablikiv and Tymashev troops. All the rest wanted to go after the Tartars.

Among those who decided to go were many bold Cossacks, including Demid Popovich, who was temperamental and never liked to stay in the same place for long. He had had his fun with the Poles, now he wanted to have some with the Tartars for a change. Among the troop chiefs, Nostugan, Pokrysha, Nevylychy, and many valiant Cossacks wanted to try out their swords and their strong shoulders fighting the Tartars.

There were also many of the best among those who were staying: there were Troop Chiefs Demetrovich, Kukubenko, Vertykhvist, Balaban, and the young Bulba, Ostap, and many, many Cossacks who had been all over—had raided the shores of Asia Minor, had ridden over the Crimean salt marshes and steppes, knew well all the rivers, large and small, that flow into the Dnieper, knew all the fords and all the islands, had raided Moldavian, Wallachian, and Turkish territories, had sailed all over the Black Sea in their double-ruddered Cossack boats, had attacked with fifty boats the tallest and richest ships, sunk many a Turkish galley and used up a lot of gunpowder in their time. They had often made foot bands of the finest linens and velvets and many of them had belt buckles made of gold sequins. As to the amount of goods each of them had drunk and squandered during those years, it would have supported another man all his life. The Cossacks spent everything, treating every comer, hiring musicians, so that everyone in the world should have a good time. Even now most of them had some precious cup or casket or bracelet buried somewhere or concealed under the reeds in case the Tartars managed to raid the camp. And it is unlikely that a Tartar would have discovered any of these private treasures because even their owners often forgot where they had hidden them.

Such were the Cossacks who decided to remain behind to avenge their faithful comrades and the Christian faith insulted by the Poles! And old Bovdug also decided to stay among them, saying:

"I'm too old nowadays to run after Tartars. And why should I, since there's plenty of room here for me to die a decent Cossack death? I have been praying God for some time now that, if my life has to end, it may be in a war for a holy Christian cause. And this seems to be it. There can be no better end for an old Cossack."

When they had all divided up and were aligned in two parallel rows, troop by troop, the headman walked between them and said:

"Well, brothers, is everyone satisfied?"

"We are, headman, we are!"

"Fine! Then kiss one another farewell, for God knows whether we'll meet again in this life. Obey your chiefs and do as your Cossack consciences dictate."

And all the Cossacks, every last one of them, embraced one another. First the two headmen, holding their mustachios out of the way, kissed each other crosswise and then squeezed each other's hands hard, as though wondering whether they would meet again. They did not utter a word and they lowered their old gray heads. And the other Cossacks were taking leave of one another knowing that they all had many things to do. They did not part immediately but waited for night to fall so as not to attract the enemy's attention to the reduction in their numbers. In the meantime, they dispersed by troops and sat down to dinner.

After dinner they lay down and fell into a deep sleep as though they felt this might be the last they would enjoy in safety. They slept until the sun was completely down, and, as it grew dark, they began to grease the wagons. When this was finished, they sent the wagons on ahead, and, with a last wave of their fur hats to comrades staying behind, they quietly followed. Then those on horseback, without shouting or whistling at the horses, trotted behind with muffled hoofbeats. And soon they had all dissolved in the darkness. And only the dull echo of a hoofbeat and the occasional screech of a wheel that was still stiff or had not been properly greased in the dark flew back out of the night.

For a long time after they had lost sight of the last rider, the remaining comrades waved their hats into the darkness. And when they returned to their places and saw under the starlight that half the wagons were gone, that many friends were no longer with them, sad thoughts possessed them, buzzing in their downcast heads.

Taras saw how troubled his troops were, and, although he knew that it was not good to allow fighting men to be gloomy, he said nothing for a while, giving them time to overcome the sadness of parting with friends and comrades. In a little while he planned to snap them out of it with a Cossack reveling cry, which would bring their gaiety back and, with it, an even stronger determination. He was relying on that resilience of which only the Slav soul is capable, a soul compared to which others are what shallow rivers are to the sea. When it is stormy, the sea roars and thunders and lifts its waves into the air, as the weak rivers cannot do, but when it is calm, it is brighter and shinier than any river, stretching out its brilliant surface in a limitless delight to the eye.

And Taras ordered his men to unpack one of his wagons that stood apart by itself, the sturdiest and the biggest in the entire train. Its strong wheels were rimmed with double bands of iron, it was heavily laden and covered with oxhides and horse blankets tied with taut, tarred ropes. It contained all the kegs and barrels of the best wine from Bulba's cellars. He had brought it along for some great occasion, for the important moment preceding an action destined to be remembered by their descendants—at that time the Cossacks would drink this precious wine and be equal to the occasion. On their colonel's command, the men ran to the wagon, slashed the ropes with their sabers, removed the covers and the oxhides, and unloaded the kegs and barrels.

"Take all you want," Bulba said, "help yourselves. Grab whatever you can lay your hands on, a jug, your horse's buckets, or what have you, a gauntlet, a hat, and, if you have nothing, just cup your hands!"

Every Cossack did as he was told and Taras's men walked among them and poured wine out of the kegs and barrels. But they had to wait to down it until Taras gave the signal because he wanted them to drink it all at the same time. And, first, he intended to say something to them. He knew well that even the very strongest and noblest wine, that strengthens and cheers a man's spirit, becomes stronger, even twice as strong, when it is accompanied with the appropriate words.

"I am treating you, brothers and gentlemen," Bulba said, "not to thank you for the honor you showed me by making me your commander. Nor is it on the occasion of our parting with our comrades. No, at other times both these occasions would be worth a drink, but things are different now. We are faced with the utmost exertion and the greatest glory! And so, let us drink, friends, first of all to the holy Orthodox Church, to the time when it will have spread all over the world and be the only faith, the time when every single pagan and Moslem on earth will have become a Christian! And while we are at it, let us drink to Camp Zaporozhe too, may it stand firm against the undoing of the infidels, and, every year, may ever more splendid warriors come out of it! And then, let us drink, too, to our own glory, so that our grandchildren and their children shall say that . . . that, yes, there were men once who never let down their friends. So, to our Church, gentlemen, to our Church!"

"To the Church!" shouted those in the front rows. "To the Church!" shouted those behind them and they all drank to the Church.

"To Camp Zaporozhe!" Taras said and raised his hand high over his head.

"To the camp!" the front rows boomed deeply. "To the camp," the old ones said quietly, stroking their gray mustachios. "To the camp!" intoned the young ones, stirring like young hawks. And the voices of the Cossacks drinking to Camp Zaporozhe resounded far afield.

"And now the last, friends—to the glory of every Christian living in the world!"

And all the Cossacks present took the last swig out of their jugs to the glory of all the Christians of the world and for a long time the phrase rolled from troop to troop: "To every Christian in the world."

The wine was gone but the Cossacks still stood with hands raised, and, although their eyes sparkled merrily, they were wrapped in thought. They were not thinking of the possible booty, of pieces of gold, costly weapons, embroidered garments, and Circassian stallions. They were looking into the future like eagles perched high on a rock, scrutinizing the boundless sea with its galleys, ships and vessels of all sorts that look to them like little gulls on the water, seeing the remote narrow coastlines on which the towns show like tiny insects and the trees of the forests like blades of grass. Like eagles, the Cossacks scrutinized their oncoming fate. They saw the whole plain, with its unfilled fields and its paths strewn with blanching bones; soon, very soon, it would be drenched with Cossack blood and covered with broken wagons, shattered swords and splintered spears.

And scattered all over would be Cossack heads with their tangled tufts stiff with dried blood and their mustachios drooping; and the eagles would swoop down and claw and peck at their Cossack eyes.

But there is much to be said for a common grave! Not a single noble deed would be lost as a grain of powder disappears in the barrel of a gun. There would come a day when a lute player, his beard waist-long but, perhaps, still full of manhood's fire, would compose strong, resounding words to describe their deeds. And their

glory would cross the world like a wild horse and whoever was born in the future would talk about them, for
a strong word carries far and wide and is like a church
bell into which the maker has put much pure silver so
that its clear peals should carry farther and reach towns,
villages, hovels, and palaces, calling everyone to join in
holy prayer.

9

Those in the besieged city did not realize that half the
Cossacks had departed in pursuit of the Tartars. The
sentries on the city tower noticed some wagons moving
into the forest, but they decided that the Cossacks were
laying an ambush. The French engineer concurred. In
the meantime, the headman proved right when he had
said that the defenders would soon be short of food
again. As has happened throughout the centuries, the
army had underestimated its needs. They tried to make
a sortie, but half of those who risked it were slain by
the Cossacks and the rest returned empty-handed. Some
Jews from inside the city, however, took advantage of
the sortie to find out everything: where and why a part
of the Cossacks had left, which commanders and which
troops, how many men had departed and how many had
stayed, what they intended to do. In brief, in a short
while, everyone in the city had heard the news. The two
colonels cheered up and decided to give battle.

Taras Bulba guessed this from the movement and
commotion going on in the city and acted quickly and
efficiently. He went around issuing orders and giving instructions. He decided to deploy the troops in three
rows, each flanked by wagons as protection; the two remaining troops were sent into ambush and a section of
the field was planted with splintered spears, broken
swords and sharp sticks—Bulba planned to lure the
enemy cavalry over them. A battle formation of this type
had always been eminently successful for the Cossacks.

And when all the dispositions were taken, Taras addressed his men. He did so not to cheer them up, not
to give them courage, of which he knew they had plenty,
but simply to share what he had in his heart:

"I'd like to talk to you, friends, about the ties that unite our brotherhood. Your fathers and grandfathers have told you how greatly respected our land used to be by one and all: our strength was felt by the Greeks, Constantinople had to pay us tribute in gold coin, our cities were prosperous and so were our churches—and our princes were of our own Russian blood, not Catholic heretics. All this the heathen took away from us. We were left orphaned and our native soil was like a lonely widow after her husband has been slain. That, friends, was when we joined hands and that is how our brotherhood originated. There are no ties more sacred than the ties between us. The father loves his child, the mother loves her child, the child loves its father and mother—but it's not the same thing, brothers. A wild beast also loves its young. Only man is capable of a kinship of the spirit, as opposed to blood kinship. There have been faithful comrades in other lands too, of course, but not comrades such as are found on Russian soil. Many of you have spent time in foreign lands. You know the people there are also God's creatures and, on occasion, you can even pass the time with them. But when it comes to matters that touch you deeply, you find it's no good—he may be a sensible man but he's different, a man just like you but not really the same.

"No, brothers, no one can love like a Russian, love not with the head, nor with any one part of him, but with everything that God has given him. Ah, you know!" And Taras waved his hand, twitched his mustachio and shook his white head to indicate the absurdity of comparison. "No, I say, no one can love like that! And I say this although I am fully aware of the despicable things that are taking place in our land. There are among us those who think of nothing but filling their barns with grain, owning large herds and keeping a stock of sealed casks of mead in their cellars; those who adopt the devil knows what heretical ways; those who are ashamed of their language, so that, even among themselves, they will not speak their own tongue. There are those who are willing to sell their kinsmen in the market like dumb beasts. The favors of some foreign king—and not even of the king, but of some stinking Polish nobleman, who on occasion kicks them in the face with his yellow boot—is more important to them than brotherhood. But even the lowest of these bastards, even if he's spent his whole life groveling in dirt and subservience—even he has at least a tiny scrap of a Russian heart and one day that scrap will come to life and the miserable creature will beat his breast and tear his hair, and, cursing his villainy, will be prepared to redeem himself through any suffering. So let's let these people know what we mean by the brotherhood of the Russian land! And if we have to die, let 'em realize that none of them will die like us! None, none! Their rabbit's nature prevents it."

And when Bulba was through speaking, he still shook his head, whitened in Cossack campaigns, and everyone around was moved by his strong words. The older Cossacks stood immobile, their gray heads lowered, and many among them wiped away a tear with a sleeve. Then, as if obeying a secret signal, they all stirred, shrugged and shook their seasoned old heads. Probably Taras had stirred in them many a noble feeling, familiar to those who had become inured to sorrow, hardship and adversity. As to the young ones, they understood him instinctively, the way children do, who are an eternal joy to their old parents.

Meanwhile, with drums beating and trumpets blowing, the enemy host emerged from the city gates. The Polish knights, surrounded by large retinues, rode out sitting astride their horses nonchalantly. The big colonel was shouting orders. In tight ranks, the Poles moved on the Cossack wagons, threatening, aiming their pistols, their eyes and their brass armor flashing.

But when they were within pistol range, the Cossacks opened up a continuous fire. The crackling of the shots spread all over the surrounding fields and meadows, merging into one great din. The two forces floated in a cloud of smoke as the Cossacks kept firing without interruption and those behind kept reloading the pistols and handing them to those in the front, completely bewildering their foes who could not understand how the Cossacks managed to fire without reloading. Soon the smoke grew so thick over everything that neither side could see when comrades, one then another, disappeared

from their places in the ranks. However, the Poles felt
that the bullets were too thick, that it was becoming too
hot for them. They moved back out of the smoke and
looked around—of their people, many were missing. On
the Cossack side, on the other hand, only very few had
lost their lives. And they still kept firing without pause.
Even the French engineer marveled at this style of fighting which he had never witnessed before. He said out
loud, for everyone to hear:

"Wonderful fighters, these Cossacks. Their fighting
methods should be emulated by those in other coun-
tries." And he advised the Poles to aim their cannons
at the Cossack wagons.

A thundering roar came out of the wide, iron throats
of the cannons, the earth stirred and shook, the smoke
grew thicker than ever and the tang of gunpowder
spread across the countryside. But the gunners had
aimed too high and the red-hot cannonballs, describing
steep arcs, screamed horribly over the Cossacks' heads,
and, cutting deep into the ground, hurled columns of
black earth into the air. The French engineer tore his
hair at the sight of such poor gunnery and went over to
aim the guns himself, disregarding a shower of Cossack
bullets.

Taras saw from a distance what the cannons would do
to the Nezamaikovsky and Stablikiv troops and shouted
very loudly:

"Get out from behind your wagons! Everyone on
your horses!"

Still, they wouldn't have been able to obey his order
in time had it not been for Ostap, who appeared amidst
the Polish gunners and struck the fuses out of the hands
of six of them. But there were four more gunners and
four more fuses which Ostap did not have time to attend
to. The Poles succeeded in pushing him back and, in the
meantime, the Frenchman himself took a fuse to set to
a cannon bigger than any they had seen before. Its mon-
strous mouth gaped at them horrifyingly and they felt as
though a thousand deaths were staring at them straight
through it. Then it roared and its incredible thunder
mingled with the roars of the other three cannons. The
soil trembled and terrible havoc was unleashed. Many a

Cossack mother would weep at the news of her son's death, beating her thin chest with her worn hands, and many a Cossack wife from Glukhov, Menirov, and Chernigov became a widow through that blast. But she would not know it and she would rush out every day to the market place, grab the passers-by by their coats, look into their eyes, searching for the one dearest to her; and many, many fighting men would pass through the town and never would she find her loved one among them.

And it was as though one-half of the Nezamaikovsky troop had never existed! They fell like rich, heavy, shiny wheat, flattened by hail in the field, and the Cossacks went mad with fury. They tore forward ferociously to the attack. Kukubenko, the commander of the Nezamaikovsky troop, realizing that better than half of his men lay dead, broke into the Polish ranks, raving and raging, followed by the survivors of his troop. In his anger he cut to pieces the first Pole that he came across as if he were shredding cabbage. Then he upset several horsemen, reaching with his spear for man and beast, and, coming up with the gunners, captured a gun. Turning, he saw that the commander of the Uman troop, Stepan Guska, had already captured the big cannon, so the Nezamaikovsky troop wheeled and barreled back through the Polish ranks, leaving behind them an avenue of corpses. Then they turned to the left and laid out a street. The enemy ranks were noticeably thinning; the Poles were falling like mown grass.

Then up to the attack came Vovtuzenko, from behind the nearest wagons, and Degtyarenko, from those on the far side. Degtyarenko had already speared two Polish noblemen and was trying to do the same to a third, a shifty, stubborn one. The Pole wore rich armor and had with him at least fifty men-at-arms. He was gaining the upper hand against Degtyarenko and finally knocked him off his horse and, swinging at him with his saber, shouted:

"There's not one of you Cossack dogs can overcome me!"

"Here's one to start with!"

It was Shilo. He rushed forward. He was a strong Cossack, a man who had gone through much in his life and

had commanded many a Cossack seagoing expedition.
He and his men had been captured by the Turks at Treb-
izond and had been taken as galley slaves, wrists and
ankles shackled, with no food and only horrible sea
water to drink for two whole weeks. But the poor captives bore it and all refused to renounce their Orthodox
faith. That is, all except Shilo, who trampled underfoot
his holy faith, rolled an unholy turban around his sinful
head, gained the special trust of the Pasha, and was put
in charge of the captives. The prisoners were sad, knowing that when a man betrays his faith and joins the op-
pressors, he becomes even harsher than any infidel. And
this was the way it turned out. Shilo had them shackled
in heavier chains, three in a row, and he had the shackles
made so tight that their flesh was cut to the bone. And
he walked among them, laying out blows on the backs
of their necks. The Turks were pleased to have found
such a servant. They organized a celebration and, forgetting their religious laws, drank themselves drunk. Then
Shilo took his sixty-four keys, went down to the hold,
handed the keys to the slaves, who unlocked their shackles, grabbed sabers, rushed out and slashed the Turks to
death. The Cossacks returned home with a lot of booty
and for a long time the flute players celebrated Shilo's
exploit. Probably he would have been elected headman,
but he was a peculiar Cossack. There were times when
he could put an operation together that even the wisest
Cossack could not have thought up, while at other times
he would do the stupidest, most irresponsible things. He
had drunk everything he possessed, was in debt to everyone, and, worse still, he had committed a theft as low
as that of any street thief: one night he had crept into a
barracks and stolen a harness and all the equipment of
another Cossack, giving it as a pledge to an innkeeper.
So they tied him to the pillar of shame and put a cudgel
at his feet for every passer-by to hit him with as hard
as he could. However, no Zaporozhe Cossack would lift
his hand against Shilo because of his past service. That's
the kind of Cossack Shilo was.

"You'll find that there are men who can wallop you,
you dogs!" Shilo shouted, throwing himself on the Pole.

Then the two swung at each other wildly. Soon their

shoulderplates and breastplates were thoroughly dented under the blows. The Pole succeeded in cutting through Shilo's coat of mail and reached his body with his blade. Shilo's Cossack shirt turned crimson but he paid no attention to the sound, swinging his sinewy arm, famous for its strength, and striking the Pole a blow on the head. The brass helmet shattered, the Pole fell stunned, and Shilo continued to rain down blows on him, slashing him crosswise with his saber. It would have been better if, instead of finishing off his enemy, he had turned around. But he did not, and one of the vanquished knight's men buried a knife deep in his neck. Even so, when Shilo did turn he would have reached his assailant had it not been for the thick smoke which enveloped the other. Now the crack of the guns sounded on all sides. Shilo covered his wound with his hand; he sensed that it was a mortal one and shouted to his comrades:

"Farewell, gentlemen, brothers and comrades! May Holy Mother Russia live forever and may her glory never pass!"

He screwed up his weakening eyes, and out of his rough body flew his Cossack soul.

And here Zadorozhny and his men joined the battle and Vertykhvist and Balaban with their troops were toppling the Polish lines.

"What do you say, gentlemen?" Taras shouted to his troop chiefs. "Do you still have plenty of powder in your flasks? Is the Cossack force still not weakening? Are our Cossacks still standing firm?"

"There's still plenty of powder, headman, and the Cossacks are as firm and unyielding as ever."

And they thrust forward and wrought confusion in the Polish ranks. The smallish colonel had the rally sounded and up went eight bright-colored standards to call together the widely scattered forces. The Poles rushed toward their standards, but before they had time to re-form their ranks, Kukubenko and his Nezamaikovsky troop were in among them pushing toward the big fat colonel. The fat colonel was isolated from his men, and Kukubenko's assault was too much for him. He turned his horse away and Kukubenko chased him across the field, preventing him from rejoining his men. Stepan

Guska watched this chase for a while and then moved fast on the fat Pole from another side, his head lowered till it touched his horse's neck, a rope in his hands. Choosing just the right second, he cast the noose over the Pole's neck in a single movement. The colonel turned purple, clutching the rope with his hands, trying to break it, but a spear, hurled with tremendous force, drove into his belly, threw him down and pinned him to the ground. Guska did not have long to live himself—as the Cossacks turned their eyes from the dead colonel, they saw him raised in the air on four spears. The poor man shouted: "Death to our foes and long live Russia," and then he breathed his last.

The Cossacks looked around: over on the Metelitsa flank, they were giving it to the Poles, stunning them one after another; and on the other flank Nevylychy at the head of his troop was pushing them back; and by the nearer wagons, it was Zakrutiguba who was on them, while by the farther wagons it was Pisarenko; and, over by the very furthest wagons, they were fighting hand to hand, standing on top of the wagons.

And Taras, the acting headman, rode out in front and called:

"Well, gentlemen, have you still enough powder in your flasks? Is there still strength left in your arms? Can the Cossacks still hold out?"

"There's still enough powder, headman, and enough strength; the Cossacks won't give way."

At that moment old Bovdug fell from a wagon. A bullet had struck him under the heart. The old one took a deep breath and managed to say:

"I'm not unhappy to leave this world. No one could wish for a better death and may our Russian land be glorious forever and ever!"

And Bovdug's soul soared high above the earth to tell those who had died long ago how well the Russians were still fighting, and dying even better, for the Orthodox faith.

And soon after, Balaban, the troop chief, fell. He had received three mortal wounds, one from a spear, one from a bullet, and one from a heavy broadsword. He had been one of the most famous Cossacks and had commanded many a naval expedition, of which the most glorious was his raid on the shores of Asia Minor. They had captured many pieces of gold then, many Turkish fabrics and ornaments and valuables of all sorts. But, on their way home, they had come under the cannons of a Turkish man-o'-war and a salvo had landed among their boats. Half the boats spun wildly around and capsized and many were drowned. But the reeds tied to the sides of the Cossack boats kept them afloat. Balaban ordered the boats rowed as fast as possible and placed in a straight line between the sun and the man-o'-war so that the Turks would not be able to see them. The whole of the following night they spent bailing out with pitchers and hats, stuffing holes, and making sails out of their wide Cossack trousers. And the next morning they managed to lose the fast Turkish ship. And not only did they reach home without further trouble, they even brought with them a gold-embroidered chasuble for the Archimandrite of the Mezhigorsky Monastery in Kiev and a setting of pure silver for the icon of their church in Camp Zaporozhe. And for a long time afterward the successes of this Cossack leader were sung by the lute players. And now he lowered his head in mortal pain and said quietly: "It seems to me, brothers, that I am dying a proper death. I've slashed seven to death, nine—pierced with my spear, trampled many of them with my horse, and I can't even remember how many of them my bullets have reached. . . . So, may the Russian earth prosper forever!" and off flew his soul.

Cossacks, Cossacks! Do not lose the cream of your army! Now it is Kukubenko who is surrounded. He has only seven men left of his troop and they are finding it hard to stay alive and there is blood on their chief's clothes. Headman Taras Bulba, seeing this, rushed to his rescue. But it was too late: a spear reached Kukubenko's heart before the rescuing Cossacks could get to him and push back the surrounding foes. And he sank into the arms of the Cossacks and his bright young blood streamed out like expensive wine carried from the cellar in a decanter by careless servants who slip and break their precious load by the dining-room door. And the master, seeing the wine all over the floor, holds his head in despair, because he has been keeping this wine for the great day when, in his old age, he would meet a friend of his youth and they'd remember the old days together, when men partook of different and stronger joys. . . .

And Kukubenko half-opened his eyes and said:

"I thank God that I died before your eyes, brothers. May people live after us even better than us and may the Russian land, beloved by Christ, flourish forever. . . ."

And as his young soul left his body, angels took it in their arms and carried it up to heaven. And this soul would be happy there.

"Sit there, on my right, Kukubenko," Christ would say, "you did not betray the brotherhood, you never acted dishonestly, never sold out a comrade, you always upheld and defended My Church."

Kukubenko's death saddened all the Cossacks. Their ranks were thinning terribly. Many, many brave ones had left them, but they still held out.

"What do you think, gentlemen?" headman Bulba inquired of the surviving troop chiefs. "Is there still enough powder in the flasks to go around? Aren't the sabers getting blunt? Aren't the Cossacks exhausted? Can they still hold out?"

"We're all right, headman, there's enough powder, the swords are still sharp enough, the men are not so tired and they can hold out."

And the Cossacks again rushed into the fray as though they'd never suffered a loss. Only three troop chiefs remained alive now. A whole net of scarlet rivers covered the plain and the piles of Cossack and Polish bodies were like bridges over them. Glancing up at the sky, Taras saw a flock of hovering vultures, sensing a feast. And, over there, he saw Metelitsa raised on a spear; and the cut-off head of one of the Pisarenkos spun in the air, its eyelids beating; and then the mangled body of Okhrim Guska fell to the ground.

"Now!" Taras Bulba shouted and waved his kerchief.

Ostap Bulba was waiting for this signal. He leaped out of ambush, and, at a full gallop, he and his men hit the enemy cavalry. The Poles toppled under this fierce assault and Ostap pushed them into the sector of the field where the splintered spears and sharp stakes had been planted. Many of the Polish horses began to stumble, their riders flew over their heads, and Cossacks by the furthest wagons, within range now of the hard-pressed Polish cavalry, opened fire.

The Poles seemed defeated and the Cossacks exulted: "Victory, victory—we have them!" rang through their ranks and the Cossack victory banner was unfurled while the defeated Poles were still trying to flee and to hide.

"No, no," Taras said, looking at the city gates. "Not quite yet. We haven't finished yet."

And he was right.

The gates opened and out rode a regiment of hussars, the pride of the Polish cavalry. Every horse was a dun-colored Caucasian stallion and at their head rode the handsomest and the boldest rider of them all. As he rode, a black lock escaped from under his shining helmet and lay across his brow; a rich kerchief embroidered by the most beautiful lady in the kingdom fluttered in the wind behind him.

Taras was stunned when he recognized Andrei.

And Andrei, fretting for battle, eager to honor the light scarf tied to his arm, came dashing forward like the youngest, the swiftest, the handsomest greyhound of the whole pack, which, unleashed by the hunter, flies off in a straight line, its feet hardly touching the ground, its body slightly twisted, tossing up the snow as it changes direction, outrunning the hare in a burst of speed.

Old Taras stopped and stared, watching Andrei blast a passage before him, raining blows, slashing right and left, trampling men under his horse.

Suddenly he could stand it no longer and shouted:

"What are you doing? Can't you see, you son of a dog, that you're killing your own people?"

But Andrei no longer knew who were "his people" and who were his foes. He could only see hazel tresses, a swanlike neck and breast, and white shoulders that had been fashioned for his wild caresses.

"Lure him into the wood! Get him over there, lads!" Taras called out to the Cossacks.

And immediately thirty of the fastest Cossacks volunteered. Setting their tall sheepskin caps firmly on their heads, they darted out to cut across the path of the hussars. They hit them from the flank, cut the Polish riders in two and started pressing on the two halves, while Golokopytenko fetched Andrei a blow in the back with the flat of his broadsword. Then, at a signal, the Cossacks turned and galloped off as fast as their horses could carry them. Andrei rose in his stirrups and his young blood rushed to his head. He spurred his horse and flew after the Cossacks without looking back to see how many of his hussars were up with him, not realizing that there were only about twenty of them. And the Cossacks rode at full speed and turned into the wood. Andrei had almost caught up with Golokopytenko when a powerful hand grabbed the bridle of his horse. He looked up and saw Taras.

His whole body began to tremble then and he turned white. He was like a schoolboy who has been hit on the forehead with a ruler by a classmate and, jumping from his seat, red with rage, pursues his frightened friend, preparing to take him to pieces, when he stumbles on the teacher who has just entered the room. Within a second the wild rush stops and the fire of rage goes out. And now it was the same—Andrei's fury disappeared as though it had never existed. And all he saw before him was the terrifying figure of his father.

"What shall we do now?" Taras said, looking him straight in the eye, and Andrei said nothing and just looked down at the ground.

"Where are they now, your damn Poles, son? Why aren't they helping you?"

Andrei said nothing.

"The way you sold out! You sold your religion, you sold your people! Get off your horse!"

Obedient as a child he dismounted, and, neither dead nor alive, stood before Taras.

"Stand still and don't move! It was I who begot you and so it is I who must kill you!" Taras said, stepping back and taking his gun in his hand.

Andrei was white as linen and his lips moved slightly, forming someone's name. But it was not the name of his native land, nor his mother's name, nor the name of one of his comrades—it was the name of a beautiful Polish lady. And Taras fired.

Like a stalk of corn cut by a sickle, like a young lamb feeling the deadly steel under its heart, Andrei dropped his head on his chest and fell onto the grass without uttering a word.

The murderer of his son stood for a long time looking at the lifeless body. Even in death he was magnificent: his manly face, which only a few minutes earlier had been full of strength and irresistible charm for women, was still incredibly handsome and his black eyebrows framed his pale features like mourning cloth.

"What a Cossack he could've been!" Taras muttered. "So tall and black-browed and with the features of a nobleman and an arm so strong in battle . . . and now, now he's finished, dead ignominiously, like a dog. . . ."

"Pa! What have you done! Was it you who killed him?" Ostap cried, riding up.

Taras nodded.

Ostap looked intently into his dead brother's eyes and was filled with pity for him.

"Let's bury him properly, Pa," he said. "Don't let's leave his body to be jeered at by his enemies or torn to shreds by the buzzards."

"Don't worry about that," Taras said, "they'll bury him without us and he'll have many women to weep and mourn for him."

Nevertheless, for a minute or two Bulba stood there, hesitating whether to leave his younger son's body to be torn by wolves and buzzards or to spare his warrior's honor. But then Golokopytenko rode up at a gallop.

"Bad news, headman, the Poles have been reinforced, a fresh Polish force has arrived to relieve them."

And before Golokopytenko had finished, Vovtuzenko rushed up shouting:

"Things are bad, headman, Polish reinforcements are pouring in."

And then Pisarenko, horseless, came running:

"Where were you, headman? The Cossacks are looking for you. Troop Chief Nevylychy's been killed. Zadorozhny, killed. Chervichenko, killed. The Cossacks are holding but they don't want to die without seeing you, they want you to see them in their last hours."

"Mount your horse, Ostap," said Bulba, in a hurry to get to his Cossacks while they were still alive and to let them see their headman. But even before they were out of the forest, enemy riders armed with spears and swords appeared among the trees around them.

"Ostap, Ostap, don't let them take you," Bulba shouted as he drew his saber and started swinging it right and left.

Six men had suddenly fallen upon Ostap. But soon the head of one of them flew off. Another one toppled over as he backed away. Ostap's spear pierced the flank of a third. The fourth was more daring: rushing forward, he dodged Ostap's bullet, which, however, hit his horse in the chest. It fell, crushing its rider under it.

"Good boy, good boy, Ostap!" Taras kept repeating. "Wait, I'm coming . . ."

And while he kept fighting back his assailants, slashing away, dealing blows to one Polish head after another, he kept an eye on Ostap. And so he saw that about eight of them were on him.

"Ostap, Ostap, don't let 'em . . ."

But now they were overcoming his resistance. Already one of them had succeeded in passing a noose around his neck, already they were tying him up, taking him. . . .

"Oh, Ostap, Ostap!" Bulba howled, trying to make his way toward his son, cutting, slashing everything around him. "Oh, Ostap, Ostap . . ."

But a heavy stone hit Bulba and everything swayed and turned before his eyes. For one second he saw in a haze heads, spears, smoke, sparks, twigs with leaves on them, flashing before his very eyes, and then he crashed to the ground like a felled old oak and a black screen veiled his eyes.

10

"I must have slept for a long time," Taras said as he came to his senses. He felt as if he had been in a heavy, drunken sleep and looked around him, trying to recognize things.

He felt a terrible weakness all through his body and could only vaguely make out the walls and corners of an unknown room. Finally he realized that his friend Tovkach was standing near him, listening intently to his every breath.

"Yes," thought Tovkach, "it looked as if he'd gone to sleep for good." But he said nothing and just shook his finger.

"But will you tell me where I am, after all?" Taras asked, striving to recollect what had happened.

"Keep quiet for God's sake. What else would you like to know?" his friend said roughly. "Can't you see you're all slashed up? We've been riding for two weeks now, and, in your fever, you haven't stopped rattling on—all sorts of nonsense. This is the first time you've fallen properly asleep. So you'd better keep quiet if you don't want to kill yourself."

But Taras kept making desperate efforts to remember.

"But . . . but I was completely surrounded and the goddam Poles were about to grab me. How could I possibly have worked my way out of there?"

"Shut up, I tell you, you offspring of unholy demons," Tovkach shouted at him like a nurse made frantic by an impossible child. "What difference does it make how the hell you got out? The main thing's that you did, isn't it? There happened to be some people who didn't let you down and that should be good enough for you. Besides, we've plenty of night riding to do, because I hope you don't imagine that they rate you as a rank-and-file Cossack. No, sir! There's a reward of two thousand pieces of gold on your head."

"Ostap, what about Ostap?" Taras shouted. It had all suddenly come back to him. He tried to rise. He remembered clearly now how they had been binding Ostap before his eyes and he realized that he must be in enemy hands. A terrible despair came over him. He started tearing the bandages from his wounds, throwing them all over the place and then began raving again. Fever and delirium took possession of him and wild speeches flew from his mouth. And his faithful friend stood over him, swearing and reproaching him endlessly for his madness. Finally, Tovkach took him by his arms and legs and swaddled him in bandages like an infant. Then he rolled Taras into a cowhide, picked him up, tied him with ropes to his horse, jumped onto his own and set off once more at a fast gallop.

"Dead or alive, I'll get you back," Taras's friend said to himself. "I won't let the damned Poles insult your Cossack body, tearing it into little pieces and tossing them to the fish one by one. And if it's your fate to have an eagle peck out your eyes, let it be one of our steppe eagles and not a Polish one. Even dead, I'll get you back to the Ukraine."

And Tovkach galloped without rest and brought the unconscious Taras all the way back to Camp Zaporozhe. And there he nursed him patiently back to health with herbs and poultices. He found a Jewish woman who knew about potions and she fed them to Taras for a whole month and at last Taras showed signs of getting better. Whether because of the drugs or his own rocklike constitution, in six weeks he was on his feet and healed and only deep scars bore witness to his terrible wounds.

But he was much gloomier than before. Three deep furrows appeared on his brow and never went away again. And as he looked around the camp, everything seemed different to him. It seemed that all his old comrades were dead. None of those who had gone with him to uphold and vindicate their faith against the Poles were there. Nor any of those who had elected to follow the old headman in pursuit of the Tartars. They too had all perished some time before, some had been killed in open battle, while others had died of thirst or hunger in the Crimean salt marshes. Others must have died in captivity, unable to bear slavery. And the old headman, too, had been dead for some time. None of Taras's old comrades was still alive and grass grew over what had once been boiling Cossack energy. All Taras knew was that there had been a feast, a noisy feast, that all the glass and hardware had been smashed, that not a drop of wine was left, that the guests and the servants had stolen all the gold and silver goblets and left the sad host standing alone wishing there had never been a feast at all.

In vain did people around him try to cheer him up.

In vain did gray-bearded lute players, two, even three at a time, sing to him about his own Cossack feats of arms—he sat there indifferently, staring at the world around him and repeating with his head lowered:

"Ostap, Ostap, my son . . ."

The Cossacks left on a sea raid. They lowered two hundred boats into the Dnieper and Asia Minor got a glimpse of their heads, shaven except for the tuft, wreaking death and havoc on its fertile shores; it saw the turbans of its Moslem inhabitants strewn like flowers over its blood-soaked fields or floating along its coasts. Asia Minor saw many tar-stained Cossack trousers, many muscled arms wielding knouts. The Cossacks ate or destroyed all its grapes; they left mosques heaped with dung and wrapped costly Persian shawls around their soiled coats. For a long time to come, people would find short Cossack pipes along that coast.

The Cossacks sailed back in a happy mood. They were given chase by a ten-gun Turkish man-o'-war and its salvos dispersed their flimsy craft and one third of them perished in the depths. But the rest reassembled and reached the mouth of the Dnieper with twelve barrels of gold sequins.

But Taras was indifferent to it all. He walked off into the steppe as though to hunt, but his gun remained unfired. And he would put it down and sit on the shore and, hanging his head, repeat again and again:

"My boy! Ostap, my son!"

The Black Sea stretched out sparkling all around him. A seagull screamed in the reeds. Taras's white mustachio gleamed like silver as his tears were caught in it one by one.

And finally he could stand it no longer.

"Whatever happens, I must find out whether he's still alive or if he's in his grave or, even, no longer in the grave. . . . I must find out, no matter what. . . ."

And within a week he appeared in the city of Uman. He was on horseback and fully equipped for campaign: spear, saber, canteen, traveling kettle, powder flask, ammunition and all. He rode straight to a dirty little house with windows that could hardly be made out because they were covered with soot or God knows what; the chimney was stuffed with a rag and the roof was full of holes and teeming with sparrows. A heap of refuse was piled up before the entrance. A Jewish woman in a head-dress decorated with discolored pearls appeared in the window.

"Your husband in?" Bulba asked, dismounting and tying his horse to an iron hook by the door.

"He's in," she said. She disappeared inside the house and almost immediately reemerged at the door carrying a bucket of grain for the horse and a beaker of beer for the rider.

"Where is he then?"

"He's praying," she said, bowing and wishing Bulba good health as he lifted the beaker to his lips.

"Stay here and give my horse a drink while I talk to your husband alone. I have private business with him."

The husband was none other than Yankel. He had been living there for some time, renting land, running an inn, and gradually making all the local gentry and aristocracy dependent upon him by draining them of practically all their funds, thus making his presence strongly felt in the area. Not a single house in good repair could be found within a three-mile radius of Yankel's house; everything was left to go to ruin and every penny was spent on drink, until all that was left was poverty and rags as though a fire or a plague had swept over the place. And had Yankel remained there another ten years, he certainly would have succeeded in spreading misery over the entire province.

Taras entered the room where Yankel was. The Jew was praying covered by a rather stained prayer shawl, and, as he turned round to spit for the last time as his religion demanded, his eyes met those of Bulba, standing by the door. The first thought that rushed to Yankel's head was of the two thousand gold pieces placed on Bulba's head, but he was ashamed of his own greed and tried to suppress the everlasting obsession with gold that torments the Jewish soul.

"Listen, Yankel," Taras said, interrupting him as he greeted him and at the same time rushed to close the door lest anyone see them together. "Remember, I saved your life once; without me they would have torn

you to pieces in Camp Zaporozhe. Now it's your turn
to render me a service."

"What service?" Yankel said, pursing his lips slightly.
"If I can render this particular service, why shouldn't I?"

"Don't say anything to anyone and take me to
Warsaw."

"Warsaw? Did you say Warsaw?" Yankel's shoulders
jerked up in surprise.

"Don't say anything and take me to Warsaw. Whatever happens, I want to see him once more and say one
last word to him."

"Say a word to whom?"

"To him, to Ostap . . . to my son."

"Is it possible, Colonel, that you haven't heard that
they . . ."

"I know, I know, there's a price of two thousand gold
pieces on my head. What do those stupid fools know
about its worth? I'll give you twelve thousand. Here's
two to start with. . . ."

And Bulba poured two thousand in gold pieces out of
a leather bag.

"You'll get the rest when I'm back."

The Jew seized a towel and threw it over the gold.

"Nice stuff, noble stuff," he kept saying, turning a coin
in his fingers, then trying it with his teeth. "I bet the
man you relieved of this gold, Colonel, was unable to
go on living, deprived of these lovely coins: he must have
gone to the river and drowned himself."

"Look, Yankel, I wouldn't have come to you . . . I
would perhaps have managed to find the way to Warsaw
by myself, but the damn Poles might recognize me and
then I am not so good at thinking up clever ways of
getting around things, while you Jews, you're just made
for it. You can hoodwink the devil himself and you know
all the ropes. That's why I came to you. And even if I
got to Warsaw, I couldn't get what I want by myself. So
hitch up the horses and let's go!"

"Do you really imagine, sir, that I can just harness my
mare and shout 'git up' and take you unconcealed to
Warsaw? Is that it, sir?"

"Hide me if you want, put me in an empty barrel
or something. . . ."

"Colonel! Do you really think that an empty barrel is such a good place when people expect to find vodka in it?"

"Let them think. . . ."

"What are you saying? Let them think!" the Jew exclaimed, grabbing his sidewhiskers and pulling them upward with both hands.

"Well, what's come over you?"

"Hasn't it occurred to you, sir, that God created vodka so that it should be tasted by everyone? And around Warsaw, they all know what's good and a Polish squire would be prepared to run behind the cart for five miles to try and steal some by piercing a little hole in the barrel and then, when he saw that nothing came seeping out, he'd say to himself: 'Whoever heard of a Jew carrying an empty barrel around. There must be something hidden in it! Let's grab him, confiscate his money and clap him in prison!' And that's because everything is blamed on the Jew, because the Jew is treated like a dog, because people believe that a human being is not human if he's a Jew."

"All right, hide me in a cartload of fish."

"Impossible, impossible, sir, I swear it can't be done. People all over Poland are hungry as dogs and when they steal the fish, they'll be bound to feel you under it."

"Well, I don't care how, but take me there."

"Listen, listen, Colonel," Yankel said. He stuck his thumbs behind the lapels of his coat, spread out his fingers fanwise and, coming very close to Bulba, said:

"Here's what we're going to do. There's plenty of building going on, fortresses, castles, that sort of thing. French engineers have come from abroad especially for it. And so there's lots of brick and stone being transported all over the place. You'll lie flat on the bottom of the cart and I'll cover you with bricks. You look in good shape, Colonel, and I'm sure you won't mind if it feels a bit heavy. It won't hurt you. And I'll make an opening in the bottom of the cart, for food, you know. . . ."

"Do as you wish, just take me to Warsaw."

And an hour later, a cart loaded with bricks and pulled by a couple of nags left Uman. On one of the nags sat Yankel, tall and thin as a signpost. His sidelocks had escaped from his skullcap and bounced up and down as he jogged along.

11

At that time there were no guard posts or customs officers on the frontiers such as were later to become the plague of enterprising people, and so anyone could carry around anything he liked. And if by chance someone insisted on inspecting a load, he did so mostly for his own edification and usually because he suspected the load consisted of attractive items and the circumstances were propitious for him to emphasize his personal weight and authority. But few such inspectors were interested in bricks and the cart drove unmolested through the city gates of Warsaw.

Confined in his narrow brick cage, Bulba could hear nothing but the rattling of wheels and the shouts of drivers. Yankel, bouncing up and down on his short, dust-covered nag, chose a roundabout way toward a dark, narrow street known as Muddy Alley or Street of the Jews, because actually it housed almost all the Jews of Warsaw. This street looked very much like a backyard turned inside out. It seemed that the sun never managed to reach the level of the lower floors. Poles stretching across the street, from window to window of the blackened wooden houses, further added to the general gloom. Here and there the reddish wall of a brick house, gradually turning black, could be seen and now and then the sun would light up the top of a stucco wall which seemed dazzlingly bright amid the surrounding bleakness. The street was littered with chimney pots, rags, vegetable peelings, broken utensils. . . . Whatever was discarded was flung out into the street as an offering to the esthetic feelings of the passers-by. A man on horseback could almost reach the various objects dangling from the poles across the street: the long stockings Jews wear, their short pantaloons and smoked geese. Sometimes the rather pretty head of a Jewish woman, adorned with discolored beads, would appear in a ramshackle window. Curly-haired children, dirty and tattered, were playing noisily in the dust. A redheaded Jew with freckles all over his face making him look like a sparrow's egg peeped out of a window and immediately got into conversation with Yankel in an incomprehensible tongue, whereupon Yankel turned into a courtyard. Another came in from the street and joined them. All three went into a huddle, talking heatedly until Bulba finally emerged from under his bricks. Then Yankel turned toward him and told him that everything would be done, that Ostap was in the city jail, and that, although it would be very difficult to persuade the guards, he hoped to arrange for Bulba to see his son.

Bulba followed the three Jews into a house. They again started jabbering something and he kept glancing at each of them in turn as he spoke. Something seemed to have snapped Taras out of his deadness and a flame of hope, the hope that sometimes comes to a man driven to despair, appeared in his rough, indifferent face, and his old heart was set beating in the cadence of youth.

"Listen," he said excitedly, "nothing is impossible for you Jews; you can lift a thing from the bottom of the sea and there's even a saying that a Jew can steal himself if he only wants to. Set my Ostap free! Give him a chance to escape from the devil's clutches. I've promised this man twelve thousand gold pieces and now I'll add another twelve thousand, everything I possess, all my costly goblets, all my buried gold, all my houses. . . . I'll sell my last shirt and I'll sign a contract with you by which, as long as I live, one half of everything I bring from the wars will be yours. . . ."

"I'm afraid it can't be done, dear sir," Yankel said with a sigh.

"Impossible," one of the other Jews said.

The three of them looked at one another.

"Still one might try," the third one said. "Maybe, with God's help . . ."

The Jews then started speaking German and try as he might Taras could only make out one word that kept recurring and which sounded like "Mordecai," and nothing else.

"Sir, we must talk it over with a man the like of whom there has never been in this world," Yankel said after a while, turning toward Taras. "He's as wise as King Solomon and if he says he can't do it, no one can. Wait for us. Here's the key. Let no one in."

And they walked out into the street.

Taras locked the door and stood staring out the window onto the dirty street. The three Jews stopped in the middle of it and started another rather heated discussion. A fourth joined them. Then a fifth. Again, the oft-repeated word, "Mordecai, Mordecai," reached Taras's ears. They kept glancing across the street at one of the dingy houses and finally from out of its door there appeared a foot in a Jewish shoe, flashing from under the fluttering skirts of a long coat. A tall, thin Jew, not quite as tall as Yankel but much more wrinkled and with a huge upper lip, approached the group and all of them shouted, "Mordecai!" and started in turns to tell him something. And since Mordecai kept looking toward the little window behind which Taras stood, it was obvious they were talking about him. Mordecai gestured with his hands, listened, spat sideways, lifted the long skirts of his coat to get some trinkets out of his trouser pocket, displaying thus a very shabby pair of trousers. Before long all the Jews were shouting so loud that the one who seemed to be keeping a lookout started making them signs to keep quiet. Taras was already beginning to be concerned for his safety when he remembered that Jews can only discuss matters in the street and that since, anyway, no one, not even the devil himself, could understand their lingo, he had nothing to worry about.

A few minutes later, all the Jews entered his room and Mordecai approached Taras, patted him on the shoulder, and said:

"When we and God decide to do something, don't worry—it gets done."

Taras looked at this new Solomon, the like of whom did not exist in the world, and felt some hope and, indeed, his looks might well have inspired hope: the man's upper lip was simply awe-inspiring, although its thickness was undoubtedly partly due to outside causes. The beard of this Solomon consisted of fifteen hairs and, even so, all of them were on the left side. And his face bore so many marks of the beatings he must have received for the risks he had taken that he himself must have lost count of them and no longer been able to tell them from his birthmarks.

Then Mordecai left, followed by his friends, who were brimming over with admiration for his wisdom.

Left alone, Bulba found himself in an extraordinary situation: for the first time in his life he felt fear. He was in a feverish state. He was no longer his old self, the unbending, unyielding, immovable oak. He was cowardly and weak. He started at the slightest noise; he started every time a Jew appeared in the street. He stayed there like that till the end of the day: he neither ate nor drank and his eyes never left the window for more than a minute.

It was quite late in the evening when Mordecai and Yankel returned. Taras's heart stood still.

"Well? Did it work?"

He was as impatient as a wild horse. But before they had time to answer him, Taras realized that one of Mordecai's untidy sidelocks was missing. Then the man tried to tell Taras something but Taras could make neither head nor tail out of it. As to Yankel, he held his hand over his mouth all the time as though he were suffering from a cold.

"Oh dear, sir," Yankel said finally, "it is quite impossible to do anything now. I swear it's out of the question. Such a vile breed, these people, I'd like to spit in their nasty faces! Let Mordecai tell you. He tried to do what no man has tried, but God was not willing: there are three thousand soldiers to guard them and tomorrow all the prisoners are to be executed."

Taras looked at them and there was no impatience or anger in his eyes.

"If you want to see him, it must be done before sunrise tomorrow. The guards seemed amenable and their officer promised to help. But—may they be unhappy in the next world—what a greedy breed! You won't find the likes even among us. I had to give fifty pieces of gold to each guard and to their officer. . . ."

"All right, take me to him," Taras said, regaining his self-possession.

He agreed to let himself be disguised as a foreign

count from the German lands. The provident Jew had already procured clothes for this purpose. Night had fallen. The owner of the house—the freckled Jew—had pulled out a thin mattress covered with a sort of sackcloth and spread it on a bench for Taras. Yankel lay on the floor, on a similar mattress. The red-haired Jew downed a glass of something or other, removed his coat, and, looking somewhat like a chicken in his stockings, climbed with his wife into something that might have been a closet, outside which two children lay down like a couple of puppies. But Taras could not sleep. He sat up, softly drumming on the table with his fingers, smoking his pipe and puffing out so much smoke that one of them kept sneezing in his sleep and pulling his blanket over his nose. And scarcely had the pale forewarning of dawn appeared in the sky, when Taras poked Yankel with his foot and said:

"Come on, get up and give me my disguise."

In a few minutes he was ready. He blackened his mustachio and his eyebrows, placed a little dark cap on the crown of his head, and none of his friends would have recognized him. One would hardly have thought him more than thirty-five now, so rosy were his cheeks, and the scars on his face gave him an even more commanding air. The gold-embroidered coat looked very good on him.

The streets were still asleep. There was not a single merchant around with his basket. Bulba and Yankel arrived at a building which looked like a crane sitting on its nest. It was low, wide, and blackened, and on one side of it a sort of tower with a projecting roof jutted upward, the whole thing sticking out like the neck of a crane. This building served many purposes: it was used as a barracks, a jail, and even as a court of criminal justice. Taras and Yankel passed through the gate and found themselves in what was either a vast hall or a roofed courtyard. About a thousand persons were asleep there. Directly opposite the entrance was a little door, next to which two guards were playing a game in which one of them kept flicking his fingers against the other's palm. They paid little attention until Yankel approached and said:

"It's us! Do you hear, gentlemen, it's us!"

"Go ahead," one of the guards said, opening the door with one hand while presenting the other to his colleague to be flicked at.

They entered a dark, narrow passage that took them to a hall similar to the first, with little windows high up under its ceiling.

"Who are you?" several voices shouted at the same time, and Taras saw armed guards looking at them. "We were told to let no one through."

"But it's us. I assure you it's us, gentlemen!" Yankel shouted.

Still, they wouldn't listen to him. Luckily at that moment a fat man came along. He had all the marks of seniority—that is, he used fouler language than the others.

"But, sir, it's us. You know me already and the count will show his appreciation. . . ."

"Let 'em through, you goddam mother-eating bastards! And don't you let anybody else through, you so-and-sos, and wear your swords and stop making this filthy mess on the floor. . . ." Taras and Yankel didn't hear all the eloquent instructions to the guards, and to everyone they met Yankel kept saying:

"It's us, we're friends, it's us."

When they reached a door at the end of the corridor, Yankel asked the guard standing near it: "All right?"

"It's all right with me," the guard said, "but I wonder whether they'll let you through into the jail itself. Jan has been replaced by another guard."

Yankel moaned softly. "It looks bad," he said to Taras.

"Go ahead," Taras said stubbornly, and Yankel obeyed.

By a door with a pointed top, which led to the dungeon, stood a soldier with a three-storied mustachio: the ends of the top story turned upward, those of the second were parallel to his lips and the bottom ones turned down, all of which made him look very much like a tomcat.

Yankel shrank into himself and came up very close to the soldier.

"Your Grace, excuse me, Your Grace. . . ."

"You talking to me?"

"Yes, Your Grace. . . ."

"Hm . . . I'm . . . see, just a soldier," the man with the three-storied mustachio said with an amused twinkle.

"I'm sorry, sir, I took you for the Military Governor himself," Yankel said, shaking his head and spreading his fingers wide apart. "You do look like a colonel, sir, I swear, exactly like a colonel! Just a little something, sir, and you'd be exactly like a colonel. Then if they gave you a stallion fast as a fly and regiments to drill . . ."

The soldier smoothed the bottom story of his mustachio and his eyes looked very merry.

"What wonderful people, the military," Yankel went on. "What wonderful people! Those gold lacings, those spangles, all those shiny things like sunlight. . . . And the ladies . . . whenever they see a soldier . . . ah, dear me. . . ." Yankel again wagged his head admiringly.

The soldier now gave a twist to the top story of his mustachio and let out a sound like the neighing of a horse.

"I would like to ask you for a favor, sir," Yankel said. "You see, this count has come from far away, hoping to have a look at the Cossacks. He has never seen what sort of people the Cossacks are, what they look like."

Foreign counts and barons were no rarity in Poland. They often went there to have a look at that remote, almost semi-Asiatic corner of Europe. They considered Muscovy and the Ukraine as part of Asia itself. And so the mustachioed soldier, bowing rather low, thought it appropriate to put in a few words himself:

"I really don't understand, Your Grace, why you'd want to look at them. They're not human, just a bunch of dogs, and they have a peculiar sort of religion that everyone despises. . . ."

"You're lying, you damn bastard," Bulba said. "You're a dog yourself! How dare you say that our faith isn't respected? It's your heretical faith that isn't."

"Well, well!" the Pole said. "Now I know who you are, friend. You're one of them, one of that lot sitting in there. Just wait while I call our men. . . ."

Taras realized his blunder, but his anger and stubbornness prevented him from trying to retrieve it. Fortunately Yankel managed to come up with something immediately.

"My noble lord," he said, addressing the Pole, "how could you possibly imagine the count to be a Cossack? Supposing he were a Cossack—how could he be dressed like a count, and look like one too?"

"Keep talking," the soldier said and opened his wide mouth to call.

"Your Royal Highness, Your Royal Highness, please, please, quiet," Yankel shouted. "Be quiet and we'll reward you as you've never been rewarded before. We'll give you two pieces of gold!"

"Yes? Two pieces of gold? I'm not interested in two pieces. I give that much to the barber for shaving only one half of my whiskers. Hand over a hundred, Jew!" The soldier gave a twirl to his top mustachio and added: "Otherwise I'll start calling."

"Why so much?" Yankel said bitterly, untying his leather purse. Still, he was glad that it did not contain more money and that the soldier couldn't count beyond a hundred anyway.

"Let's go, let's go, quickly," Yankel said to Taras, noticing that the soldier was fingering the money, perhaps regretting not having named a larger sum. "Hurry. What a horrible lot, the people of this country."

"What are you waiting for, you damn Polish swine?" Bulba suddenly said to the Pole. "You took the money all right, do you think you'll get away with not showing us the prisoners? No, you've got to go through with it. Once you've received the cash, you've no right to refuse."

"Get out of here, both of you! Move or I'll report you and then . . . Take yourselves out of here, I tell you!"

"Sir, sir, let's go. Believe me, let's get out of here!" Yankel said, trying to convince Bulba. "The hell with him. May he see horrors in his dreams. . . ."

His head sadly lowered, Bulba slowly walked back along the passage. Yankel trotted behind him, bitterly regretting the wasted pieces of gold.

"What need was there to provoke him! Let the dog swear! These people can't do without swearing. Why is

God so kind to some? . . . That pig earned a hundred gold pieces just for kicking us out, while they would tear out a Jew's sidelocks and push his face in so that nobody'd care to look at him and, have no fear, no one ever offers him a hundred. Oh God, oh merciful God!"

But the failure seemed to have a much deeper effect upon Bulba. There was an all-consuming flame in his eyes.

"Come," he said suddenly, as though trying to snap himself out of a nightmare, "let's go to the square. I want to see how they torture him."

"Why, sir? Why go? We can't help him that way."

"Let's go," Bulba repeated stubbornly and Yankel, sighing like a patient nurse, followed him.

It was impossible to miss the square where the executions were to take place—people were pouring into it from every side. In that savage age, not only the ignorant masses but the aristocracy as well regarded executions as a choice spectacle. Numerous old ladies of great piety, timid maidens and easily frightened women never missed a chance to attend, though throughout the following night gory corpses might obsess them and make them cry out in their sleep using words one would expect only from a drunken hussar. And many of them would scream hysterically that it was horrible and turn away from the tortures and still stay standing there for hours. And some, mouths gaping, arms widespread, looked as though they were about to jump on top of the heads of those around them, to get a better view.

The fat face of a butcher stood out among the ordinary, medium-sized heads. He observed the whole procedure with the expression of an expert and exchanged monosyllabic remarks with a gunsmith whom he addressed as "pal" because they got drunk in the same inn on holidays. Some engaged in heated arguments and occasionally even made bets, but the overwhelming majority were those who gape at everything that happens in the world and go on picking their noses. In the first row, just behind the mustachioed municipal guards, there stood a young Polish aristocrat, or at least he looked like one. He was dressed in military attire and was wearing absolutely every item he possessed—all that

was left in his lodgings was a tattered shirt and an old
pair of boots. Two chains, one on top of the other, with
some sort of gold coins dangling from them, hung round
his neck. He stood there with his sweetheart and kept
glancing around to see that no one stained his silky garments. He had explained everything to her so thoroughly
that there was definitely nothing to add.

"You see, Juzysya dearest," he said to her, "this
whole crowd has come to see the criminals executed.
And the one over there, see, dear, the one with the ax
and the other instruments, that's the executioner—he's
the one who carries out the executions. And when he
begins to break them on the wheel and puts them
through other tortures, they'll still be alive, but when
the head's chopped off, then, sweet, the criminal will die
immediately, understand? So at the beginning you'll hear
them shout and move but as soon as they chop his head
off, the criminal won't be able to shout or to eat or
drink, because, of course, my sweet, he won't have any
head left."

And Juzysya listened to all this, at once horrified
and curious.

The roofs of the houses were teeming with people.
Extraordinary mustachioed physiognomies in what
looked like bonnets peeked out of little windows. On
the balconies, the aristocracy sat under awnings. The
sugar-white hand of a laughing lady lay gracefully on a
railing. Majestic and rather fat aristocrats looked around
with an air of great dignity. A footman in beautiful livery
with flowing sleeves went around with a tray of refresh-
ments. Often some bright, playful thing with black eyes
would seize a piece of pastry or perhaps some fruit in
her light little hand and toss it into the crowd below.
The throng of underfed knights held out their caps to
catch the morsel and some tall member of the gentry in
a faded red doublet covered with tarnished golden cord,
with his head sticking up above the others, would stretch
out his arm and, thanks to its length, be the first to
snatch it. He would kiss the prize and put it in his mouth.
Another spectator was a falcon in a golden cage that
hung under a balcony. His beak turned sideways and his
claw raised, he too was staring intently at the people.

Suddenly a shiver passed through the crowd.

"They're bringing 'em! They're bringing in the Cossacks!"

The Cossacks' heads were bare, their long tufts swaying in the wind as they walked. They did not look particularly frightened or dejected and there was in their bearing a sort of quiet cockiness. Their coats, made of expensive cloth, were torn and hung in rags. They looked straight ahead without turning their heads toward the crowd. Ostap walked out in front.

What did old Taras feel when he saw his Ostap? Standing among the crowd, he kept his eyes glued on him and the smallest of his son's gestures did not escape him. When they reached the place of execution, Ostap stopped; he had to go through it first. He looked at the other Cossacks, raised his hand and said loudly:

"May God grant that none of the heretics gathered here shall hear a complaint from a tortured Christian! May none of us utter a single word!"

Then he stepped up to the scaffold.

"Good boy! Good, my son!" Bulba said very quietly and hung his old head.

The hangman tore off Ostap's rags. They tied him by his wrists and ankles onto a frame made especially for the purpose and . . .

But why describe the hellish tortures that made one's hair stand on end? They were the product of that crude, cruel age when men led lives of violence and blood and their hearts were closed to human feelings. In vain did a few exceptional men try to oppose these beastly acts; in vain did the King and some enlightened knights insist that this cruelty would only arouse the Cossacks to vengeance. The authority of the King and of intelligent men counted for nothing, in the chaos of the day, against the arrogant will of the Polish aristocracy, who, through their thoughtlessness, incredible lack of foresight, childishness, and petty vanity, had turned the Polish Sejm into a parody of government.

Ostap bore the tortures and torments like a Titan. No cry, no sound, escaped his lips when they started breaking the bones of his arms and legs, and even when the sinister cracking of his bones was heard in the remotest corners of the square, when the Polish ladies turned away their eyes, he did not let out a moan and his face remained immobile.

Taras stood in the crowd, his head lowered but, at the same time, his eyes were raised and looked with a sort of proud approval at his son, while his lips kept muttering: "Good boy, you're doing well. Good, son. . . ."

But when they started taking him through the last set of tortures, it looked for one second as if Ostap's strength was coming to an end. His eyes swept around and all he saw, oh God, were strange faces. If only someone close to him could be there as he died. He was longing, not for the desperate sobs of a weak mother nor the hysterical screams of a beloved, tearing her hair and smiting her white breasts—what he was searching for, hopelessly, with his eyes, was a strong, stern man whose calm encouragement would have eased his suffering and helped him to die. His forces were fading and finally he could stand no more and shouted in agony:

"Father! Father! Where are you? Can you hear? . . ."

"I hear, my son!"

The shout rang out in the silence and the whole huge crowd shuddered. Some mounted guards rushed to scrutinize the faces in the crowd. Yankel went deathly pale. But when, after having made certain that there were no guards near, he looked around for Taras, he could not find him. Taras was gone.

12

But he was heard of again soon enough. A Cossack army a hundred and twenty thousand strong massed on the border of the Ukraine. This was no small force, no detachment preparing for a profitable raid or setting out to chase Tartars. No, this time the whole nation was up in arms, the patience of the people was at an end. They were thirsting for vengeance—their rights had been flouted, their customs scorned, their faith insulted, their churches desecrated. The savage excesses of alien overlords, the attempts to force allegiance to the Pope, the disgraceful rule of the Jews over a Christian land—all these things had been stored up for long years and had caused fierce hatred to grow in the Cossack people.

Their young and intrepid headman, Ostranitsa, was in command of this vast Cossack force. At his side was Gunia, his experienced friend and adviser. Eight colonels led regiments of twelve thousand men each. Three staff officers rode behind the headman. The chief standard-bearer carried the principal standard and others fluttered farther back. There were people with all sorts of ranks and functions, quartermasters, scribes, and specialists in transportation. The army had its cavalry and infantry and there were many volunteers in addition to the registered Cossacks. They had come from all the corners of the Ukraine to join—from Chernigov, from Pereyaslav, from Baturin, from Glukhov, from the lower and upper reaches of the Dnieper and from all its islands. Countless horses, wagon trains, and carts stretched over the fields. And among all these Cossack regiments, the crack regiment was led by Taras Bulba. Everything made it stand out from among the others: the age of its commander, his experience in open warfare, and his unmatched hatred. Even his own Cossacks felt that his cruelty and ferocity were at times excessive. His prisoners were doomed to fire and the gallows, and, in a war council, this gray head would always insist on ruthless annihilation.

There's no need to dwell on the battles in which the Cossacks showed their mettle nor to describe the general course of the campaign. All this can be found in the chronicles. We all know what a war in defense of the faith is like in the Russian land. There is no stronger force. It is immovable and stern like a wild crag jutting out of the unquiet, ever-changing sea, its jagged sides rising to the sky from unfathomable depths. It can be seen from far away, facing unmoved the rolling breakers, and woe to the ship that is hurled against it: splinters fly, everything inside is smashed and crushed, and the startled air is filled with the heartbreaking appeals of the drowning.

The pages of the chronicles describe in detail the flight of the Polish garrisons from the liberated towns, the hangings of unscrupulous Jewish contractors; the helplessness of the numerous Polish force under the King's hetman, Nicholas Potocki. The chronicle tells how, routed and pursued by the invincible Cossacks, many of Potocki's crack troops were drowned in a small river; how the Cossacks then besieged him in a small place called Polonnoye, and how, finding himself driven into a tight corner, the Crown hetman promised under oath that full satisfaction would be given to all Cossack demands by the King and his government and that all their former rights and privileges would be restored. But the Cossacks knew only too well what a Polish promise was, and it is certain that Potocki would never again have been seen swaggering on his Caucasian stallion, valued at six thousand pieces of gold, attracting the eyes of aristocratic Polish ladies and the envy of noblemen, or making so much noise in the Sejm, or giving sumptuous banquets to the senators, had it not been for the intervention of the Russian Orthodox priests.

The Russian Orthodox clergy went out to meet the Cossacks in their gold chasubles, carrying crosses and icons, with the bishop, cross in hand, marching at their head in his miter, and all the Cossacks lowered their heads and removed their hats. To no one else except the king himself would the Cossacks have shown respect at that moment. But they did not dare disobey their church. Hetman Ostranitsa and his colonels agreed to let Potocki go, after he had sworn to let the Orthodox churches practice their faith unmolested, to forget the ancient feud, and to commit no act that could cause prejudice to the Cossack army. Only one of the colonels would not accept this peace. This was Colonel Taras Bulba and he tore a wisp of hair from his head and raised his voice:

"Hetman and colonels! Don't be a lot of old women, don't trust the damn Poles! They'll doublecross you, the dogs!"

And when the scribe presented the treaty and the hetman signed it with his firm hand, Taras unbuckled his costly Turkish saber, drew out the flashing steel blade, snapped it in two like a reed, tossed away the pieces, one to the left and one to the right, and said:

"Good-bye then! Just as these two splinters will never be fused again into one saber, so you and I will never meet again in this life. Remember my parting words. . . ."

Here his voice suddenly grew in volume, rose, acquired an uncanny strength, and all were awed by his prophetic words:

"You'll remember me before you die! You think you've brought peace and quiet? You believe you'll live like squires from now on? Well, I see different things in store for you. You, Hetman, they'll take the skin from your head and stuff it with chaff and for a long time it will travel from fair to fair throughout the country! And you, gentlemen, won't get away with your heads either. You'll perish in damp dungeons, immured within stone walls, if you are not stewed alive like sheep in a caldron. And you, lads," he said, turning to his own regiment, "which of you will die a proper death, not by the stove or in bed like a woman, not lying drunk in a ditch outside an inn, but a true Cossack death, all together, in one field, like newlyweds in their bed? But maybe you're going home to become heretics and let the Polish priests ride on your backs?"

"We're with you, we're with you, Colonel. We'll follow you!" shouted Taras's entire regiment, and many others besides hastened to join them.

"Well, if you're coming, come on then!" Taras said, pulling his hat down fiercely over his brow and looking defiantly at those who stayed behind. He mounted his horse and shouted to his followers:

"Let no one reproach us or say a slighting word about us! Off we go, lads—let's pay a visit to the Catholics!"

Thereupon he lashed his horse and a hundred wagons moved off behind him and, behind them, many Cossacks on horseback and on foot. Then he turned back once more and threw a threatening look at those who had stayed behind—a look full of wrath. No one moved to stop him. The regiment marched off in sight of the whole army and for a long way Taras kept glancing back threateningly.

The hetman and the colonels stood there greatly disconcerted, sunk deep in thought. It was as though they felt some sinister foreboding. And Taras's prophecy was correct. Everything turned out exactly as he had said.

Soon after the treachery of Kanev, the hetman's head was stuck on a pole, as were the heads of many of his foremost lieutenants.

And Taras? Taras swept over Poland with his regiment, burning eighteen villages, about forty churches, and almost reaching Cracow. Many of the Polish gentry were slaughtered. Many a rich and beautiful castle was looted and mead and wines, a century old, were poured out on the ground. They slashed and burned sumptuous clothes and materials and broke and scattered provisions in the larders. "Spare nothing," was all old Taras would say. And the Cossacks did not spare the black-browed damsels either—the white-bosomed, fair-faced maidens could find no safety even by the church altar. And afterward the flames consumed them and their altars. Many a white arm rose toward heaven above the tongues of flame, amidst shrieks for pity which would have touched the damp earth itself and made the steppe grass bow in compassion. But the callous Cossacks heeded nothing—they speared infants in the streets and tossed them into the same flames.

"That's for you, you goddam Poles. A requiem for Ostap," was all Taras would say. And this requiem was repeated in every Polish village and settlement, until it dawned on the Polish government that Taras's exploits were going well beyond the ordinary raids, and they commissioned the same Potocki, at the head of an army of five regiments, to overtake and capture Taras at any cost.

For six days the Cossacks evaded their pursuers, using lanes and byways, and their horses were hard tried by these forced marches. But this time Potocki was equal to the mission entrusted him. He pursued them relentlessly and overtook them on the bank of the Dniester, where Bulba had halted to recuperate in the deserted ruin of a fortress.

The broken ramparts of the fortress loomed above the steep bank of the river. Rubble and broken masonry, strewn along the top of the wall, looked as if they would fall at any moment. At this spot, Potocki concentrated his attack from two sides of the field. For four days the Cossacks fought, struggled, defended themselves with

bricks and stones. But their stores and their strength
were running low and Taras decided on an attempt to
break out. And the Cossacks broke out all right and
their swift horses would have carried them away from
their foe once more, but suddenly Taras stopped in full
gallop and said:

"Hold on, brothers! I've dropped my pipe and my
tobacco pouch. I don't want those Polish dogs to get
even that much!" And the old chief leaned over and
started looking in the tall grass for his pipe, his insepara-
ble companion on sea, on land, on campaign and at
home. At that moment, a wave of the enemy swept over
them and Taras was grabbed by his heavy shoulders. He
twisted his whole body as hard as he could but those
who had grabbed him did not fall away as they used to
in the olden days.

"Damned old age," he said and began to cry. But it
was not a question of old age. Strength was overwhelmed by strength; maybe thirty of them were hanging
onto his legs and arms.

"The old crow is caught!" the Poles shouted. "All
that's left is to decide how best to honor the dog."

And with Potocki's permission they sentenced him to
be burned alive in sight of everyone.

A bare tree that had been struck by lightning stood
nearby. They bound him with iron chains and dragged
him to it. They nailed him by his hands to the trunk,
after lifting him high so that he could be seen from far
away. Then they began to build up a fire. But Taras did
not look at the firewood and it was not of the fire that
he was thinking. He was looking to one side, where the
Cossacks were still firing back at the Poles, and from his
height he could see everything quite well.

"Occupy it, occupy, occupy the hillock," he shouted,
"behind the wood. They won't be able to approach
it! . . ." But the wind did not carry his words to them.
"My God, they'll be lost for nothing," he said in despair,
and looked down toward the gleaming Dniester. Joy
gleamed in his eyes. He saw the sterns of four boats
sticking up among the reeds and, gathering all his
strength, he shouted:

"To the river, lads. Take the path to the left. There

are boats hidden there. Take them all, so they can't follow you!"

This time the wind was from the other side and the Cossacks heard his words. But his advice brought him a blow from the blunt end of an ax and everything swayed before his eyes.

The Cossacks raced full gallop downhill with the Poles at their heels. But the path twisted and turned and they saw that it ran parallel to the bank too much of the way.

"All right, brothers, down we go, we've nothing to lose," one of them shouted.

They stopped for a second, raised their whips and whistled. And their Tartar horses detached themselves from the ground, stretched themselves out like dragons, flew through the air, and dropped with a splash into the Dniester. Only two of them failed to reach the river. They fell from the heights, hitting the stones, and were lost forever with their horses, without even having time to let out a cry. But the rest were already swimming in the river with their horses and untying the boats. The Poles stopped on top of the precipice, wondering at the incredible Cossack feat and trying to decide whether to leap or not.

One young Polish colonel, with hot, boiling blood, the brother of the beautiful Polish girl who had bewitched poor Andrei, was not long deciding. He threw himself with his horse in pursuit of the Cossacks. Rider and mount spun around three times in the air and were hurled straight upon the jagged rocks. He was torn by the sharp stones and his brain, mixed with blood, bespattered the bushes that grew on the uneven edges of the cliff.

When Bulba came to after the blow, he looked down at the Dniester and saw the Cossacks already rowing away in the boats, while bullets rained down on them from the cliff, missing them. And the eyes of the old chief sparkled with joy.

"Farewell, comrades!" he shouted to them. "Remember me sometimes, and, when spring comes, come back here and have a damn good time! And you, what do you think you have gained, you Polish dogs? Do you think there is anything in the world that'll frighten a

Cossack? Wait, the time will come when you'll find out what the Russian Orthodox faith is like! Even today nations far and wide are beginning to feel that a tsar will arise on the Russian land, and there'll be no power on earth that won't submit to him!"

In the meantime, the flames were rising and lapping around his legs and now the whole tree burst into flames. . . .

But are there in the world such fires, such tortures, or such forces as could overcome Russian strength?

The Dniester is no minor river and it has many backwaters, thick reed banks, shallows, and deep pools; the river's mirror glitters, resounding to the ringing cry of swans, and the proud golden-eye skims swiftly over it. There are many snipe, red-breasted sandpipers, and other birds in its reeds and on its banks. The Cossacks rowed swiftly in the double-ruddered boats; steering skillfully, then carefully avoided the shallows, raising frightened birds from the reeds, and talked about their chief.

Afterword

"We have the marvelous gift of making everything insignificant."

—N. V. Gogol

Gogol, as Vladimir Nabokov wrote, is the strangest prose-poet Russia ever produced. Never married, secretive, writing falsehoods home to his mother, fleeing Russia when he felt his work to be ill received, burning the manuscript for the second volume of his novel *Dead Souls,* and starving himself to death at the age of forty-three with the help of his inept doctors, Gogol in his life as much as in his work defies any typology of personality, biography, or literary school. His Petersburg stories may at first seem to be only satire aimed at man's obsession with rank, money, clothing, and mustaches, but Gogol uses all this misplaced devotion to the trivial to reveal a terrifying spiritual vacuity.

Gogol was born in Sorochintsy, Ukraine (then part of the Russian Empire), on April 1, 1809. He grew up on the small family estate of Vasilievka and spent eight years at a boarding school in Nezhin, Ukraine. Feeling destined for greatness, although uncertain of what kind, he moved to Petersburg in 1828, where he eventually, if briefly, became a civil servant and then a teacher of history. In 1830, Gogol began to write short tales set in the Ukraine, a fashionable genre at the time. A first group was published in 1831, under the title *Evenings on a Farm near Dikanka,* followed the next year by a second set; in 1835, he published another

pair of volumes of Ukrainian stories entitled *Mirgorod* that
included "Taras Bulba." *Arabesques,* a volume containing
stories set in Petersburg, appeared the same year.

In the 1820s, the theme of the Ukraine had become a
way of celebrating Russian national history; the Cossacks'
battles with the Poles provided, among other things, an occasion to elevate Russian Orthodox Christianity, which
Russians considered the essence of Russian national iden-
tity, over Roman Catholicism. In composing his historical
novella "Taras Bulba," Gogol drew from histories of the
Ukraine and collections of Ukrainian songs, combining local lore with the manner of the historical novels of Walter
Scott and James Fenimore Cooper and *The Iliad,* all of
which were very popular in Russia at the time. Sources for
the scenes of parting with the mother, the image of the
dead Cossack, the portrait of the bonds of Cossack brotherhood, and the poetry of battle can be traced to the "Songs
of the Ukraine," about which Gogol wrote an article (1834),
while the comic Jew resembles the stock character from the
tradition of the Ukrainian puppet theater, the *vertep,* for
which Gogol's father wrote plays. The history in "Taras
Bulba" is approximate; Gogol sought to present "the spirit
of a bygone age," but mixes up the fifteenth and the six-
teenth centuries, while some details (the historical figures
of Potocki and Ostrianitsa) belong to the seventeenth century.

The Ukrainian stories have little to do thematically with
the Petersburg ones, based as they are in a rural, oral cul-
ture, yet the two groups are closely related. Part of the rep-
ertoire of the Ukrainian puppet theater was the Herod
plays, which were performed on two-level stages, with the
divine story played physically above the secular one. The
opposition between two worlds — whether the sacred and
the profane, the magical and the everyday, or in keeping
with German Romantic Neoplatonism, the real and the
ideal — is essential to all of Gogol's work, however disguised.

Gogol's Ukrainian tales are full of devils and supernatural terrors, while his Petersburg stories take place against
such a quotidian background that they were taken as social
satire by contemporaries. But elements of Ukrainian diab-

olism appear in masked form in the Petersburg tales: traces of the supernatural are carried by, for example, the odd interference of animals (the "adult suckling pig" who knocks over the policeman in "The Overcoat"), or sudden outbursts of motion (Kovalyov breaks into a Ukrainian dance when his nose reappears on his face). Things associated with the transcendent in the rural setting are comic and mundane when moved to the urban milieu, allowing Gogol to imply the ideal through its travesty in the real.

The three Petersburg stories in this volume share the ostensible theme of the ambitions of the petty clerk, a topic popular in the early 1830s. When Peter the Great founded the city in 1703 (it became the capital in 1712), he established a table of fourteen ranks for the civil and military service; Gogol's heroes belong to the lower ones, and this shapes their obsessions. Kovalyov is intimidated by his own nose because it is of higher rank; Poprishchin believes his rank deprives him of all the blessings of life; and Akaky Akakievich is almost subhuman in his role as a copying clerk. Gogol makes fun of Petersburgers' pretensions, ambitions and limitations, but rank is a form of concern with the trivial (medals, uniforms, boots, noses) that reveals the absence of spiritual meaning he finds in Russian life, from the capital to the provinces.

"The Nose" was written between 1833 and 1834. The absurdity of how Major Kovalyov's nose detaches itself from his face and zips around Petersburg causes some critics to agree with the Nose, who says "I understand absolutely nothing" (p. 32), and consider the tale a parable about the impossibility of interpretation. Yet "The Nose" begins and ends with an evocation of Christian faith: March 25, according to the old Julian calendar, is the same date as April 7 in the new Gregorian one, which is Annunciation Day in the Orthodox church. What could have been a conversion tale, about gaining faith through catharsis, turns out instead to be about failure to change: Kovalyov is the same person before and after his nose loss, just as March 25 and April 7 are the same day on two different calendars, and the miracle of divine birth, parodied by the nose in the loaf, goes unremarked. A conversion is hinted at by the barber's reformed behavior: after Kovalyov's "tragedy" has been happily resolved, Ivan Yakovlevich is a changed man, asking himself, "What can it mean?" He is "embarrassed as he had never been embarrassed" (p. 49) and learns to shave Kovalyov without holding on to his nose. Kovalyov's mock tragedy leads to his double's mock reformation. Ivan Yakovlevich lives on Voznesensky (Ascension) Prospect; Ascension Day, the fortieth day after Easter, marks Jesus' ascent to heaven. The reappearance of Kovalyov's nose on his face can be understood as a parody of that miracle, displacing the resurrection of the spirit and thereby revealing the appalling emptiness of the hero's concerns.

God and the devil appear only as epithets in "The Nose." Kovalyov has no fear of either, invoking the devil nine times in twenty-odd pages, but using God's name only on four occasions, twice in tandem with the devil's. He projects his own lack of godliness onto the Nose, of whom he says "for this person nothing was sacred" (p. 34). Only when trying to convince the newspaperman that he has no nose does Kovalyov suggest respect for the Lord: "I swear to you, as God is holy" (p. 37). When the doctor offers to buy the nose, Kovalyov screams, "No, no! I won't sell it for anything! . . . better let it disappear" (p. 45). With his pitch-black sidewhiskers, the doctor is a parodic devil trying to buy Kovalyov's soul; as Kovalyov says, his nose is "almost the same thing as" Kovalyov himself, (p. 37) a mock representation of his spiritual essence.

Kovalyov's absence of faith is displayed in the Kazan Cathedral. As the place where the earthly and the divine conjoin, the church is the proper setting for Kovalyov's encounter with his nose, possibly possessed by unclean powers controlled by Madam Podtochina. His soullessness is signaled by his preoccupation with fleshly appetites—food, women, tobacco: in church he sees an ethereal beauty, whom his noselessness prevents him from courting, accompanied by a tall footman, who is opening his snuffbox. Gogol associates tobacco with the diabolical because it obscures vision, whether through sneezing, a haze of smoke, or the distraction of snuff taking, and Kovalyov's vision of the divine is obscured by his preoccupation with the woman, his missing nose, and its uniform. After Kovalyov's nose is restored, another image of tobacco shows his unregenerate nature—"deliberately taking out his snuffbox, kept stuffing his nose at both entrances for an extremely long time" (p. 50)—and he resumes his womanizing with new gusto: "And after this [he] could be seen ... pursuing absolutely all the pretty ladies" (p. 50). The tale of Kovalyov's absurd loss reveals the terrifying meaninglessness of Petersburg daily life.

"The Nose" parodies the supernatural tale, replacing uncanny events with absurd mundanities—Kovalyov is worried at the beginning and end of his ordeal about a pimple. Gogol originally intended that the whole story be a dream, and the fact that the story begins and ends on the same date hints at the possibility. Kovalyov wonders whether he is dreaming when he discovers the absence of his nose: "Isn't he asleep?" (p. 29). After his visits to three officials, Kovalyov returns home, and trying to explain the event by the usual devices in supernatural tales—sleep or drunkenness—he hopes: "This, probably, is either a dream or simply a daydream" (p. 40). He pinches himself, which convinces him "that he was acting and living in a wakened state" (p. 40).

Kovalyov is infuriated by the indifference of his servant Ivan, whom he finds spitting at the ceiling, and indeed, all of Petersburg is indifferent to Kovalyov's extraordinary predicament, quite immune to amazement. Only the narrator reacts. He is outraged. But not at divine injustice. The narrator (but who is he?) is angry at the unlikelihood of the events described (but by whom, then?), at their indecency, and by authors choosing such subjects, which are of no use to the fatherland. The epilogue of "The Nose" shifts the mock moral of the tale to the literary world's relationship to the fatherland, explicitly opening out its implications to all of Russia. Gogol transposes the supernatural horror tale into the world of Petersburg, rendering it apparently secular and playful but giving "The Nose" a profound uncanniness.

To contemporary readers, "The Nose" looked like a parody of the tales of E. T. A. Hoffmann, whose comic supernatural tales were widely read at the time in Russian translation. Gogol's characters suffer from clouded vision in a city where all becomes clouded with fog during events that can only be supernatural, but we are able to glimpse the unrealized transcendent world behind Kovalyov's comic fear of Podtochina's witchcraft. The spiritually anni-hilating gaze of Ukrainian folkloric monsters in the earlier tales is recast as the socially humiliating look of—a nose. Instead of exorcising demons by prayer, Kovalyov goes on a quest for his nose through the (corrupt) civil agencies of Petersburg—the newspapers, the officials, the police. Hav-ing glimpsed the supernatural forces that Gogol has recos-tumed in Petersburg dress, we can no longer read "The Nose" as either a social satire, a parody of the supernatural genre, a sexual fantasy, or absolute nonsense. Instead the danger of ensnarement by meaningless exteriors threatens us at every turn.

Like Kovalyov, the hero of "The Diary of a Madman" (published in *Arabesques,* part II, 1835), is obsessed with rank. The petty clerk Poprishchin (whose name can be as-sociated with the Russian for "pimple," *prishchik,* or *po-prishche,* "calling") is infatuated with the boss's daughter Sophie precisely because she is the daughter of a general; his idealization extends to her "aristocratic" (p. 5) handker-chief. The tale parodies Romantic stories about the obses-sions of mad musicians, but as usual, Gogol lowers the subject matter, changing the artist to a lowly clerk and the object of his obsession from great art to rank in the civil service.

The dog's-eye view of civil servants, from Poprishchin at the lowest rank to the general at the top, shows them all to be absurd. In their letters, Madgie and Fidèle, whose senti-mental effusions over "spring" and "love" parody the epis-tolary novel, compare canine and human suitors, and evaluate the ribbon the general is so proud of by smell and taste, revealing the arbitrariness of rankings, awards, and the social status Petersburgers are shown to value. The only way Poprishchin can compete with the court chamber-lain who is to marry Sophie is to attain higher rank than all of them, and so he imagines himself to be the King of Spain. Poprishchin knows from the newspaper *The Northern Bee* about the actual conflict over the Spanish succession after the death of Ferdinand VII in 1833, and he echoes Ferdi-nand's brother Don Carlos, who disputes the right of Ferdinand's daughter to the throne, in saying "a donna can't ascend the throne" (p. 16).

The final entry in "The Diary of a Madman" attains a pathos that is then undercut by a sudden shift to the comic: "And did you know that the Dey of Algiers has a bump right under his nose?" (p. 23). Just as Madgie diminishes the general's bureaucratic award by sniffing it (no aroma, only a little salty), Poprishchin reduces the potentate to an absurd physical detail. If the greats of this world have noses just like everyone else, can there be any meaningful power on earth?

Set neither in the Ukraine nor in Petersburg, "The Carriage" (1835) is a prelude to Gogol's novel, *Dead Souls* (1842); along with his great play, *The Government Inspector* (1836), it conveys his idea that a provincial town is inanity carried to the highest degree. Leo Tolstoy called "The Carriage" "the peak of perfection in its kind." The plot is modeled on an actual event involving the legendarily absentminded Count Vielgorsky, who once invited the entire diplomatic corps to a large dinner in Petersburg, but forgot about the invitation and went to dine at his club as they were arriving, in all their medals and ribbons, at his empty house. Chertokutsky resembles both the braggart Nozdriov and the unctuous Chichikov (characters in *Dead Souls*), and the description of the town is a forerunner of that of the town of NN with which *Dead Souls* opens.

"The Overcoat" (1842) is Gogol's masterpiece. It contains a vast universe in a tiny space. The narrative voice moves from the tone of a chatty acquaintance at one extreme to the eternal, distant judge of humankind at the other. Between the lowly and the elevated, the narrative tone grades from matter-of-fact reportorial ("He needed to acquire new pants" [p. 79]) to lyrical ("Even at those hours when the gray Petersburg sky completely darkens" [p. 71]), to pathos-filled ("in these penetrating words rang other words: 'I am your brother'" [pp. 69–70]).

More than most artists, Gogol was a scavenger, and suffered constant anxiety about his ability to produce his art. Desperate for a subject, he would beg Pushkin to tell him an anecdote that might inspire a story. "The Overcoat" is based on an anecdote Gogol heard (we don't know where)

about a poor clerk who scrimps to buy a rifle but loses it the
first time he goes hunting. Gogol sees in this everyday tale
the mad devotion to an insignificant object; he creates an
equally insignificant hero, mocked by his very name and
patronymic, which repeats the child's word for excrement,
kaka. The touching passage in which one clerk repents his
mistreatment of Akaky is undercut by Akaky's almost subhuman limitedness—he is incapable of recasting the first
person into the third, and can barely utter a coherent sentence.

Gogol found a fruitful resource in the stories of E. T. A.
Hoffmann, whom his contemporaries were pillaging regu-
larly, appropriating his themes, images, intonations, and
word usage. Akaky the copying clerk is related to the copy-
ist Anselmus from Hoffmann's "The Golden Pot." But
while Anselmus transcends mere copying to become a
scribe in the medieval religious sense, instead of the meaning of the word, Akaky loves the letters of the alphabet
themselves, and the rank of a document's addressee. He
fails the test of the scribe associated with the transmission
of the divine Word, just as he fails the test of the martyr
Saint Acacius, against whom he is implicitly measured.

Furthermore, Akaky accepts the diabolic temptation to
buy a new overcoat. The tailor Petrovich, whom we first
glimpse in clouds of smoke, acts as the devil's agent, the go-
between bridging the worldly and the transcendent. His all-
consuming devotion to the "idea of the overcoat" parodies
devotion to a beloved woman; Akaky's beloved "life companion" (p. 80) is—an overcoat. The coat, which should be
no more than a reasonable necessity, becomes an emblem
of the mundane obsessions of Petersburg life that displace
awareness of a higher world.

Akaky's obsession leads to his demise, but he triumphs
in the afterlife when he seizes the Important Personage's
overcoat. Gogol turns the theft of an overcoat into a supernatural event, but even the supernatural is lowered; Akaky
becomes a "clerk-corpse" (p. 95)—not even a ghost—who
steals to wreak revenge. Akaky briefly lives on as one of
several thieves in the afterlife, which apparently teems with
them. Akaky, who received his name from his father and
not from any saint, does not understand his calling and, liv-

ing in godless Petersburg, cannot become a saint or an artist, or even a romantic lover. After his death he finds neither heaven nor the eternal life of the spirit, but a miserable parody of sinful everyday life. "The Overcoat" combines Hoffmann's romanticism and the Russian Orthodox genre of the lives of the saints with the low realism of the Naturalist school.

For Gogol, following the Platonic tradition, beauty is a means to absolute truth, a source of all that is good, capable of transfiguring man. But the world abounds with false images of beauty that are diabolic deceptions. Divine intention is disguised, and Gogol's characters are ruined by their inability to discern it, while the reader is made to work to unveil a higher truth concealed in the everyday. The grotesque collision of these ideals with Gogol's comic genius produces the "laughter through tears" that he intended.

—PRISCILLA MEYER

Classics of
Russian Literature

THE BROTHERS KARAMAZOV
Fyodor Dostoyevsky
Four brothers, driven by intense passion, become
involved in the brutal murder of their own father.

CRIME AND PUNISHMENT
Fyodor Dostoyevsky
The struggles between traditional Orthodox morality
and the Eurocentric philosophy of the intellectual class
are the potent ideas behind this powerful story of a
man trying to break free from the boundaries imposed
upon him by Russia's rigid class structure.

WAR AND PEACE
Leo Tolstoy
In this broad, sweeping drama, Tolstoy gives us a view
of history and personal destiny that remains
perpetually modern.

ANNA KARENINA
Leo Tolstoy
Sensual, rebellious Anna renounces respectable
marriage and position for a passionate affair which
offers a taste of freedom and a trap of destruction.

Available wherever books are sold or at
signetclassics.com
facebook.com/signetclassic

READ THE TOP 20
SIGNET CLASSICS

ANIMAL FARM BY GEORGE ORWELL

1984 BY GEORGE ORWELL

THE INFERNO BY DANTE

FRANKENSTEIN BY MARY SHELLEY

BEOWULF (BURTON RAFFEL, TRANSLATOR)

THE ODYSSEY BY HOMER

THE FEDERALIST PAPERS BY ALEXANDER HAMILTON

THE HOUND OF THE BASKERVILLES
   BY SIR ARTHUR CONAN DOYLE

NARRATIVE OF THE LIFE OF FREDERICK DOUGLASS
   BY FREDERICK DOUGLASS

DR. JEKYLL AND MR. HYDE BY ROBERT LOUIS STEVENSON

HAMLET BY WILLIAM SHAKESPEARE

THE SCARLET LETTER BY NATHANIEL HAWTHORNE

LES MISÉRABLES BY VICTOR HUGO

HEART OF DARKNESS AND THE SECRET SHARER
   BY JOSEPH CONRAD

WUTHERING HEIGHTS BY EMILY BRONTË

A MIDSUMMER NIGHT'S DREAM BY WILLIAM SHAKESPEARE

NECTAR IN A SIEVE BY KAMALA MARKANDAYA

ETHAN FROME BY EDITH WHARTON

ADVENTURES OF HUCKLEBERRY FINN BY MARK TWAIN

A TALE OF TWO CITIES BY CHARLES DICKENS

Penguin Group (USA) Online

What will you be reading tomorrow?

Tom Clancy, Patricia Cornwell, W.E.B. Griffin,
Nora Roberts, William Gibson, Catherine Coulter,
Stephen King, Dean Koontz, Ken Follett, Nick Hornby,
Khaled Hosseini, Kathryn Stockett, Clive Cussler,
John Sandford, Terry McMillan, Sue Monk Kidd,
Amy Tan, J. R. Ward, Laurell K. Hamilton,
Charlaine Harris, Christine Feehan...

You'll find them all at
penguin.com
facebook.com/PenguinGroupUSA
twitter.com/PenguinUSA

*Read excerpts and newsletters, find tour schedules
and reading group guides, and enter contests.*

Subscribe to Penguin Group (USA) newsletters
and get an exclusive inside look
at exciting new titles and the authors you love
long before everyone else does.

PENGUIN GROUP (USA)
us.penguingroup.com

S0151

PO #: 0003296802